PRINCESS GRACE OF EARTH

THE ZEROT INFESTATION

A K LAMBERT

SERIES EDITOR - ELLEN C CAMPBELL

To my long suffering kids!

PROLOGUE

The Japanese Giant Hornet.

It just takes one scout to find a colony of European honeybees, mark it with a pheromone, and invite thirty of his buddies over.

These killing machines are capable of destroying a colony of thirty thousand bees in the space of a few hours.

Then, they take the spoils. They gorge themselves on the honey and carry off the larvae to feed their young.

(National Geographic)

* * *

PREMIER GOR SAT in his circular office staring up and frowning at the portrait of himself hanging over the grand stone fireplace. He would move it soon, but not just yet. He activated the virtual screen again and rechecked his notes. All in order, just as they had been a short while earlier. He deactivated it, looked at the portrait and sneered.

He had assumed this political position two years ago and

enjoyed the trappings of the top job. But today, he was nervous and apprehensive.

She was coming.

Everything was in order, though. She would find little to criticise. As usual, Gor had carried out his job expertly. She had known his worth from their early academy days—the master planner.

Within four years he had embedded himself into this society and assumed the highest political position. Phase one was now complete. The rest of his Cadre was about to arrive, signalling the commencement of phase two.

Things were about to get interesting.

This new world presented an excellent challenge—technologically advanced and strong-willed; they would not be easy to break. All of the dynasties would wager grandly in this high stakes game.

She would be pleased.

The receptor plate on the floor to his left started to shimmer. She was coming. An opaque globe formed over the plate then evaporated to reveal her standing there—tall and with her usual imperious look.

Gor stood up. 'Madame.'

'Carffekk.' she paused briefly. 'Premier Gor. Happy to see you again, though your appearance is somewhat fragile looking.'

'This is a copy of an elderly specimen. I assure you, I am very much here.' They both grinned.

'Good. Food and drink first, then show me your plans. I'm eager to get underway. And, after that journey, I need satiation.' Again, she grinned, baring sharp, needle teeth. 'And what will be my role in this world's downfall?'

'I have two powerful women in leading positions for your consideration. Both are close. So once you've chosen, we can invite her over.'

'Excellent.'

PART I
THE ADOLESCENT YEARS

CHAPTER 1

*T*he *Ventar Designation*
Preenasette - Bala Verceti - 2000

PRINCESS TAURIAR WAS ATTENDING her very first Decennial Ceremony. But unlike the event of ten years ago where she was the centre of the nation's attention, this was the turn of the Ventar designation.

Within the majestic grounds of the Bala Verceti Palace of Ancestors, the ceremony was underway to replace the outgoing High Council Elder and introduce a new baby boy as Prince. There on the rosewood stage, surrounded by the gently fluttering flags of the nine provinces, the young princess proudly sat next to the three older Royal Trainees.

Tauriar wore her new white robe, made especially for this occasion, with the Vercetian Life Vine delicately embroidered on it, a green serpent weaving its way around her, with explosions of red and yellow flowers.

On the stage next to her sat Prince Camcietti. Ten years her elder, the prince was now a young adult. He turned to her and smiled, and then pulled a face, eyes crossed and lips puffed out. Tauriar tried to keep her composure—this was, after all, the most important event she had ever attended—but the young prince was relentless in his quest to make her laugh. She soon succumbed, lifting her hands to her face to hide her giggling, her powder blue cheeks turning dark sapphire.

They both looked up to see a hover-cam close in on the prince's antics. The shock on Tauriar's face at being caught on camera in such a manner, and on such an occasion, was evident. The prince, however, just sat back, crossed his legs and gave the enthralled watching millions a broad smile and a cheeky wave. The two older Royal Trainees to his left looked on with resigned exasperation, but their faces couldn't hide the fondness they felt for this roguish young man.

The little princess regained her composure and looked past the three elder Royals to Bakta, who looked anxious to get the ceremony started. He sat on his ornately jewelled throne, positioned centrally on the stage, his hands caressing the golden shape of the High Council Coat of Arms on his Overseer Amulet. She saw Bakta most days and was sure he was looking much older lately. He introduced the four High Councillors, the Vercetian heads of state. These were the rulers of Bala Verceti. One day, thought Tauriar nervously, she would be seated there.

The audience was soaking up the sun on this perfect day, and she tried her best not to worry about how many would be watching from the country's provinces.

Finally, all was quiet. Bakta the Overseer stood up and stepped forward to welcome everyone.

'The four Great Houses: Camcietti, Tauriar, Ventar and Domeriette welcome you all to the 29th Decennial Ceremony —The Ventar Designation.

Goodbye to our Ventar Elder.
Congratulations to our new Ventar Councillor.
Greetings to our new Ventar Prince.
The Council balance is reaffirmed today.'

PRINCESS TAURIAR silently recited the traditional opening to the Decennial Ceremony. She had learnt and now understood how it all worked, and her place in the ruling dynasty. Her Life Team had looked after her and trained her for ten years and would do so for another thirty. She would then join the High Council and serve for forty years, the last ten of which she would be Council Elder—the most powerful Vercetian in the land. This system of governing ensured the viewpoint of all age ranges and genders were equally represented in all decision making. Today the Council Elder would retire and a new prince selected. She would cease to be the youngest Royal.

The ceremony slowly proceeded throughout the morning. Tauriar's mind kept wandering. Interesting as this was, her thoughts kept returning to Krankel, the wolf puppy she had gotten the day before. A gift from the Life Team to celebrate this occasion. She wanted to pick him up and cuddle him.

She snapped out of it when it was Prince Camcietti's turn to move on. She giggled to herself at the thought of him tripping over as he walked the three steps to the seat on his right. But he stood up and bowed to the audience and strolled to Bakta's throne, grandly sitting down and giving the crowd his trademark smile and wave. The auditorium erupted in laughter yet again at the prince's antics. Bakta, with a rare genuine smile on his face, quickly shuffled him back to his correct seat.

At last, it was Princess Tauriar's turn.

This simple act of standing up, bowing, walking three steps and sitting down again had been practised in her mind a thousand times.

Bakta the Overseer called to her, 'Princess of the great

house of Tauriar, stand before your nation and celebrate your onward journey.'

Tauriar froze. Her brain and legs felt in complete disharmony. A million eyes pinned her to her seat. She could feel her world falling apart.

Then Prince Camcietti appeared in front of her. He reached for her tiny hand and with his thumb and forefinger gently raised it, drawing her into a standing position. He then bowed to her, so deeply his forehead was on the rosewood floor, and remained there still as the night.

Princess Tauriar looked forward, bowed deeply to the assembly, took three steps and sat gracefully down in the next chair. The crowd clapped and cheered the youngest princess.

Bakta approached and stood behind her, his hands resting lightly on her shoulders. He waited for quiet.

'And now the part of the ceremony that I know many of you have been waiting for—the selection of the new Prince to occupy the vacant seat. It seems like only yesterday we named this lovely young lady,' Again, Tauriar's pale complexion darkened. 'And here we are today celebrating her first step towards our ruling council,' He moved back to the centre of the stage and the ceremony continued.

Tauriar smiled as ghostly images appeared around her on the stage, proud parents with beautiful baby boys from around the provinces. The holograms zoomed in so only the babies' heads were in view. She reached out to touch the one closest to her, who was showing his frustration at being awakened at what must have been nighttime in his province.

Bakta walked to the front of the stage to make the final decision known.

'And, the new Prince Ventar will be... Kalter of family Camerra!'

The holograph of the happy parents glided to the front of

the stage with the same frustrated baby who now, as though working to a script, ceased crying and started smiling.

Everyone was on their feet now, cheering for the new prince, as was Tauriar, though this time she had managed to stand up on her own.

With the ceremony over the Princess sat back in her seat and watched as everyone started mingling—a mixture of small talk, laughing and hugging. She was perceptive for a ten-year-old, though, and could see cracks in the glossy veneer the leaders of her country were trying to maintain.

Everything was far from okay.

Bala Verceti was at war with Trun Rizontella.

The two nations of Preenasette had been for hundreds of years—Princess Tauriar knew this. Her Life Team had taught her the history of it. The shameful period in Bala Verceti's history. The creation of the High Council, all those years ago by the very first Elder, Lord Camcietti, so that those mistakes could never happen again.

But over the last year, the war had turned ugly. Tauriar had overheard her elders referring to it. Even Bakta had said the Royals were in danger.

But today wasn't the day to worry about such things. And, what could she, a ten-year-old girl, do anyway? She had a puppy that needed her attention. Leave the war to the adults.

She turned to see Prince Camcietti pulling another face at her. She laughed loudly and pulled a face back at him.

* * *

AMDORMA COULDN'T BELIEVE IT. They had chosen. The result would be the biggest coup in the KBS's three hundred year history. And it was all down to him.

Too old am I? Should be put out to pasture? I'll show you all at

11

*tonight's meeting, and this news will prove that I, Amdorma, am still
an important, influential officer.*

He was too excited to go straight home. He went to the
Feathered Fig and ordered a dark ale, drinking it much too
quickly. He ordered another.

Two hours later and he was bragging about the great,
mysterious news he had had today. Annoying everyone
around him.

He sat down, feeling dizzy.

Oh dear, too much ale.

He was feeling a burning in his chest, tightness. Then pains
in his arms, neck and jaw. The realisation something was
wrong came over him.

But the feeling didn't last long. The old man rested his head
in his arms on the table, took one more short breath, and
was gone.

It was a while before the folk around him noticed something was amiss.

Poor old Amdorma was dead. And, for the time being at
least, his great news would go to his grave with him.

CHAPTER 2

𝒯he Council Decision
Preenasette - Bala Verceti - 2000

THE BALA VERCETI HIGH COUNCIL sat facing each other around
the circular graphite table in the Pre-eminent Chamber, high
up in the south tower of the Palace of Ancestors. The old cream
marble walls and floors tried hard to give this forbidding room
a simple and unpretentious feel, but didn't quite make it. Not
even the fantastic view through the curved glass recess in the
southern wall could get their interest today. The view of the
town sweeping down to the sea, with the Needles stretching
out to the horizon, would need to wait for another day.

'We must decide, council. The Trun now hold the upper
hand. The threats we are facing are tangible and many. We can
delay no longer.'

Bakta sat back, fingers caressing his Overseer's amulet. His
gaze moved around the table, fixing slowly on each of the other
six assembled council members. To his right, the Military High
Commander, Kam Major and to his left Cascan Ofier, first

minister of the Civil Council. Opposite him the four High Councillors, decision makers of Bala Verceti.

Bakta turned to Kam Major, giving her the floor.

'The Overseer is correct.' The weight of the decision in front of them was draining her; the proud officer being chosen as High Commander of the Vercetian military seemed a distant memory. 'My forces are stretched to the limit. The status quo we have been maintaining for decades has shifted violently against us. We are in grave danger of losing this war. They are blatantly targeting our Royals. They want to destabilise our system of government. Two attempts in the last month alone thwarted, but we were lucky, incredibly lucky with the attempt on the young prince. The explosive device was found by pure chance. We now suspect the Trun of having infiltrated nearly every aspect of our society. We don't know who to trust. I cannot, hand on heart, guarantee their safety in the current climate.' She dropped her head even further.

'This is not your fault, Kam Major.' Bakta placed his hand on his friend's shoulder. 'We, collectively, are responsible for the plight Bala Verceti now faces. Our enemy has shown an unprecedented level of ingenuity and brutality over the last couple of years.' He moved his hand away, and turned to his left, looking at Cascan Ofier.

'The Civil Council also believes the time has come for action, though I think it is a disastrous idea to consider sending the Royals off world.' The politician's superior tone grated on Bakta as usual. 'Many think talk of this is premature, but the vote to ratify this decision—should the High Council decide this path of action—has been carried.'

The room went silent for a moment. Kam Major looked back at Bakta, her moment of weakness now ebbing away and she forced a grim smile. Bakta's attention turned to the four High Councillors opposite. Bana Domeriette, the eldest and newly elected leader of the council. Bana Camiette, now only one step away from wearing the white robe and assuming leadership. Bana Tauriar. And Bana Ventar, the youngest councillor and only a few days into the job.

The four Councillors sat with hands clasped and eyes closed, readying to debate telepathically. Only Bakta joined the group, capturing their thought packages for public record.

"SURELY, we cannot consider letting the Royal Trainees out of our influence? Mine is only a baby, chosen only three days ago," thought Ventar.

"You still have much to learn. The Royals won't be completely out of our minds sight." Tauriar replied.

"Correct. Our focus here must concentrate on what the possible outcomes are likely to be during the next decade and the safety of our Royals. The Trun spy network in our country is more entrenched and active than we had ever thought. The Royals do not yet possess the skills we have. They must be protected and allowed to develop and learn in readiness for the High Council," Domeriette added.

"And we must focus on how we can use our psychic abilities to redress the balance of the war," Camcietti said.

Tauriar continued, "We aren't ready for that, the necessary skills still need much work. And should we even use this power? We haven't concluded the ethical debate yet."

"We need to complete both of these tasks, and quickly," Domeriette replied.

"Precisely. Our long-term efforts to broker peace lie in ruins. This latest aggression is unlike any previous Trun campaign. Kam Major is correct, the tide is turning irretrievably against us. We need to prepare. Plan a strategy and implement it. Domeriette, as our new Elder, the final decision rests with you," Camcietti concluded.

"Thank you for reminding me, Camcietti. We have debated this for many months, and we know our outgoing Elders thoughts on the matter. Now is the time to take action. I have decided, and I recommend to you all, that we dispatch our three youngest Royals to safe and secret off-world locations. Princess Domeriette, our eldest princess, will remain here. We need her psychic abilities. The two princes and the younger princess must be sent away for their protection, and to preserve our culture if the worst was to happen. Eight to ten years should suffice. We will have stabilised the situation we are in by then. Are you in favour, councillors?" Domeriette asked.

"Agreed. Though I will miss helping my young prince grow up," Ventar said.

"Agreed. The time has come for decisive action. In the right location and with a skilled Life Team their training can be every bit as thorough as if they were here," Tauriar offered.

"Agreed. Though I'm glad I don't have that decision to make yet. The Royals' journeys and the planets they will settle on could be fraught with dangers," from Camiette.

"Ten more years and you will, and yes, there will be dangers. But there may be great adventures as well. We must now be decisive and push on. I'm confident we will be able to bring this conflict to a peaceful conclusion. But as Ventar said, more work is needed. We just need more time." said Domeriette.

CHANCELLOR BANA DOMERIETTE opened her eyes, placed her hands in her lap and smiled. 'Thank you for your patience.'

'Bakta, Have you captured our complete discussions?' He nodded. Domeriette continued, 'We want you to prepare the three youngest Royals for evacuation to safe havens.' The look of relief was evident on Bakta's face, but he remained silent.

'Kam Major. You shall continue to marshal the defence of our nation. We need to keep the Trun at bay for the foreseeable future. There is no one in the realm more suited to this task,. Kam Major's face gave nothing away, but her posture and shoulders straightened noticeably. 'Please implement as soon as possible the second of the three evacuation plans you have proposed to us. The element of surprise is imperative.'

'Cascan Ofier, please relay our decision to the Civil Council and thank them for their support.'

'In the meantime, we shall evaluate possible new strategies for the defence of Bala Verceti.'

CHAPTER 3

he Attack
   Preenasette - Trun Space - 2000

THE SPACE DOCK ATTARRI 6 duty officer rubbed his eyes and looked at the screen again.

Still there.

A wave of craft heading from Vercetian space in numbers not seen in his twenty years at this station.

He glanced around the control room of the ageing maintenance and overhaul space dock, seeing his colleagues moving away from their stations to view mimic screens, the quiet now turning into a low hum.

He hit the analysis button, and his screen started lighting up with little orange tags attached to the white dots that were marching relentlessly towards him. Three battle cruisers were tagged. The first one was spearheading the Armada and the others moving to each flank. The next tags identified twelve bifighters: six deployed to the spearhead cruiser and three each to the flanks. Finally, fifteen delta spheres were bringing up the rear. He hit the second button to confirm what he already suspected. The orange projection lines from the cruisers slowly moved off in three differing directions, but the predictive arcs they followed all converged at the same point—Attarri 6.

The duty officer opened communications. 'Central Command, do you see this?' The space dock commander and a small group of his co-workers now standing over his shoulder, also trying very hard to take in the current situation. 'A Vercetian fleet comprising thirty vessels, three of which are battle cruisers. The current course confirmed as being inbound to Space Dock 6.' One of the cruisers now erupted with a plethora of tiny white dots cascading from its core. 'Wait, the left flank cruiser is now deploying arrows.' He paused and looked at his commanding officer who gave him an approving nod. He continued, 'Awaiting your instructions.'

* * *

CENTRAL COMMAND DUTY OFFICER ANTON PILZ viewed the flurry of information bombarding the peripheral screens in the Main Control Hub—the heart of the massive space station in geosynchronous orbit over Trun.

His team was rapidly transferring information onto the 3D holo-projection system. Segments of the display came into focus, occupying the centre of the hub, processing massive amounts of data. With the view of the Vercetian armada came the darkness of the surrounding space, contrasting with the lightness of the peripheral work zones. An amphitheatre was playing out a drama in space with a ring of technicians as the audience. First, the central battle cruiser appeared, a floating grey image quickly finding its definition, a technological sculpture enacted at blindingly fast speed. Moments later the other shapes appeared, replicating the vessels thousands of miles away. Soon the whole picture was complete.

The spaceport officer's assessment appeared accurate, thought Pilz. 'Launch your fighters to engage the arrows, then lock down the station. Full defensive mode. A squadron will be with you shortly.'

'Understood, central command.'

Pilz hastily gave the orders to dispatch the standby squadron. Another quick message appraised his superiors of the situation. The Supreme Commander was on the space station carrying out a scheduled review. He would be much too close for comfort.

In no time at all the Supreme Commander's voice broke through the flurry of activity in central command. 'Officer Pilz, report current status.'

'A Verceti armada is on course to arrive at Space Dock Attarri 6 in twenty-five minutes. Three battle cruisers, twelve bifighters and fifteen delta spheres. Fifteen arrows have been already launched by one of the cruisers, with the other two deploying more as we speak. I've instructed the station to dispatch all available 3W fighters to engage and then proceed with lockdown protocol. Squadron XB3 is readying for immediate deployment. Estimated time of arrival thirty two minutes.' Pilz took a deep breath, feeling that he'd been efficient enough in his assessment of the situation. Supreme Commander Zander ruled with a rod of iron, and everyone felt his wrath at some point or another.

'I'll be there presently,' Zander said.

A few minutes later he entered the hub, his bright red cape flowing gracefully behind him, exposing the ebony black lightweight body armour he always wore. His head cap captured the dancing lights emanating from the peripheral screens and brought out the hue dark of aquamarine that most Trun naturally had.

Pilz handed his control station to one of his sub-officers and stood up for a better view of the fleet. The vessels appeared to be stationary, the only movement being the smaller ships drifting away from the cruisers. He watched Zander stroll into the swirling mass of ghostly apparitions perhaps to try and get into the head of the Vercetian commander and fathom out the real intent of the attack formation. All around him the arrows were leaving the cruisers, blinking out of existence as they reached the outer limit of the holographic domain. Pilz watched him stop and contemplate a bifighter tactical twin-cannon ship. Zander waved his hand gently through it, perhaps with admiration. These were formidable ships, light, agile and heavily armed. The Trun would have them soon; their spy network in Verceti had recently stolen the plans. The remainder of the fleet was made up of silver delta spheres, fifteen of them. *An odd choice*, Pilz thought. They were modestly armed and not what you would consider attack ships. More suited to long range reconnaissance. He wondered if the Supreme Commander would pick up on that.

Zander joined Pilz and instructed him to recalibrate the holographic view to include the space dock. Pilz sent a whispered message via his face communicator and the view of the fleet pulled back until the complete saga could be seen unfolding.

Commander Dori Mancer appeared on the other side of the Supreme Commander.

'What is happening, Domantry? This aggression is most unlike the Vercetians. And why on this facility?'

Zander's number two clasped the barrier rail with large calloused hands that had seen more military action than any other Trun. He leant forward, struggling to focus on the armada, well aware that his old body was failing him in so many ways. But he still had the respect and admiration of his men and was determined to see his young prodigy succeed in the top military job. That job had never interested him. He was a leader of men and an astute strategist, but in his heart, he was a fighter, happy to be in the thick of it with his troops.

'What is their intent? I can't see the rationale behind this attack.'

'I agree,' replied Zander.

Pilz couldn't resist joining in; it was rare to be in such company. 'Why so many delta spheres?' He kept his gaze straight forward.

'My thoughts exactly,' the Supreme Commander replied and then went completely silent. A minute later he turned to Pilz. 'How many of our TW Spheres have we available for immediate deployment?'

After another whispered message, Pilz replied in a very nervous voice. 'Six, sir,' desperately aware that he had given the order to proceed with some unscheduled maintenance work and many were unavailable.

'Only six!' roared Mancer, turning to confront Pilz directly. 'Is that all?'

'Dispatch them immediately,' Zander interrupted, 'and let's hope for your sake that that is enough!'

he First Trials 1
Zerot - 200 Years Earlier

BIRJJIKK STRODE into the combat arena and glared up at the Elders. They were ignoring her, talking in small groups, backs to her. Their murmuring created a dull drone that reverberated around the cavern.

She was sure they were enjoying having her fate in their hands, deciding who would fail and who would progress forward in the First Trials of Academy 188.

She continued into the centre, stepping around chunks of flesh and patches of blood.

My comrades have been busy. But I shall be busier. I shall drench this cavern in blood. The Elders shall no have reason to fail me.

She stood there in the silence.

How long will they keep me waiting?

The celestial monoliths that adorned this place of death looked down on her. They would wait. They had watched and waited for thousand of years. Today's carnage would be a tiny drop of what they had witnessed.

But, they haven't seen me.

Birjjikk's concentration sharpened as the Elders began taking their seats and a hush fell over the arena. Judgment would now begin.

She checked her weapons and took a deep breath. She was ready.

* * *

THE CREAKING of rusty hinges broke the silence. In semi-darkness, Birjjikk's opponents were herded into the pens, gates slammed shut behind them. She couldn't make out the shadowy figures, but she could smell their fear.

The pen on her left opened and into the light a white beast appeared—a Shantra Bear.

It immediately moved back into the shadows and sauntered around the perimeter of the arena, its eyes fixed on her. It moved slowly in the oppressive heat. The beast stopped at an object previously unseen by Birjjikk, and with its massive paw flicked it from out of the shadows into the light.

It was the mutilated body of one of her Academy. Judging by the slim torso, it looked like Garkkikk.

Had the bear done that?

Blood was still evident on the fur around its mouth and long white fangs.

Is it showing me my fate?

A second gate opening to her right caught her attention.

Four small feline animals entered the arena: Tagras. The animals' prominent burning red eyes locked onto her; their yellow fangs bared. One began stalking her with the others following its lead, black and white striped fur looking magnificent and menacing against the dull granite walls.

Birjjikk was aware of her vulnerability, positioned directly between the felines and the bear. She stepped backwards bringing both into view, and in doing so exposing the line of sight between the bear and the Tagras. The first of the felines paused momentarily, assessing this new threat.

The pause was all Birjjikk needed.

She sheathed her sword and unclipped the scissor blades from her belt. With one eye still watching the bear, she coiled her body, then threw the blade set at the lead Tagra. She watched its trajectory and willed a minor directional adjustment. As the point of contact approached she initiated the scissor action, the blades flashing together in the dull light, slicing off its leg.

Perfect technique—that will impress.

As the Tagra crashed to the ground, howling, Birjjikk drew her sword and set her stance. The remaining Tagras were momentarily in disarray. The bear was still pacing, moving into the arena now, trying to get to her blind side. The three remaining felines regrouped and charged at her.

Birjjikk pointed her left arm at them and from her forearm armour guard released a spray of small steel darts. Not designed to kill, but to disorientate and infuriate. With the same hand, she reached for her dagger.

My speed is my greatest weapon.

A dart close to its eye had severely impeded one of the Tagras, but the others, now wilder with fury, were in full flight. They leapt. But Birjjikk jumped higher. From above she drove her dagger straight down at the one nearest to her. The blade struck its neck but lacked penetration; she had misjudged the distance. Cursing her sloppy technique and sure that the Elders would have noticed, she landed back on her feet, facing the impeded feline that had only just reached her. It met the fury of her sword. She spun around and drove her sword into the staggering Tagra, hoping the Elders would think that was her plan all along. The third Tagra had overrun, directly towards the advancing bear. It tried to turn but, lacking purchase, couldn't escape the bear's lunge.

Birjjikk stared into the bear's eyes, then at the feline pinned under its massive paw. The bear stared back, baring its teeth, challenging her.

Kill it then, beast, was her first thought, thrown at the bear with raging venom.

The bear started. There'd been a reaction, its eyes widened, then narrowed again.

A perceptive animal? *Am I in your mind, beast?*

She focused. *Kill it.* She pointed straight at the struggling Tagra.

The bear looked down at the stunned feline, then back at Birjjikk. It stood up on its back legs and roared.

Birjjikk wrestled with the beast's will, sweat forming on her forehead.

Kill it, beast.

It roared again, louder.

Kill it, beast. Now!

It slammed its paw down hard, talons sinking deep into the Tagra's neck. The Tagra screamed. A scream that slowly abated as the life left its body.

The bear looked at Birjjikk again, this time, a questioning stare.

Stay. Get down.

The bear relaxed. A puppet with its strings severed, the tension gone from its body, its front paws remaining draped over its limp trophy.

You are mine.

She recovered her dagger, then strode to the whimpering Tagra with the missing leg. She kicked it to one side, enjoying the feeling of inflicting extra pain on the pitiful animal, picked up her scissor blades, attached them to her belt and returned to the centre of the arena. She looked defiantly at the Elders, awaiting the next challenge.

CHAPTER 5

*T*he Battle
Preenasette - Trun Space - 2000

PILZ WATCHED the Vercetian armada close in on the spaceport like the three pronged claw of the Rizontella desert scorpion. The Trun fighters and the arrows were playing cat and mouse with each other, bright flashes blinking on then off as they took hits on their protective shielding—dancing hors d'oeuvres as the prelude to the approaching heavy artillery.

He was still standing with Zander and Mancer, desperately hoping that the delta spheres had little importance in this unfolding game. The three-pronged attack was centred on the far side of the spaceport, forcing the Trun squadron to travel further before joining the battle. They would also be met by a flanking cruiser before they could engage with the main force.

The bifighters broke off from the cruisers and began attacking the spaceport shield. The cruisers were yet to join the fray.

'This isn't right,' exclaimed Zander. 'There's no conviction in the Vercetians attack.'

'None at all,' Mancer added.

Pilz moved to the side as the two men delved into the enemy's tactical errors. 'The cruisers should be firing now.'

'The space dock's shield generators are vulnerable, but they're ignoring them.'

'The bifighters aren't coordinated.'

'The spheres are playing no part.'

A sub-officer came running up to them and addressed Zander. 'Supreme Commander. We are getting unconfirmed reports from Bala Verceti of unusual activity around the Life Teams. Nothing firm just yet, but it appears they may have left the planet.'

'It's a ploy,' Zander said through clenched teeth.

One of the delta spheres peeled off and headed away from the spaceport and the planet. Twenty seconds later another followed it.

'The Life Teams may be aboard the Delta Spheres,' said Mancer.

'They're heading for wormhole Prefaxi 3.' Pilz was relaying information from his sub-officer. 'Estimated time of arrival of first ship ten minutes at current speed.'

By now there was a row of spheres all following the same path at regular distances apart. Their positioning now revealing a sophisticated subplot—chaos into order—en route to the wormhole.

'It appears that all fifteen are entering.' Pilz knew he was stating the obvious. Zander gave him a sharp look. 'Twenty-eight minutes and they'll all be through,' he continued lamely.

'Get our spheres through there immediately,' Zander growled. Nothing else was small enough and appropriately equipped for wormhole travel. 'Who is first Sphere Commander? Get him, now! And make sure Squadron Commander Dag gets our spheres through safely.'

The Trun Squadron approached the space dock. Dag now with new orders to deposit the spheres safely into the wormhole. Pilz could now see that the Vercetian cruiser's primary role wasn't spearheading the attack, but was to back up whichever flank the Trun squadron took. Clever. Now Dag was on screen discussing tactics with Zander and Mancer. Pilz knew his position was redundant with both his bosses here. He could see their squadron begin to sweep to the aft side of the space dock, following a path that would skirt around the flanking Vercetian battle cruiser. He glanced up at one of the trajectory screens, which confirmed what he was anticipating. They were forming a corridor, by pinning the Vercetian fleet against the spaceport. It allowed the Trun spheres to travel around the outside and pick up the route to the wormhole.

The one problem with this, or any other strategy that he could think of, was that soon the two fleets would be broadsiding each other, and the result of that could be messy. The spheres would never have made the wormhole in Trun space without this impressive backup, and the Vercetian cruisers and bifighters were there to make sure they did, at any cost. He picked up on a conversation between the sphere commander and Zander.

'Commander Courtier reporting, sir. What are your instructions?'

'Are your ships and your officers ready for some possibly long term interstellar space travel?' Zander asked bluntly.

'Yes, they are, High Commander.' Courtier replied.

'Good. Commander, get to Prefaxi 32 as quickly as the squadron can get you all through. You are then to follow six of the Vercetian spheres. We suspect four of them are carrying the high council Royals. The rest are decoys. We anticipate that they will all, ultimately, head in differing directions, to confuse and randomise their ion trails. You're playing a numbers game, but, providing the Royals are in separate ships, the odds are in your favour to pick at least one of them.'

Mancer added, 'The Vercetian fleet are going to throw everything they have at ours to slow your progress. Be patient, when you do get through you should have time to pick up their trails. Trust in your judgment when choosing. Good luck.'

* * *

THE TRUN SQUADRON XB3 consisted of two TC cruisers—slightly smaller than the enemy's, but much more manoeuvrable, and ten TB carriers—half the size of a cruiser, but highly weaponised and each carrying four 3W fighters. The six TW Spheres were now in pursuit, rapidly playing catch up with the squadron.

All ten of the carriers launched their fighters. A swarming mass of flying bugs forming a spearhead in the direction the corridor would take. The space dock fighters broke off from their personal encounters with the arrows and headed to join them.

The two TC cruisers and seven of the carriers veered away to follow the swarm of fighters. They would ultimately form the corridor wall. The remaining carriers held their ground to ward off the now advancing Vercetian arrows and also, so Pilz assumed, pick up the TW Spheres when they arrived and shepherd them towards the wormhole. Further into space, the lead Vercetian sphere was approaching the wormhole. It slowed down just before entering. There was a small flash as it opened and blinked closed.

Zander, Mancer and Pilz stood looking down at the slow motion jigsaw puzzle forming before their eyes. Pilz could see that the delta spheres were nearly safe and well on their way to escaping. The Vercetian armada could retreat now, but instead, they were setting themselves up for a fight. They must need more time, he assumed, not just for the escape, but maybe more time for the spheres to affect some dispersal plan at the far end of the wormhole. Or, they had become aware of the Trun spheres and were trying to stop them. As the remaining vessels moved into place, the scene was set for one of the largest space battles any of them—except Mancer—would have ever witnessed. The three of them would now have little influence on the action, the vessel commanders, space station techs and the raft of tactical computers now taking full charge.

The Trun squadron was ready first. The TC cruisers and TB carriers creating a two tier wall from the spaceport away in the direction of the wormhole. Between the two levels, an infill of fighters hovered in anticipation, their main work still to be done. Finally, the three remaining carriers, each with two TW Spheres under shield protection, started their dangerous journey through the makeshift turkey shoot. The central command centre techs held their nerve, not yet wanting to provoke the enemy. The longer the Vercetians held off firing the further the three surrogate mother ships would be able to advance safely with their precious cargo.

The Vercetians must have thought the same, for as soon as the second of its enormous battle cruisers slotted into its designated place, broadside on, it opened fire. A perfect line of twenty small glowing red globes released along its length, lime green tails forming behind them. The vivid colours began to light up the holo-deck. The cannon banks discharged immediately and again a third time. Pilz watched the rows of globes form, the second and third globes desperately hanging on to the tails in front. They grouped into three distinct spearheads, directed at the nearest TC cruiser and two carriers. The pedestrian speed at which they appeared to travel within the holo environment belied the spectacular colour show that ensued when they eventually smashed into the target ships. Streaks of

35

red and green lightning forks shot in all directions, briefly displaying the full expanse of the protective shielding around each ship.

Pilz could make out the canon banks on their vessels glowing red, an ominous precursor to their participation in the battle. Moments later triple volleys of bright red energy globes with the same characteristic green tails were making their way towards the Vercetian battle cruiser. Within moments the fighters and the arrows filled the void between the two protagonists' artillery, ignoring each other now, their role being to destroy the globes, targeting the lead ones first with decisive blue laser strikes. These attacks, together with the flashes of exploding globes produced a silent orgy of colour on the holo-deck.

The Trun battalion was forced to hold its rigid defensive formation, unable to break the barrier of shields in front of the advancing three carriers. The Venetians however, were much more flexible. The bifighters, able to roam at will, were targeting the shields of the ships that were actively protecting the carriers. And the fighters were far less efficient in neutralising their firepower.

The shield levels on each side were slowly decreasing. Zander kept looking up at the screen showing the status of the Trun fleet's shields, now getting seriously low. Its forced defensive posture, and the sheer firepower of the Vercetians was sealing their fate. He turned to Mancer. 'Our shields will fail first. I think we're going to lose this.'

Mancer paused, studying the holographic battle a few moments longer. 'Just hold on.' He looked up at the same screen Zander had been studying. 'I think our cruiser commander is trying something. Watch, he's changing his formation.'

* * *

Squadron Commander Dag Fallas shouted at Tech 13, 'Are you sure this will work?'

Forester Jerramii, designated Tech 13 replied, 'My tactical computer has confirmed my strategy, but we must act now.'

'Proceed. Please don't let me down, Forester.'

Forester gave an order to the tactical control matrix. 'Tactical computer 13 taking full control of all ship-wide manoeuvring. Authorisation Dax Fallas.' He could see Dax confirming the command as he finished punching in the interface request. Tactical 13 uploaded the new instructions.

* * *

Pilz watched the formation of the Trun Squadron alter subtly. The three carriers protecting the spheres formed a tight circle. The other ships moved around them. Rather than a thinly spread, two-dimensional, flat target for the Vercetian ships to attack, they were forming an elongated egg shape, with the pointy end facing the Vercetians, giving them a much smaller target to aim at. This narrow target meant only the nearest two Vercetian ships could mount an offensive—the other ships were hopelessly positioned and scrambling to get back in the game. Meanwhile, the Trun fighters surrounding the squadron were being very effective at neutralising the Vercetian's missiles.

It was smart, but Pilz doubted it would change the outcome, just prolong the waiting. The Trun held out for a surprisingly long time before the shielding finally began to fail.

First to fail was the lead cruiser and one of the carriers, both of whom had been taking the brunt of the recent offensive. The Vercetians attack immediately turned to both ships' weapons arrays, smashing into them with a previously unseen ferocity. The spectacular light show had changed to something far more sinister, as lightning white explosions sent chunks of weaponry flying off in all directions.

The other Vercetian vessels had finally taken up decent flanking positions and were bombarding the next wave of Trun carriers. The 3W fighters were in chaos, flying aimlessly about, firing with no conviction.

All seemed lost. But the Trun tactic had managed to buy enough time for the three rear carriers to position themselves such that they could release the six TW Spheres safely. Their natural speed would now ensure they got to the wormhole unmolested.

Pilz could make out a noticeable pause in the Vercetian attack. With the TW Spheres now lost to them, Pilz nervously awaited their next move. They had the Trun squadron at their mercy. To his surprise and relief, the Vercetian armada ceased all weapons fire and turned towards their space.

The light show in the centre of the central command hub was no more. The only sign of life now was the Vercetian arrows scuttling onto the three large cruisers. Zander signalled one of the technicians to shut down the holo-deck, and the images disappeared one chunk at a time.

CHAPTER 6

*J*on O'Malley
    Earth - The Republic of Ireland - 2002

JONATHAN O'MALLEY'S dream world began to disappear as he drifted into the start of a new day. He became aware of a piercing light invading his senses and buried his head in his pillow to shut the intruder out. Moments later his brain began to prise open his eyelids until he finally realised it was the sun's rays squeezing through a gap in the curtains. He jumped out of bed and flung them open. The weather had finally brightened up. The first week of the school summer holidays had been awful—wet and windy—but now the sun was shining, and the sky was blue.

He raced downstairs to where Moira was making breakfast. She was his nanny, or had been when he was younger, looking after him during the many times his parents were away working. Her job description nowadays was undefined, but she loved working there, and in Jon's mind she was part of the family.

He sat down and started devouring the scrambled eggs and bacon Moira had placed in front of him. She joined him, and they ate in a comfortable silence before she asked, 'So, where are you going today now the weather has changed? Football with the boys?' She knew the answer before she'd even asked the question.

'I think I'll be heading off on my bike. Any chance of a sandwich to take with me?'

'Already done and in your backpack,' she smiled.

* * *

JON LOVED HIS BIKE; it set him free.

Oh, he liked his schoolmates and was popular with them. It was just, well, they were always playing football, and it wasn't his thing. He wasn't a team player; always happier in his own company. And never more so than when he was riding his bike.

He made his way to the highest point of the woods on the eastern side of Harewood Hall. He loved it there. This Irish countryside was as dramatic as it was beautiful. His choice of routes to the valley below could be exhilaratingly fast, technically demanding or downright dangerous.

Jon looked down to see the old hall in the distance. He put his helmet on and closed his eyes for a moment. A gentle breeze kissed his cheeks, and the warmth of the rising sun radiated through his clothing. He visualised the route he was going to take: the gradients, the technical sections, the fast sections where he would let his machine fly free. He entered his cycling mindset. As he started down, he rose out of his saddle and felt his bike begin dancing over the rocks and tree roots, all carefully placed there by Mother Nature to unseat less worthy riders. His part in this addictive partnership of man and machine, was to choose a line, feather the brakes and trust in his bike.

Jon kept his body fluid in readiness for the steeper terrain. The obstacles trying to bring him off his bike came towards him at blindingly fast speed. He relaxed his arms and legs and could feel the bike's Marzocchi suspension begin to show its pedigree. His DiamondBack bike may have been a little dated but when new it was the best money could buy. His father had told him that the suspension was the same as that used in the Ferrari Formula 1 racing cars. It certainly was the most well balanced bike he'd ever ridden, and it felt like a Ferrari right now. The technical section eased off, and the route became a flatter but fast single track. He powered through the bike's gears to get maximum speed for an upcoming jump. As he hit it, he lifted off and floated through the air—time seeming to slow down as he felt tree branches flash by on either side of him. He sighted his landing point and relaxed further, letting his body and the Ferrari suspension cushion his landing. Before he knew it, he was at the bottom, the time taken to get down having now dissolved into a fusion of senses. His only desire now was to do it again.

By midday, he needed a break as three-quarters of his time was spent working hard to get back up the hill. The last effort had left his quads burning. Some food and rest were in order at his favourite relaxation place. Swan Pool, a lake within the grounds of the Harewood Hall.

CHAPTER 7

*A*manda Walker
Earth - The Republic of Ireland - 2002

AMANDA WALKER STOMPED out of the hall in a mood.

Nobody had any time for her. Grace had lessons. Her mum and dad were in deep discussions with the Squire—god knew about what. If they were old friends, why did they seem to be always working? Everyone else was busy with one thing or another. She'd heard Helen and Gordon promising the Squire that everything would be fully operational by this evening—whatever that was. She couldn't even play with Krankel; no one knew where he was.

She went to the workshop and found Peter busy at work on something electrical looking. She pulled out a chair next to him dramatically and slumped down onto it, sighing loudly.

'Good morning, Amanda. Did you get out of the other side of the bed today?' Peter asked.

'Wrong,' she replied.

'You did not?'

'No. Wrong side of the bed.' He was looking at her quizzically. 'It's, "did you get out of the wrong side of the bed," not other side.' He was always getting things slightly wrong.

'Ah, sorry. I'm still perfecting your language. We say other in Norwegian.' He smiled at her. 'And why are you in such a mood, young female?'

'Lady. Oh, forget it,' said Amanda. 'I'm bored. Everyone is busy.'

'We're all on a deadline to get the security system complete. The Squire says we're taking too long.' Peter pointed at her bike. 'Gordon has finished repairing your bicycle. Why not go for a ride on it?'

'Could do, I suppose. I could head down to the lake.'

'Good idea,' said Peter. 'You may bump into the young man who tends to visit the lake after he has been cycling in the woods.'

'The local boy?' said Amanda. 'You've mentioned him before. I'll be careful.'

Her bike was one of some old ones left here by the previous owners of Harewood Hall. Gordon had fixed one of them up for her—he'd even put a basket on the front. That, she liked.

She set off, gently to start off with, getting used to the bike. The paths near the hall were in good condition, but as she ventured further away they deteriorated, and she needed to be a little more careful. She could see the lake in the distance. She was enjoying her ride now.

As she approached the water, she noticed the boy. He was sitting on a grassy hill, gazing across the lake. He must have heard her as he turned around and looked straight at her. All she could make out at this distance was his untidy black hair. She decided to ride by him and give him a scornful look. She might even challenge him to find out what he was doing here on private land.

Unfortunately, she was watching him and not where she was going.

She felt the front wheel dip down and stop instantly, a large pothole making her grind to a halt. With the rear of the bike starting to rise, she found herself looking down towards the pothole. She felt her body rising above her, her legs now high in the air and her hair fanning down towards the ground. Her only thought was, *this is going to hurt.* And it did. After a complete pirouette in the air, which must have looked quite dramatic to the boy, she landed on the ground with a thud.

A moment later she opened her eyes and was greeted with a view of a blue sky full of little fluffy clouds. Spoiling the view, was the silhouette of the boy looking down at her, his scraggy hair plain to see, but his other features unclear.

'That was spectacular,' Amanda muttered, more to herself.

'Are you okay?' he asked.

'Yes, I think so.' For the moment she felt more embarrassed that physically hurt, but it didn't take long to realise she was. 'My ankle—ouch.'

He tentatively reached out his hand. 'Here, let me help.'

She sat up, reached out, took his hand and managed to get up, bearing her weight on her good foot. She carefully tried her other foot, but it was having none of it. 'Sorry, I can't walk. Let me sit down for a while and try again in a bit.'

He stepped back, and she was able to get a better look at him. He was tall and slim, though he looked strong. He wasn't what you would call handsome. His mouth sloped to one side, and his nose had come second best in a fight or something. His jet-black hair seemed to have a mind of its own, growing in all different directions. But his striking blue eyes brought it all together, making him not altogether unpleasant looking.

He knelt down and started undoing the laces of her shoe. 'I'm Jonathan. Pleased to meet you.' She winced as he gently removed her shoe.

She looked directly at him. 'Amanda,' she said. 'I'm staying up at the hall. My parents are visiting. They're old friends of Squire.' She looked down at her foot. 'You should have left my shoe. It stops the swelling.'

'Mmm, you're probably right. I can put it back on if you prefer.'

'No, that's all right,' she liked his singsong Irish accent. 'What are you doing here? This land is private, and you've caused me to crash.'

'I may have distracted you, but this fellow,' he pointed at the hole in the ground, 'is the bad boy here. So why didn't you try to ride around it?' His wry smile softened the crookedness of his mouth.

'You should be aware, sir, that I am a guest here, and you are trespassing,' Her rigid posture was now looking a little staged. 'And you still haven't answered my question.'

'I ride in the hills over there,' Jon replied.

'On that old thing?' Amanda looked down at his mud stained bike. 'It doesn't even have a basket on the front.'

'No, but it does have two wheels that work.' He was looking across to Amanda's very poorly-looking front wheel. 'I slip through the fence to relax and enjoy this view. God's work, I think, not the Squire's.'

* * *

JON RIGGED up his bike with a sling hanging from the handlebars to support Amanda's leg. He helped her on, slipped her injured leg through the support and started to walk her back to Harewood Hall.

'This will be the closest I've ever been to the hall, what's it like inside?'

'It's big,' Amanda replied. 'And full of old fashioned furniture and paintings everywhere. My father's friend bought this place at the beginning of the year. He comes from Norway, or somewhere, with his wife, daughter and servants. Their daughter's name is Grace. She's a year or so older than me, but she's not allowed out yet. Been ill or something.

Jon listened as Amanda chatted away about this and that. He was getting tired. The path to the hall was slightly uphill. He noticed one of the groundsmen putting up what appeared to be a lamppost. 'Strange place to put a light,' he said.

Amanda looked over to where it was being erected, in the middle of a small thicket of trees. 'Who knows. They've been putting them up everywhere, she said. 'Oh, there's Krankel.'

Jon froze. Standing directly in their path was the biggest dog he'd ever seen. It had the look and colouring of an arctic wolf, mostly white, but flecked with dark hair, giving it a dirty appearance. Its ears pointed upwards, showing acute attentiveness, and it had extraordinary sapphire blue eyes. It must have been taller than a Great Dane. It stared at Jon, apprehensiveness bordering on aggression. Jon stepped back instinctively, exposing Mandy to the dog.

'Krankel, you great big ball of fluff. Come here.'

Krankel's gaze softened, and he lumbered over to Mandy. Jon could now see more grey-brown wispy streaks in his white coat. Mandy leant over and put her arms around the dog's neck and hugged him. 'Did the naughty boy frighten you Krankel? Yes, yes, he is a mean naughty boy.' She looked back at Jon with a big smile on her face.

'What is that?' Jon asked. 'It's massive.'

'His name is Krankel. He's Grace's dog. Apparently, he's a rare breed from northern Sweden or somewhere like that, and he's one of the biggest ever seen. Aren't you Krankel? You're a big boy, aren't you? Stroke him, Jon.'

Jon stroked the dog's off white crown, an action that seemed to please them both, then continued leading Mandy to the hall.

As they approached the grand arched door with faded brass fittings, it opened, and a couple appeared that Jon guessed were Amanda's parents. Krankel, seeing the door open, sloped inside.

'Amanda, darling, what have you done?' her mother asked.

'I fell off my bike. My foot is swollen... it hurts.'

Amanda's father picked her up in his arms. 'There, there, darling, we'll soon get you sorted. Who is the young man?'

'Careful with her dear.'

'I'm Jon, sir.'

A short man with short spiky hair came out. His stocky demeanour gave him an air of authority. His penetrating stare made Jon feel guilty. He remembered he'd been trespassing.

'Thank you, Jon,' Amanda's father said.

The short man's manner softened. 'And I thank you too, Jon. That was excellent of you to bring Amanda back here. I'd invite you in but I'm afraid the house is in chaos at the moment with work going on, but if you'd like to pop over tomorrow at lunchtime we can thank you properly for rescuing Amanda, and you can meet my daughter Grace as well.'

'Thank you, sir. I'll look forward to it.' Jon's immediate and confident reply surprised even himself. 'Amanda's bike is still down by the lake. The wheel is rather buckled.'

'I can get that, Squire,' offered a man who was standing no more that two metres directly behind Jon. As Jon turned, the man's gaze met his. His smile was broad, but there was a look— just for an instant—was it suspicion, or was it something more?

'If you would Peter, please do,' the Squire said. 'And take it to Gordon to see if he can repair it. Will one o'clock be all right, Jon?'

Jon nodded and jumped on his bike a little too quickly, nearly stumbling. 'One o'clock it is.' And with a final glance at Amanda he headed off back into the woods.

CHAPTER 8

*P*rof. *& Mrs. Walker*
Earth - England - 2002

THE DOOR CLOSED BEHIND THEM, and Professor George Walker carried Amanda away to find Lady Gwyneth to attend to her ankle.

'Just a local boy.' Ann Walker turned to Squire Douglas Faulkner. 'Shouldn't be of any concern.'

'I agree,' he said. 'The work to secure the hall and grounds will be finished by this evening.'

Ann smiled and went to find her injured daughter, leaving Douglas Faulkner in the grand entrance hall. He looked around at the flurry of activity and paused to reflect on the last four months since they'd arrived in this system. In a few hours, they would finally be secure and fully hidden within Earth's society. The hall and grounds' cloaking system would hide any trace of their alien nature, acting as a defensive shield against any assault and entirely concealing the sphere that had brought them here, visually and from any Trun detection methods.

They wouldn't have got to this point without the help of Prof. and Mrs. Walker.

* * *

PRIME REMEMBERED their arrival in this solar system. After a cramped two-year journey, they had made a base near a giant asteroid about 60,000,000 miles away and began studying Earth. They dispatched two probes. One was positioned close to the planet, attaching itself to a redundant satellite. This probe was a data gatherer and would start sweeping the world's databases. The second was a relay booster positioned halfway between the planet and the sphere.

The first thing they needed to address was their physical differences from Earth's indigenous population. Earth was not the first possible destination on their journey. Their direction of travel had taken them past several planets that had suitable ecological conditions. They had spent time at two of them but decided they were undesirable. Earth was the first that had evolved on a similar course to Preenasette, with Homo Sapiens becoming the dominant species. Near identical atmospheric pressures meant they were of similar stature. Many of their differences—their slender form, smaller nose and ears, and their head cap—could be altered with some solid holographic manipulation. A padded suit that would look and feel like the real thing. Hiding protruding bits was a whole different game and thankfully would not need addressing. But the holographic process was only able to deal with primary colours and a few subgroups. Replicating the wealth of colours that made up skin tone would require serious effort to find a solution. Then, and only then would they appear human.

While the Life Team looked into refining their appearance, the ship's Artificial Intelligence began the task of gathering vast amounts of information. Languages, cultures, history, economics, everything required to form a gigantic snapshot of this planet. Pertinent information was then filtered and compressed into manageable data packages, tailored to the specialities of each of the Life Team members. The data packets —the size of a fingernail—were surgically inserted into the back of the neck. Tiny, preprogrammed access conduits then weaved their way to the requisite parts of the brain, allowing neural access to the database. It required some weeks for the information source to be entirely integrated. Unfortunately, all the information in the world wouldn't produce a human replica that would merge seamlessly into Earth's society. They were still missing many characteristics—the human touch. Anyone seeing their first attempts would find them decidedly comical. Downloaded entertainment such as 'Mork and Mindy' had shown them that. They needed more help to become, or appear to become, human. That's where Prof. and Mrs. Walker came in.

Bala Prime, or Douglas Faulkner as he would come to be known, leader of Princess Tauriar's Life Team, set the parameters for an algorithm the ship's AI would use to select possible candidates to help them. 'Find me a male and female couple of a mature age range, say between thirty-five and fifty-five of their years. I want proof of compassion towards their fellow humans. Reasonable IQs, in the seventy to eighty percentile. A reasonable level of affluence, same percentile range. Proceed.' Moments later the AI responded. '0.4652% of population: 16,457,000 couples,' Prime scratched his chin; they must be very cramped down there. 'Continue filter. An interest in astronomy.' *After all, they would be meeting real aliens*, he thought. 'And political influence would be useful. Narrow down percentile bandwidth further as well, to get to fifty couples.' The AI duly accommodated and data packed their information into a temporary link. Prime leisurely reviewed each couple and shortlisted eight candidates. There was little to choose between them, but one couple stood out. They had something that none of the others had and that he should have filtered into his search much earlier on but didn't think to—a daughter of similar age to the Princess and a potential friend.

* * *

GEORGE WALKER, a professor of astrophysics, was always a believer. A believer that we are not alone. His study of the stars told him that there was life out there—the maths of probability confirmed it. An estimated two hundred billion stars in our galaxy. And of the nearly infinite number of planets circling them over four billion capable of sustaining life. The chances of a planet following the development path of Earth were close on endless. Life must be out there. But he was also a scientist and understood the vast distances between the stars and the limitations on travel within a lifetime. He believed they were out there, but that they were never destined to meet.

He met Ann Sotherby in Africa, during a gap year after he'd completed his doctorate. He was travelling, doing voluntary work and entered the Meheba refugee camp in Zambia and there she was. She was also travelling after having finished her Masters degree in Political Studies. They left there together three weeks later, and were never separated again.

* * *

ANN AND GEORGE WALKER were in the kitchen of their four-bed farmhouse in Ottershaw. just southwest of the M25. It was the first day of the Easter recess of the Houses of Parliament, and Ann Walker MP was enjoying a lovely day doing nothing and being as far away as possible from her London bolthole. She was reading the Times while George started their supper.

Their thirteen-year-old daughter Amanda was away having a weekend sleepover at a friend's house.

George finished preparing the meal and popped it into the oven, and was tidying when the doorbell rang. 'I'll get it,' he said. 'Are you expecting anyone?' Ann shook her head. He opened the door and saw no one. He went outside and looked either way. Nobody. He thought he heard a buzz above him, but when he looked up, saw nothing.

'Who is it dear?' asked Ann.

'There's no one here, must be the doorbell on the way out.' George pressed it a couple of times, then walked back through the hallway into the kitchen and returned to the tidying up. There was a noise behind him followed by a low humming. They both turned towards the sound and were shocked to see a ghostly figure standing in front of them. A small man, under a metre high, stood there smiling broadly at them. Ann instinctively moved closer to George.

'George Walker, Ann Walker. Please do not be alarmed. You are not in danger. I visit you in peace.' He was expansive with his arm movements. 'Please listen to me.' George put his arm protectively around Ann, and they both stepped back. The small figure looked up at George and Ann with a puzzled expression. He leant forward, touching something that was out of the holographic domain and immediately doubled in height, causing them both to step back even further. 'Sorry, scale adjustment,' he smiled.' Even the technology in our slightly more advanced society plays up.'

Ann was first to speak, as George was still in semi-shock. 'Who are you? And what do you want?'

'My name is Prime of Bala Verceti from the planet Preenasette. That is my best translation of our names into your language. We come from the Alpheratz system, as your astronomers would call it,' He looked directly at George.

'George, you've spent years looking up at the stars, dreaming of what might be out there. We are your dream come true.'

George looked into Ann's eyes and saw the same astonishment he felt. He tried to gather himself. The alien, if it was one, appeared very human, though its skin did have a slight but definite blue tint He looked at Ann. She was the professional speaker here, but it was evident she was leaving the next response to him.

'So, what is this device here?' *Was that the best you could think of?* he admonished himself. He recovered quickly, pointing to the globe on the floor projecting the image. 'A hologram transmitter? Where are you?'

'That is a transporter globe; the hologram transmitter is within it. I'm about sixty million of your miles away,' Prime replied. 'I'm on my ship, my vessel, with the rest of my party. There are eleven of us. A probe we have in your Earth's upper atmosphere is transmitting this holo message via a relay station midway between us.'

He was so polite and engaging. Ann was finding it pretty difficult to be afraid of this genie from a bottle. 'Is this your first contact? If so, why us, and not a government?'

'You will understand the answer to that question, Ann Walker, when I have told you our story. Would you care to sit down? I know you should be asking that question in your home—I have studied your customs in great detail—but, if you sit down, then so can I. And, if you don't mind, I'll revert to my natural form. Our attempts at looking like you still need a lot of work—things are pinching me here and there.' He remained standing, waiting for them to reply.

George edged another chair around, and both of them sat down, backs to the dining table. 'Yes, to both,' he said.

Prime touched a small object to the side of him, and his transformation was instantaneous. The Walkers spent a moment studying him, his features appearing recognisable in both forms.

He sat down. 'I hope you don't find *me* too scary, though the rest of my team I can't vouch for.' His smile was now mischievous. There was a rumble of muted voices from off screen.

'Are they all there?' George asked.

'Yes,' said Prime. He leant over again, touched something, and the holo-projector started to pan around. 'Temper, Seca, Jobe, Soff, Taur-Mao, Taur-Dao, Rosa, Mika, Campazee and Princess Tauriar.' As he was introducing them, they each either nodded or gave a little wave. He'd paused the projector for a bit longer on the Princess. George could see she was much younger than the others, closer in age to their daughter Mandy, he estimated. She had bright, curious eyes and was obviously trying to hold back from smiling—unsuccessfully as it happened. The 360-degree rotation ended back at Prime. 'Can I pass you onto my second in command, Temper, who will tell you our story?'

The projector moved slightly to bring Temper into view. She was smaller than Prime, with much softer facial features. An adornment on her right cheek appeared to George to be a red tattoo marking. She smiled. A warm and inviting smile. 'Hello. I'm Bala Temper, the second in command of our Life Team. But what you must understand is that I am the real force behind the team, Prime is like a father figure that we all just about tolerate.' Temper smiled and winked, though the wink looked somewhat manufactured. 'The literal translation Life Team may not sound quite right to you, but we are a team with the sole purpose of educating, training and protecting our Princess, Tauriar. We've done it from shortly after her birth and will carry on until she is forty of our years old. When that time comes, Princess Tauriar will become one of a ruling council of four that govern all aspects of the realm of Bala Verceti. It has been a great tradition in our world for the last three hundred years. There are always two princes and two princesses, or Royals—as we call them collectively—in training.

'Unfortunately, our world is at war, a war that threatens our very existence. Our ruling council has made the decision to send the three youngest Royals out of harm's way. They will only return when the real nature of the war on our planet becomes clearer. Princess Tauriar is the second youngest Royal, and we have chosen your planet, Earth, as our hiding place. But, we need help to complete this task. "Inside help," I think you would call it. That is why we are contacting you. You appear to possess the empathy, skills and knowledge to assist us. We hope you will.'

George and Ann looked at each other. The look on George's face was one she was very familiar with. It was the same look he always had when considering a new and exciting challenge.

Prime added, 'We realise what a shock this is for you and how much we are asking from you. It won't be easy. But let's not concern ourselves too much about that now. You need time to think, consider.'

Temper continued, 'We have prepared a data package for you to view at your leisure in the transporter globe. We will leave now. The holo emitter will go to standby, but if you ask it for to commence the presentation, you will learn much about our society and our predicament. Take your time. When you need to contact us again, just ask for Prime or me.'

'We thank you in anticipation,' Prime concluded. The image disappeared, and the machine went to standby mode.

* * *

'So, WHAT DO YOU SAY?' Ann asked rhetorically. 'How does one respond to this? They want our help.'

George was on another level. 'Sixty million miles away. Do you know how long it would take us to travel that distance?

And that's just where they've parked after their interstellar journey.'

'I see you've made your decision already, George Walker.'

'Well, it can't hurt to watch the slideshow. We can make any decisions later.'

And that's what they did. For the next six hours solid, only pausing to make coffee and grab a sandwich.

CHAPTER 9

*J*on, *Mandy & Grace*
  Earth - The Republic of Ireland - 2002

JON RETURNED the next day for lunch in the hall's grand dining room. Apart from him, there was Amanda, Amanda's mum and dad, Grace, her mother and father (the Squire and Lady Faulkner) and Grace's two private tutors.

Everyone was very courteous and went out of their way to make him feel at ease. The food was lovely, and he was hungry, especially after spending the morning riding in the hills, but there were a few things that he found a little odd.

He'd arrived at one pm on the dot and waited at the main entrance of the hall. It was ten minutes before Peter, the gardener who had returned for Amanda's bike, arrived, trotting over the grass from the direction of the woods, Krankel at his side. 'I was waiting at the hole in the fence for you. Didn't expect you to be this formal.' His smile was warm, with no trace of the distrust from yesterday. 'I'm Peter, by the way.'

'How did you know I came into the grounds there?' Jon asked, with a guilty look on his face.

'Oh, Ive been keeping my eye on you. You're here most weekends. I've also watched you in the woods on your bike. You looked skilled at riding. Perhaps you would allow me to ride with you sometimes if that's acceptable to you. I'm considered a good rider of bikes back home, though the bike I have here isn't a patch on yours. I'll need permission from the Squire of course, and gardening duties notwithstanding.'

'Love to,' Jon agreed suspiciously. He had rarely ridden with anyone that was able to handle the terrain and speeds he could. *Could be interesting* he thought, *but why have I never seen him?*

He decided to ask. 'Why didn't you say something when I was on the grounds before?'

'Well, you didn't seem like a cosmic threat to us. Unless I'm wrong, of course, and you have a ray gun in your backpack? Carry on using the hole in the fence. We've finished putting up some security devices, but they're more for nighttime. Come, everyone is waiting for you. You're the first official guest we've had. You should feel honoured.'

'No pressure then,' Jon sighed.

Krankel edged up to Jon's side and nuzzled his hand. Jon's fingers dug into the fur on the back of his neck. They walked along together as old friends would.

Before they entered, he saw Amanda turn the corner, riding her bike. The bike was looking as good as new. *Must be a new wheel,* he thought. When she dismounted, there appeared no sign of her injury. She bounded over to him, smiling and looking enthusiastic. She pulled up short of him, realising she might seem to be a little overly friendly. 'Hello Jon, glad you could come.'

Peter silently drifted away as Amanda took charge of their guest of honour.

'Is your foot okay?' Jon asked.

'Yes.' Amanda replied. 'Gwyneth is a wizard at first aid. Only a slight sprain, she reckoned. They've been busy all morning preparing for this lunch. You're the guest of honour.'

'Yes, so Peter said.' Jon put his bike next to Amanda's. She looked at him and smiled, then put her arm through his and started marching him through the door. Jon felt a bit weird. He wasn't used to this level of contact with girls, but she didn't give him time to worry over it. in the main entrance hall There was a reception committee lined up and waiting for him. Amanda took charge.

'Okay then, introductions.' Amanda assumed an official and most likely rehearsed role. 'These are our hosts, Squire Douglas Faulkner and his wife Lady Gwyneth Faulkner, and this is their daughter Grace.' The Squire held out his hand for Jon to shake, which he did, followed by Lady Gwyneth and Grace. In the dim light of the hallway, they all seemed to have a very slight lack of clarity to their facial features, *a trick of the light?* Jon wondered. Grace smiled brightly, with a sparkle of excitement in her eyes. 'And this is my father, Professor George Walker and my mother, Ann Walker MP.' Again, Jon shook hands. 'And finally, Miss Thorpe and Mr. Bunter, Grace's tutors.'

'Amanda,' her mother said, 'enough of the formalities. You'll frighten the poor boy away.'

She put her arm around Jon and led him into the dining room. 'I, for one, want to thank you for rescuing our accident prone daughter. Come, let's eat.'

* * *

OVER THE NEXT couple of weeks, Jon visited five more times. The three children got on well. Mandy was the theatrical one and would have the other two in stitches with her shenanigans.

Grace was still quiet but was steadily growing in confidence as each day passed. She still liked to let Mandy take centre stage. Everything she came across in the woods seemed to hold a special wonder to her.

Jon, well, he just liked being with the two lovely girls. Without thinking, they would stroll either side of him with their arms locked through his, as his tendency was to walk everywhere with his hands in his pockets, and listen to Mandy mimicking one of Grace's tutors or making up some ridiculous story. They would walk through the woods and talk as all teenagers do—utterly incomprehensible to adults. They even went swimming in the lake during his last visit, with Peter and Gordon in close attendance.

Today, Jon had finally arranged to meet Peter early for a ride. They met at the highest point of the woods on the eastern side of Harewood Hall, Jon's usual starting point. He had brought Krankel, which delighted Jon. The boy and the dog had rapidly formed a "boys only" bond that would frustrate and entertain the others in equal measure. He jumped off his bike and started play fighting. No one else seemed to do this with him. But Jon and Krankel would do it for hours.

Peter was right; his bike wasn't anywhere near as good as Jon's. It was a bog standard mountain bike that you could buy from one of the supermarket chain stores, no suspension, heavy, and no subtlety. Mass produced for the masses.

Seeing Jon eyeing up his bike Peter said, 'It was left here by the previous occupants. Not what I'd call "state of the art," but enough to put you in your place.' The gleam in Peter's eye implied the challenge had been laid down.

'Will Krankel keep up?' asked Jon.

'Will he ever,' replied a smiling Peter.

Jon smiled back. 'See if you can keep my back wheel in sight then.' And he was off.

He'd picked a route that slowly weaved its way down the

hill, not overly steep, but still fast. It contained three switch-backs where he'd be able to see how Peter was doing. He slid easily into his biking mindset, took a deep breath and started flowing effortlessly down. At the first switchback, he had turned completely through 180 degrees before sensing Peter. *He's not doing too bad,* he thought. Through the next section, he tried to go a little faster. He was aware of a white shape flashing along between the trees on his right. Krankel? At the next switchback, Peter was even closer and at the final one he was right on his heels. By the bottom, the three of them were almost side-by-side as Jon skidded to a halt.

'Wow! Good riding,' was Jon's first comment. 'And on that old carthorse of a bike.'

'As I said, I *have* done a bit of riding. But I wasn't as good as you when I was your age. And neither of us are as fast as Krankel.' They both laughed at the mud splattered dog with his tongue hanging out, asking desperately to go again.

* * *

PETERS IDEA OF 'A BIT OF RIDING' was pilot training. What Jon referred to as 'his cycling mindset' was to Peter, 'Heightening Senses' and was the primary attribute a pilot needed for worm-hole travel. One of the ways to train this sense was with technical cycling.

Before coming to Earth, Peter had thought the bicycle was unique to Preenasette. But arriving here, he saw he was way off the mark. Pondering upon it, he had realised that most bilaterally symmetric, "humanoid" races would "invent the wheel" at some stage of their evolution—that was obvious to him in hindsight—and would eventually design modes of two, three and four-wheeled transport. The early attempts at bicycle design would be crude, but would keep improving. Wheels would become lighter and stronger. Some form of tyre developed for comfort. A power transfer system and brakes. Steering. On Earth, every type and design of bike had been tried, but in the end, natural selection would always lead to the same optimum design. Be it for overcoming difficult terrain, technical courses or just for pure speed, the same design principles applied. And when technology overtakes development and tries to replace the physical deficiencies of the rider a stalemate occurs. The cyclist rebels. So they put limits on bike technical development. The only improvements were to come from rider's skill, daring and fitness, or the difficulty of the courses.

On Peter's world, riding a bike was an art form. The inhabitants of Earth were showing a remarkable aptitude as well.

'Lets go again,' Peter said, 'Something a little more challenging, perhaps?'

They spent the rest of the morning exploring all of Jon's tracks down the hillside. Peter gave little pointers here and there on subtle technicalities and the adoption of thought processes to help with heightening his senses. Peter and Krankel even made going back up the hills look easy, though he, of course, neglected to tell Jon they were brought up on a planet with a slightly higher gravity and lower oxygen level. Earth made them feel a bit like superheroes.

Jon and Peter made their way back to the hall after a great morning of cycling. Krankel had run ahead, seemingly tireless. The girls came running to greet them, alerted of their return by the dog, full of excitement.

'Hi, you two. Had a good morning?' Mandy asked.

'Great,' Jon replied.

'And what have you done to my dog?' Grace laughed, trying to fend off the affections of the giant mud pie.

'I'll take him and hose him down,' said Peter. 'And I better be off before the Squire realises how long I've been out.'

'See you Krankel... and you, Peter,' Grace called. 'Come on

Jon, Mandy's thought up a great new game,' she said, mimicking Jon's Irish accent and looking up to the heavens.

The children strolled across the grounds of Harewood Hall to the far side of the manor house.

'Okay,' said Mandy. 'There's the stream. And here are the rules...'

CHAPTER 10

The Assassin
   Earth - The Republic of Ireland - 2002

Now was perfect.

The security shield had been in place for about two weeks. Nothing could penetrate it, not a missile, not a search drone, not even somebody carrying a toy gun. The artificial intelligence controlling the shield watched anything and everyone. But it was partially down for thirty minutes. Helen was carrying out a minor calibration adjustment to the optical tracking system that they all had implanted to monitor each other's whereabouts—final tweaking. He would have time. He, like everyone else, knew the location of the Princess before the partial shutdown. Helen had activated the perimeter dome and told the children to stay near the hall. They were by the house and vulnerable and, more importantly, Krankel wasn't with them. He would never get close enough with the dog around.

A perfect opportunity.

He slipped out of a side exit and ran into the woods. The

vantage point he was heading for was excellent, with plenty of cover and damp moss underfoot. He wouldn't be seen or heard. In his pocket, he carried an AM Hover Dart, which contained a minuscule particle of grey matter in suspension. This weapon was a particularly efficient killing device. He had gone to great lengths on Verceti and here on Earth to conceal it. The DNA of its target was programmed in. The hover function allowed a midair setting, about chest height facing in the general direction of its target, where it would hang for a preset period. It would then accelerate to three hundred and fifty miles per hour and seek its target. When it got within one metre of the source of the DNA, it would explode—a small but deadly implosion consuming all living matter within a five-metre radius.

He could see the children now, about a hundred metres away, and set the hover function to forty-five seconds. More than enough time for him to get back to the place he was expected to be. He enabled the tracking system and touched the arming button. He paused for the briefest moment to confirm activation and hover stability, then turned and set off as quickly and as quietly as he could.

CHAPTER 11

he First Trials 2
  Zerot - 200 Years Earlier

THE FINAL THREE gates opened together.

Are the Elders testing me? Or punishing me?

Behind her to the right, a family was herded out by two large Grunz that slammed the outer gate shut behind them. A male, a female and a juvenile, flowing purple hair vividly contrasting with their snowy white skin The man carried a short sword, but his demeanour suggested he wasn't a fighter.

They look ridiculous. How are they supposed to test me? Or is it a test of my compassion. Ha, the Elders should know better.

Directly in front of her a giant, heavily armoured feudal warrior appeared, slow but probably skilled, with only one glaring flaw in his armour that Birjjikk could see.

Behind her to the left were three squat soldiers. She recognised them from the slave paddocks—recent additions.

The only sound in the arena was the whimpering of the

Tagra with the missing foot, desperately licking at the wound just below the severed humerus.

The three soldiers and the warrior were cautious. Any confidence born of having to battle a young girl was now tempered by her display in the arena, and the apparent hold she had over the bear.

Birjjikk wasn't going to give them time to formulate strategies or alliances, she would be the aggressor. She needed a strong performance to ensure progression to the next phase of training. Warrior caste would then be guaranteed. The darker arts of killing and mental training would be on the syllabus. She desperately wanted this. Ultimately, she wanted to become a Player—the leader of the Cadre chosen from her Academy. Then, and only then, would she enjoy the real benefits of being a high caste Zerot: a longer life filled with estivation—prolonged dormancy—ensuring more time to plot and play the killing game.

She ran directly at the warrior, sword in hand, knowing it would cause confusion. From his startled look, she succeeded. She leapt—by appearances prematurely—feeling the thrill of gliding through the air and triumph that her attack had already succeeded. The high forward thrust of her sword served to engage an upwards defensive parry from the warrior's sword, stretching his torso and exposing the breach in his armour. But, at the last moment, she withdrew her weapon and tucked into a ball, falling to the ground into a perfect forward roll. The momentum brought her to her knees in front of him where she inserted her sword surgically just below his chest, in the gap where the upper chainmail ended and the lower began.

She was pleased with herself and her perfect technique until she realised that she couldn't hold the warrior's weight as he fell towards her. He would die, that much was certain, but he hadn't yet, and his forward momentum meant he could complete a final lunge at her with his sword.

Birjjikk's hands felt welded to the hilt of her sword as she staggered backwards, now painfully aware that the arc of the Warrior's sword was destined to meet with the right side of her torso.

Turdgutter! This won't go well with the Elders.

She had no choice but to trigger her modulating force field, willing the left quadrant to activate. The dampened blow to her side still felt like a sledgehammer, and her whole body shifted from beneath the falling giant. The blow had twisted him, allowing Birjjikk to withdraw her sword, and giving her a means to rectify her error. She rolled onto her back, flipped onto her feet, then stood tall and shrieked.

She should have been wondering if she had recovered the situation, but there was something else going on inside her. A deep emotion began to flood her very being, a desperate yearning deep within her loins, a feeling unknown to her.

Is this the Brukkah?

The thought was just a vague impression floating in her mind—the feeling was now all consuming.

She shrieked again, high-pitched and piercing, reaching the far corners of the subterranean arena. The bear stood up and roared, feeling its mistress's new emotions.

The fire in her eyes was vivid, and her lips were drawn back, exposing needle sharp teeth.

The emotions eased, but the desire remained, stronger than before.

A desperate desire to kill.

Her thoughts fixed on the three stocky soldiers from a world recently subjected to a visit from her people. Faded and dirty uniforms gave her the impression that they were well trained and would work as a team. Each of them carried a small bronze coloured sword, and a circular metal shield adorned with a fire-breathing dragon.

Quick and spectacular with no mistakes was her subconscious demand. She moved her sword to her left hand and set off towards the family. With her right hand, she reached for the booster throwing knives attached to her breastplate, and with a fluid movement released them. Their trajectory was perfect. Birjjikk didn't need to will any adjustments to the three flying blades. As the knives detected their targets, the little rocket boosters took effect, accelerating them to such a speed that flesh and bone would not stop them. The results were devastating—blood and chunks of flesh everywhere, just as promised. She didn't even wait to see their stubby bodies crumple to the ground.

She was almost upon the family. The male had taken a protective stance, trying to shield his mate and offspring. She dodged the lunging father and dispatched his wife and child with two swift thrusts of her sword. The father screamed his horror at seeing his family cut down. A moment later he turned away, unable to look at his loss. Birjjikk wasted no time driving her blade into his midriff, the momentum bringing them face to face. She anticipated the pleasure of his terror and disbelief. What faced her though, as his purple hair swung away from his snow white face, was the cold, deadly stare of a determined man who managed to whisper to her, 'We know who you are, we will stop you.' She twisted the blade to one side and then the other, watching the life ebbing from his body. He remained stoic. She had lost the joy of the kill, and that annoyed her more than she would admit. She finally pushed him away, raised her arms, and shrieked once more.

She came back down, the unknown urge in her loins subsiding, and calmed herself. The only noise now was the whimpering from the injured Tagra. She turned to the bear and waved a hand at it. The beast rose immediately and pounced on whim. Lifting it high in its mouth and shaking it violently, finally enjoying the pleasure it had watched his new mistress have. It flung the Tagra against one of the cages. One final cry and it fell to the ground, silent. The beast pounced on the convulsing feline wanting to feed, but a voice in its head said, *No..* It stood up again and roared in defiance at the watching elders, then dropped to all fours and, head bowed, followed its mistress out of the arena.

The only sound now was the murmuring of the Zerot elders. Were they pleased or displeased? She wasn't sure, but once again, she had gotten their attention.

As she was leaving the arena she noticed her tutor, Master Nama-Krikk, high up to the left. He was in her head.

You have performed well, little one.

Thank you, Master

Enjoy a recovery day, and don't be late for first day of advanced training. This is where it gets interesting.

Birjjikk didn't respond. She kept on walking, a rare smile on her face that no one saw.

CHAPTER 12

he Assault
   Earth - The Republic of Ireland - 2002

JON AND GRACE walked slowly across the stepping-stones in the stream. This silly game was Mandy's latest invention. She stood on a small hillock throwing pinecones to try and unbalance them.

'You've got to stand one legged on each stone for the count of five. First to step into the water is out and then we swap over,' Mandy ordered.

Grace, as usual, took the game very seriously, and with excellent balance never wavered under the barrage of cones. Jon, however, succumbed when he turned to Mandy to moan about the number of cones thrown at him and received a direct hit right on his forehead. They both got to the far side, laughing about his wet feet, with Mandy dancing about on the small hill in mock victory.

Everything around Grace froze.

"Tauriar, quickly, stretch the moment. I cannot hold it for you much longer from here."

Grace's reaction was instantaneous. *"I have done it, taking over."*

Everything around her appeared to stand dead still. She took control of the time acceleration bubble that Prime had initially created from the hall.

"Find the danger, Tauriar."

The Princess looked around and spotted the only object moving. *"It's a small missile, a dart—moving fast. I have about... twenty seconds."*

"AM Dart, seeking your DNA. You've trained for this. Your brooch! Throw it into its path."

"But, they'll discover my identity.... no time."

She clutched at the brooch and threw it out of the bubble. It stopped just outside and hovered there, now in regular time. Because the holo transmitter and skin modifier were embedded in the brooch, she reverted to her natural self. But it also contained a strand of her DNA—that gave her hope. She only had about ten seconds to get away from the brooch and scoop up the other two. She stepped back so that the bubble engulfed Jon. He found himself facing a slightly distorted and blue skinned version of Grace. She grabbed his arm. 'Run!'

She half led and half dragged Jon across the shallow stream in the direction of a stationary Mandy. 'Grab her,' she shouted as they reached the top of the small mound and the bubble engulfed her as well. The fell to the far side of the mound as the bubble collapsed; Grace's concentration had failed. The crack of the dart behind them filled the air. The displacement of air from the acceleration rushing past them nearly lifted them off the ground. They all reached helplessly for something to cling to.

A moment later all was quiet.

The three children were lying in a heap. One rather blue Vercetian and two rather astonished humans.

* * *

THE CHILDREN FREED THEMSELVES, stood up and faced each other. For about five seconds there was a tense silence while they looked at each other in turn, trying to assess what had happened.

Then they all started shouting at once.

'What was all that about? I was dancing on the hill, and then I'm in a ditch with, with a blue person!' exclaimed Amanda.

'Please... I'm sorry. Don't stop being my friend. I wanted to tell you.' Grace was almost in tears and speaking in broken English.

'Wow! How cool is this?' Jon looked around in delight. 'An alien. Explosions! What's going on?'

Before any of them could answer, Peter and Krankel arrived and took a defensive stance, facing away from Grace. Peter had a strange weapon, and held it up in a protective manner. Krankel, head low and hackles raised, growled menacingly: both were looking for an unknown foe. Within seconds, Gordon and Helen appeared, and the three defenders formed a ring around the children, all holding the same weapons.

Within thirty seconds everyone was there.

Ann and George were hugging Amanda. Mr. and Mrs. Shaw were embracing Grace. Douglas Faulkner had both hands on Jon's shoulders looking closely into his eyes for signs of any adverse effects. William had joined Peter, Gordon, and Helen, now moving away from everyone in ever increasing circles, securing the site. It was twenty minutes before it all began to settle down. With everyone accounted for and no sign of an intruder, they all headed for the hall. Helen got back to finishing the work on the security system. William, Peter, and

Gordon remained outside until the shield was back up. Everyone else gathered in the day lounge, except Mr. and Mrs. Shaw, who went to prepare tea and some food.

Douglas accessed a computer that appeared out of nowhere. His hand glided over what looked like a mouse pad, and a holographic image appeared and displayed a small three-dimensional object. Within moments, he was able to give Grace another brooch. She clipped it on and touched it, reverting to her human form.

Jon and Amanda watched in awe at the transformation. Soon they sat next to her and started whispering and giggling. Jon's hand was within a few centimetres of Grace's cheek, and he was asking if her facial changes were real or some illusion. Mandy couldn't help admire the brooch, asking questions about it. Grace was answering Jon, 'Solid, but not real,' she said, and moved his hand closer so that he could feel it. She turned so that Mandy's already advancing finger could touch the brooch. *Zap.* She was Vercetian again. Jon and Mandy jumped back at the sight of Grace in her alien guise. Then all three burst into laughter—quite uncontrolled—causing everyone in the room to stop and stare, and after a moment, the tension in the room lifted markedly, dissipated by the innocence of youth.

But for one of the group, the torment remained. Failure combined with utter relief.

* * *

BALA PRIME SAT with Bala Temper in their private quarters. With brooches deactivated they no longer played the roles of Squire and Lady Faulkner. They were once again Team Leader and Cultural Instructor to Tauriar—the two senior members of the Life Team.

'I nearly missed it, Temper. If it had happened a few moments earlier, I would have been helping Triquo Rosa with the problem she was having accessing the shield protocols. The Princess might have been killed, and I would have failed.'

'Well, she wasn't, Prime. You sensed the danger in time, and Tauriar stayed calm and remembered everything we taught her, which, for a Royal of her age, shows excellent progress. She will make a exceptional High Councillor one day,' said Temper.

'Yes, well, what we do know is that we have a traitor within our team, and with the exclusion of Seca Rosa, you and myself, it could have been anyone. And with the artificial intelligence inactive, we have no way of investigating.' Prime was deep in concentration. 'The threat will always be with us.' He pulled up the data page on his implant viewer and pasted it to the adjacent wall. He knew this information off by heart, but somehow it helped to see it in the written form. Perhaps there was a hidden clue somewhere. Who could it be?

LIFE TEAM:

- Princess Tauriar (birth name Manjena). Grace, daughter of Squire and Lady Faulkner
- Bala Prime - Life Team leader. Squire Douglas Faulkner
- Bala Temper - Cultural Instructor. Lady Gwyneth Faulkner
- Bala Soff - Educational Instructor. James Bunter - Tutor
- Bala Campazee - Physical Instructor. Katie Thorpe - Tutor
- Dom Seca - Chief of Security, Life Team. William Smith - Accountant
- Seca Jobe - Pilot and security. Peter - Gardener
- Taur-Mao - Manjena's birth mother. Mrs Joan Shaw - Housekeeper
- Taur-Dao - Manjena's birth father. Mr Adam Shaw - Butler

Additional Security with Specialities:
- Seca Mika - Engineer. Gordon - Odd job man
- Seca Rosa - Scientist. Helen - Cook

THE LIFE TEAM had been with Tauriar since her selection at birth, except Dom Seca. He had replaced Thormin Seca eight years ago, when he fell ill with a rare form of cancer that was resisting all treatment. The additional team members had distinguished service records. No one stood out to him. With no hidden clues jumping out at him his concentration wavered momentarily. He remembered the naming process and the job descriptions given to them by the Walkers. He smiled to himself at the naming of Grace. The professor's favourite Hollywood actress who became a real life princess.

'Prime. My telepathic abilities are not the best, as you well know. What are you thinking?'

'Sorry. I see no obvious candidates for our traitor. We are going to have to be much more rigorous with our security.'

CHAPTER 13

The War Ministry
Preenasette - Trun Rizontella - 2002

NEARLY TWO YEARS on and Sub-Officer Anton Pilz was still being made to wear his formal sash to the Quarter Luna War Council meeting, visibly highlighting his demotion following his error when the Vercetian Life Teams escaped. He was here with Supreme Commander Komitry Zander and Commander Dori Mancer, to keep a record of the proceedings. He still felt, that he was being paraded as an example of an officer failing in his duties.

He despised the council building. It represented everything that was grim about Trun society. Built entirely from dark grey granite slate, it had two characterless statues of uniformed soldiers from a former age guarding the severe entrance. Just inside they were greeted by a circular stone registration desk manned by two stern looking receptionists.

They stopped there, with Pilz carrying out the duties of registration, before proceeding through a long, dimly lit corridor with portraits of Trun political leaders, each trying to look grander than his predecessor, and not a smile between them. At the end of the corridor was the Assembly Antechamber, with four quite uninviting sets of dark bronze double doors leading to the Great Debating rooms. They entered Assembly Room 3, where a fully assembled War Council awaited.

The military party settled at the north end of the great Vesica Piscis oval table, with Zander taking the northern, head position. At the southern end, immediately opposite Zander was Premier Gor. He had become premier a few years earlier, after the untimely death of the sitting leader. He went about his business quietly, but was very effective at getting results. Pilz watched Zander survey the assembly. Of all the people seated at the table, just three wielded real power. Pilz knew this as well as anyone. Gor, Zander, and the chief executive of the Space and Weapons Manufacturing Corporation, Salvia Kiy. Zander regarded Kiy as she marshaled her small entourage. The rumours surrounding her sudden rise to power were abundant, ranging from the sublime to the ridiculous. If only a quarter of them were real, then she had manipulated, slept, and poisoned her way to the top spot. Just looking at this woman sent a shiver up Pilz's spine. He knew it was just a matter of time before Zander locked antlers with her, and he hoped to not be around when that happened. Missing was the secret organisation, the Reticent Guard. They were autonomous of the council even though their commander, General Kirk-am was part of the Council Inner Circle.

The room went quiet, and the Council Head Speaker welcomed them all and started laying out the agenda.

* * *

PILZ KNEW he was in for a long evening. The agenda, as usual, covered a whole ream of subjects ranging from funding appropriations and military training, through to Gor's state of the war address. Even Zander was required to speak. He typically avoided this at all costs, but tonight had to give an update on the space battle against the Vercetians. Until recently, Zander didn't even come to these meetings, but for some reason, had started taking a keener interest. He had even taken to analysing the full transcript with a select group of military personnel the following day. Pilz's job was to record the meeting, then cut out the procedural rubbish and separate all political speech, leaving the facts for the following day's meeting and the rhetoric for Zander's private viewing. Pilz knew his Supreme Commander was mindful of something, but what? He had yet to discover.

The debate opened with Finance Minister Cammero's report. As usual, there was a shortfall in nearly all the main funding streams. The war was slowly bringing Trun Rizontella to its knees. When he'd finished, the speaker invited questions, and Salvia Kiy quickly seized the floor and the attention of the chamber. 'The sum allocated to our bifighter replication project is paltry. Surely, as this addresses one of the fundamental flaws in our arsenal, this project should be of top priority. We've had the completed plans for two years now, and the manufacturing process is now soundly developed and refined. We need to conclude development and begin!' The last sentence delivered with her usual, and now famed venom. Pilz wondered if she would ultimately get the funds she wanted. He didn't have to wait long for an answer. After a short period of bickering, Premier Gor stepped in to end the debate. 'Space and Weapons have a legitimate claim to more funds. I shall set up a subcommittee meeting with Minister Cammero and find a revenue stream for this money.' His statement was final, and Pilz knew that Kiy would get what she wanted and that this part of the debate was over.

The Council Head Speaker then moved the meeting on to the Military Training and Recruitment Committee report and handed over to Sub-commander Lysanda. This statement caused many in the room to lose focus, and the Speaker had to jump in a couple of times to restore order. The only news of note was the increase in troop numbers. But this wasn't a priority for the military. Zander didn't want more troops, he wanted modern weapons for the men he currently had. He wanted a better arsenal and had pushed for it at the last few sub-committee meetings, but seemed to be banging his head against a wall. Pilz, usually in tow, had seen how frustrated he was getting.

Zander's report was next.

Pilz knew that Zander hated this part of his job. Not that he wasn't a competent public speaker, he was. He just didn't see the need to report all of the military's activities to the masses assembled here. His reports were massaged to tell them what the inner circle of the ruling council wanted them to hear. He could keep it short. Premier Gor would follow him with the battle cry stuff.

In the weeks and months following the space battle, Pilz knew Zander had questioned the need to take any further action against the escaped Royals. 'Who cares that they have fled to some distant planet,' he had overheard him telling Mancer. 'Let them stay there and rot. Why waste valuable resources chasing after them?' They had all regretted sending in a sorely overmatched squadron against the Vercetian armada. They now had two significant assets in space dock, out of commission for a long time, as well as four spheres still on a wild goose chase.

So, this would be one of the few occasions where he could report the real facts. Because, after due consideration, the Royals' escape was of little consequence. And that's what he told them.

'...and it is, therefore, the Inner Council's decision to support the Military's policy of not committing any further resources to finding them. In conclusion, I would report that five of the Vercetian decoy ships have returned to Preenasette, as have two of our own. I will update the War Council further on this matter at the next quarterly meeting.'

He stood down to polite applause from the assembly.

Up next was Premier Gor.

As was his way, Premier Gor commanded respect in the most subtle of ways. The simple act of looking up and slowly surveying the room induced a stony silence. This particular address to the assembly was a state of the war summary. High and low points, ongoing tactics and new initiatives. Lots of rhetoric but little detail, and a rallying cry at the end. He stood up and commenced his address.

Pilz saw Mancer lean towards Zander. He couldn't hear them but saw where he was pointing. Zander was nodding. In the gallery seats surrounding the table, Pilz could see a sprinkling of Sestapol police sporting their new black military uniforms, with steep visor caps. Their primary duties were not defined yet, but rumours abounded.

Pilz's mind drifted away for a moment, and an awareness dawned on him. Sestapol were part of the Reticent Guard! What were they even doing here? Now his two bosses' interest in the Council Meeting was becoming clear.

Gor began, 'The balance of the war is slowly swinging our way. The Vercetians are in a panic. The evacuation of their Royals is a sign of this, but as Supreme Commander Zander has just told you, we aren't planning any further action. In other developmental research, I can confirm that we are making sound strategic advances.' Gor scanned the auditorium. 'Our new kinetic pulse body armour with projectile sensing shielding is in phase two testing. There are still some technicalities to be worked on, but I understand we are well ahead of schedule.

'Underground force field penetration tests are ongoing, but are hitting technical problems. I will personally look into this woeful lack of progress.

'Troop numbers are higher than ever, as Sub-commander Lysanda has just reported.

Our plan is coming together.' He paused for a rapturous ovation. Pilz, Zander and Mancer were quite aware of the Sestapol officers leading the frenzied applause, one or two even encouraging those around them to show more enthusiasm.

Gor raised his hands for silence.

'But we cannot be complacent. A full-scale ground attack will only work with a concerted space offensive as well. And for this to happen, we need bifighters. We are outgunned, and need the Space and Weapons Manufacturing Corporation to accelerate this building program.' He held the moment for just the right amount of time. 'Friends. While we develop our strategies the foe is developing quite diabolical ones of their own. During this last quarter alone, our spies have informed us of plans to create cyborg super-soldiers, and of force field penetrating missiles that will deliver horrifying biological payloads. There are no depths the Vercetians will not plumb to win this war and assure the end of our culture. That has always been their intention, and nothing has changed.' The assembly cursed and shook their fists at the absent foe. Gor continued, in full battle cry, 'We will stay strong. And we will work tire-lessly to make our home safe. Free from the tyranny of the Vercetians. For our children and their children. For Trun Rizontella!'

The crowd rose as one. The roar of approval was thunderous.

CHAPTER 14

The Holiday Ends
Earth - The Republic of Ireland - 2002

A COUPLE of weeks after the attack on Grace, things had gotten back to normal on the estate in the southern part of The Republic of Ireland. The security system was fully up and running, and the members of Grace's Life Team were back to their routines. Outside, the rain had returned with a vengeance. The summer holidays were drawing to a close, and Jon and Mandy would soon be back at school.

The children were sitting in the morning room, sprawled around a coffee table playing Monopoly. Grace was enthralled with the game and kept asking Mandy about all of the famous places in London represented on the board. She had access to everything on the database, but it was much more fun getting the point of view of a friend who lived there.

With no pretences to be kept up, Grace was in her native form. Although she still wore the brooch, otherwise she would revert to broken English.

Jon was using Krankel as a cushion, sprawled across him, his arms outstretched. He tried to flick the dog's nose, only to be greeted by the snap of teeth trying to nip his hand. Krankel pushed Jon with his back leg. Jon responded by grabbing his tail.

'Stop it you two!' Grace's patience was snapping. 'I've told you both, no more fighting.'

They regarded her like wounded puppies at the rare ticking off from Grace.

In the silence that followed, Mandy asked her about her position as princess.

'Grace. How does it all work? There are two princes and two princesses, and there's a ruling council. When will you join the Council?'

'We aren't proper princesses and princes in the way you mean. We aren't born into the role. We are selected at a very young age. It's a big ceremony, and anyone can put their babies forward for selection. The ones that meet the selection criteria best—they do all sorts of genetic tests and whatnot—are chosen.'

'And the name?' asked Jon. 'You're Grace to us, but I've heard you called Princess Tauriar and another name beginning with M.'

'Princess Tauriar is my official name, and Manjena is my birth name,' said Grace. 'It's all very complicated, I know, but only my parents use Manjena.'

'And that's Mr. and Mrs. Shaw, right?' said Mandy.

Grace nodded. 'I won't join the council until I'm forty. That's about forty-four of your years. And I will replace the eldest Councillor—Bana Tauriar—when she's eighty. The four Councillor names never change, two men and two women: Tauriar, Domeriette, Ventar and Camcietti, named after the first four elders hundreds of years ago. There's always a ten year age difference between them. With me so far?'

They both nodded. Jon stretched, his hand demolishing the houses Mandy had on Old Kent Road.

'Jon, you are the biggest oaf I've ever known. Your clumsiness has no limits.'

'It wasn't me, it was the smelly hairball,' complained Jon, digging the sleeping Krankel in the side.

As she crawled under the table to retrieve the little green plastic houses, he leant over and stole her King's Cross Station card, giving Grace a wink.

Mandy finished straightening her houses and looked up at them.

'What?' She looked from one to the other. 'Why have you turned bluer, Grace? What have you done, O'Malley?'

She studied the board—all seemed okay. Then she spotted the missing card.

'Where's my station?'

'You've got to catch me if you want it back.' And Jon went running out of the room, with both girls in hot pursuit. Krankel made to get up and join in the chase, but decided against it and flopped back down.

Just outside, Jon and Mandy missed Douglas wandering past, but Grace went straight into him. He managed to keep his balance and catch her.

'So, where is the little princess with the lightning reactions and reflexes?'

'That's only when I'm at work. I'm playing now.' She smiled and was gone.

* * *

AN HOUR later and they were all back sprawled over the floor and the sofas in the morning room. Grace's hotels on Mayfair and Park Lane had caught Jon and Mandy a couple of times each, which had effectively ended the game.

Grace was moaning.

'What am I going to do when you go back to school?'

'You'll be seeing me most weekends,' said Jon, a manufactured wounded look on his face.

'And we'll be back for the half term and Christmas holidays,' Mandy chipped in.

'I know, I know,' said a dejected Grace. 'I just feel we need some bond or oath that will seal our friendship. In our Decennial Ceremonies, we have poems that reaffirm the faith and loyalty of the nation and the Ruling Council, every ten years.'

'Come on,' said Mandy. 'Let's all try and write something. 'She jumped up and got everyone pens and paper, and they all settled down to the task. After thirty minutes and much cursing, paper screwing up, questions like "what rhymes with hunk?" Mandy exclaimed, 'I can't do this!' putting paid to any further deliberations.

'I've done two,' said Jon. 'What about you, Grace?'

'I can't do poems in English. Something to do with the translator—it's not creative enough.'

'So that just leaves Jon,' said Mandy. 'What chance have we got? Come on then, O'Malley, give us what you've got.'

'Okay then.'

'THERE ONCE WAS a girl that was blue,
  Who was stuck on a planet named Poo,
  Saved by local hunk Jon,
  She had friend number one,
  And there was also this other girl too.'

MANDY GROWLED AT HIM.

'I've another.' He jumped in. 'True Friendship.'

'TRUE FRIENDSHIP SPANS *the galaxy*
    and remains always in our heart.
    We are touched by the stars,
    And nothing will keep us apart.'

GRACE AND MANDY looked at each other in amazement. 'Perfect,' they said in unison.

Grace said, 'Stand in a circle and hold hands, and we'll recite it together.'

They all checked the words again and were ready. Grace made them in interlink their fingers and locked hands at a shoulder height, creating a perfect dramatic triangle.

She spoke again, quietly, 'True friendship.'

'TRUE FRIENDSHIP SPANS **the galaxy**
    and remains always in our heart.
    We are touched by the stars,
    And nothing will keep us apart.'

JUST AS THEY FINISHED, Krankel howled, a very rare occurrence. He wanted to be part of this moment. Jon and the dog played like a pair of kids, but Mandy was pretty sure that Grace and Krankel were communicating at a much higher level.

The children looked at each other and smiled. The start of a hopefully long and meaningful friendship.

* * *

'AND FINALLY, BIRJJIKK.' Lord High Elder Carrakk leant back in his seat and scratched one of the horns on his forehead.

'I put her third. Aggressive and resourceful, but lacks the

strength and skill of Graffojj and Denttikk. She made too many errors. And, someone needs to teach her some respect,' replied Lord High Elder Robbijj.

'Are you sure you were facing the arena, Robbijj?' Lord High Elder Sammanna snapped, continuing the bickering done throughout the Cadre 188 Academy mid-training assessment. 'Never on this planet can you even compare Denttikk with Birjjikk. She's strong, and a reasonably skilled fighter but it all ends there with her. Grant you, Graffojj is the strongest and most skilled fighter at present. But this is still early days in their training. Birjjikk's potential is prodigious.'

Carrakk jumped in before Robbijj could reply to Sammanna. 'She has contempt for authority and is hot headed, I agree, but those were the very traits of a young Robbijj I seem to recall. And she was the only one to tame the bear over the last three Cadre assessments.'

'I think that seven hundred years has muddled up your recall, Carrakk. Too much estivation,' replied Robbijj. 'I was never that bad. And the bear was a fluke.'

'Gentlemen,' Sammanna interrupted. 'I see a future Player in Birjjikk. And a great player at that.' She banged the table with both fists—not for the first time during the meeting. 'I will claim sponsorship of her right now for the Rebutti Dynasty, and will look forward to reaping your hard earned Game Tokens for many years to come.'

'We do not need to make that decision for ten years,' Robbijj stated. 'She could be dead by then, and very likely will be.' He paused for a moment, deep in thought, before continuing, 'I will claim sponsorship of Graffojj for the Accett Dynasty and bet you fifty Tokens that he will become the Cadre Player—if Birjjikk manages to stay alive long enough to contest him.'

'And I will bet twenty five Tokens with Robbijj, for the Cammaggama Dynasty,' Carrakk added with a wry smile. 'That's if you're up to it, Sammanna?'

'I accept both wagers. It will be a pleasure to top up my Dynasty's funds'. Sammanna's smile was much more pronounced, her brown and worn teeth fully exposed. 'I foresee a major power shift in the Game over the next couple of hundred years.'

'Business concluded, gentlemen.' Sammanna stood up to leave the chamber and stretched. 'A little sleep for a few years, then I'll then check up on my girl.'

PART II
THE CHANGING FACE OF THE WAR

.

CHAPTER 15

The Needles Deception
Preenasette - The Needles - 2005

JOELLEN GRAINTER WAS one of the most experienced comman-ders in the Vercetian military. He loved his job. His devotion to his career left him with no time for luxuries such as a wife or a family, but he had always wanted a soulmate. Unfortunately, he'd set his sights too high and never had the nerve to do anything about it.

Today, however, he felt pressure—for more than one reason.

Kam Major, the military commander of the Vercetian army, had decided to observe this routine mission to check an anomaly in the defensive shield surrounding their country. She often joined missions with the briefest of notice, to keep her troops on their toes. Grainter was good at his job, but it always seemed to be a lot harder when she was there. Apart from his team and the vessel crew, he also had two shield techs on board. They were threading their way through the Needles, a myriad of small islands between the two main continents of Bala Verceti and Trun Rizontella. His transport was a hover-craft—fast, quiet and cloaked. They would be undetected unless someone was specifically looking for them.

He looked with admiration at the High Commander leaning over the shoulder of the navigational engineer; small talk about the route they were taking, he presumed. The war wasn't going well, and it showed on her face. He moved closer to her and spoke. 'Do you think there is an underlying strategy, High Commander, with these continual probes to our shields?'

She looked up at him. At fifty years old, she was a fine looking woman, even though years in command of the Vercetian military showed on her face. Frown lines around her eyes and mouth gave her a perpetual faint grimace. He had never seen her smile. If she found something amusing, it would manifest as a gleam in her eye, and no more. He was sure that if she ever relaxed, a beautiful woman would be revealed. 'I'm not sure, Commander. There doesn't seem to be a pattern, but they are certainly taking an active interest in the Great Shield, keeping the shield Artificial Intelligence, and our forces, stretched in the process.'

Stretched indeed, thought Grainter. Monitoring the 1.2 million hoverpods that formed the matrix of the shield was a massive task for the AI and the support maintenance engineers. Adding in military forces to back up the current string of anomalies was a drain on resources. Worth it, though, to keep the war in space rather than on the ground.

The Great Shield was an impressive feat of engineering achieved by their ancestors. One of the techs was happy to explain it to Grainter earlier in the trip. 'Each pod has its own solar powered trilithium battery unit that operates a primary propulsion system, a small laser cannon and a trans-ionisation shield. But when the matrix of pods have linked, it becomes more, much more than the sum of it's formidable parts.' He had carried on describing the nature of the linking— laser guided locking systems and Tricadium fibre interconnecting power conduits— but it was beginning to go over Grainter's head. When he got to the alternative power sources—backup power fed into the matrix from the geosynchronous space stations and geothermal heat sinks from the oceans—he was ready to leave.

All Grainter needed to know was that the shield remained on standby power levels until an approaching vessel, a missile, or someone carrying a weapon tried to pass through it. Then it would come to life.

The hovercraft slowed down as it approached the shield. Grainter instructed the engineers to start their investigative work.

* * *

Trun Commander Mavar Hallot took up a position at the carefully constructed throat of the cave that opened out to the Sea of Needles. They had found a weak point in the Vercetian shield. There were three matrix pods adjacent to the mouth of an island cave, and due to the nature of the overhanging rock formation, the field passed through solid rock before forming a barrier at the mouth. This rock interference created a weak point in the shield. They had excavated from the far side of the island to get in the cave, behind the shield. This gave the Trun the opportunity to study and probe the field, and possibly, find a permanent pathway through it, undetected by the Vercetians.

Unfortunately, a ham-fisted engineer got too close to the shield face with a weapon in his toolkit and triggered a sensor. 'This isn't my weapon,' engineer Cobb protested. 'I've no idea where it came from.' This didn't stop Hallot from dressing him down in front of everyone. It was now a case of waiting to see what the response from the enemy would be. They had set up local monitoring and picked up what they thought to be a heavily cloaked vessel, probably coming to investigate.

Hallot looked at his concealed complement of solders and engineers. He had a total of twenty-four men and women, most of whom were in reasonably well-concealed locations. It was just a case of sitting back and seeing what transpired.

* * *

THE ENGINEER REPORTED TO GRAINTER, 'There appears to be a weak point in the field. I need to get closer to establish what exactly is causing it. The cloaking around our ship is restricting my readings.'

Kam Major cut in. 'Can you tell if there are any Trun present on the other side?'

'No, madam.'

Kam Major turned back to Grainter. 'What are your recommendations, Commander?'

'We should retreat to a safe distance to avoid vessel detection, and I will lead a small detail to investigate further. There's a tiny beach landing. The tech can work from there, and we can secure the location. A detail of ten should suffice,' Grainter replied.

'Good, I concur,' said Kam Major. He felt her eyes fix on him as she nodded agreement. A shiver went down his spine.

The hovercraft retreated and released a small, open top boat, through the shield slip cover, which avoided a breach in the vessel's shield integrity. The men onboard then glided slowly to the shore using a manually steered ghost motor. They landed on the small beach, and the tech started taking readings.

'The projection over the cave is rendering the force field below it ineffective,' the tech whispered to Grainter. 'We either move the force field forward of it,' he stepped back, imagining the distance it would have to move. 'That could mean meticulous reprogramming of thousands of hoverpods—a complicated job. The AI relies on us techs to input the change parameters. Or, we can just look into the cave and if there's a wall of solid rock, leave things as they are. I would need to deactivate three Hoverpods to do that.'

'We'll look inside,' replied Grainter, 'as we're here now.' He didn't want to load more work onto the already stretched shield technicians. He knew there was a risk that the enemy could be in there—masking their presence—it was a standard military procedure. Mini surveillance drones would therefore be ineffective. He gathered his men and quietly outlined a plan of action.

Commander Grainter approached the cave entrance tentatively, with two men either side of him. They were all armed with laser pistols and had body integrated force fields activated. He'd positioned two on either side of the cave entrance with laser rifles targeting anything that might be of threat within. Their objective would be to light the cave up. He signalled to the engineer to disconnect the three pods. His first officer produced a clamp flare and aimed it where he expected the roof of the cave to be. With a sudden whoosh the flare hit the ceiling, the automatic clamping device activated, and the flash lit up the cave.

The instant the cave lit up, a barrage of fire erupted from inside. Grainter, being in a forward position, took nearly all of the fire. Angry fingers were poking all over his body. His communications transmitter informed him his shield was at thirty percent—dangerously low. He would have been dead if not for the reaction of his adjacent comrades who jumped in front of him and shielded him, absorbing the torrent of laser fire. Modern day hand-to-hand combat was a numbers game. Body armour could only take a finite number of hits from any particular weapon. The more opponents firing at you, or the bigger the weapon, the quicker your shield would fail. There appeared to be more than twice as many Trun as his own team. The Vercetian detail had little choice but to retreat, and quickly.

Some tasty shooting from his peripheral riflemen meant that they were now the primary targets of the unseen enemy, giving Grainter and his four men a brief respite to find cover. They shuffled their way to the left side of the entrance. That provided some shelter. Some revising of the situation was desperately required, and Grainter was hoping that Kam Major would respond sooner rather than later.

Kam Major's arrival was spectacular. The craft appeared from left of the cave, turning sideways and slamming to a halt as the driver deactivated the hover function. Four soldiers and Kam Major leapt out and started laying down a volley of fire into the cave, giving Grainter and his men time to jump aboard. Two of her men ran to the far side to protect the lone rifleman, and shepherded him back and onto the craft. Kam Major, together with the four soldiers and the remaining rifleman leapt back on, and within seconds the hovercraft was away.

'Get that shield up!' shouted Grainter.

A couple of seconds later the engineer replied, 'Done, sir.'

* * *

MAVAR HALLOT WATCHED the Vercetian craft disappear into the distance and spotted the faint shimmer of the shield reappearing, sealing the cave again. A faint smile crossed his face.

Everything is going perfectly to plan.

His men were congratulating themselves on dispatching the enemy with their tails between their legs.

Hallot raised his rifle and casually shot three who were showboating and gloating. Without body armour activated they were blown off their feet to the ground. Dead. There was silence as the soldiers turned and stared at their commander, uncomprehending. Their hesitation gave Hallot chance to shoot three more before they came to their senses and tried to return fire. But their guns were inactive, as were their shields. Nothing was working. With the force field activated Hallot controlled the only exit. He concentrated his fire on those nearest to him, trying to herd the rest into the middle of the cave. Some ran for cover, while some braver ones ran at their commander, only to be quickly picked off.

The Trun soldiers gathered in the centre of the cave looked on in stunned silence at what happened next.

Hallot activated a device that hovered in midair and bathed him in green light. He felt his uniform and a layer of skin begin to fall away from him. The relief was luxurious. The final step of his transformation was the reappearance of the horns on his forehead and protruding vertebrae. He made a minuscule adjustment in the timeline they were occupying, then bared his sharp pointed teeth at the horrorstruck soldiers.

Time to make this a little more interesting.

He reached down for a weapon attached to his belt. The touch of a button and it extended, not once but twice, to become an evil-looking sword. Two soldiers seized the initiative and tried to overwhelm him, but within seconds one was dying on the ground with a wound to his heart, and the other was looking confusedly at what had been his arm, now lying on the ground.

Hallot roared!

The sixteen remaining men and women gaped at the terrifying creature.

'Deity help us,' one of the solders whispered.

And the mayhem began.

* * *

SUPREME COMMANDER ZANDER walked into the cave and stared. His furrowed eyebrows nearly covered his eyes, such was the carnage he was facing. Thirty men and women slaughtered by the Vercetians, and only one survived. Commander Hallot.

Commander Mancer followed him in, stopping dead in his tracks.

'What the hell happened here?'

They both moved slowly through the sea of bodies. Phaser burns were evident, but most died from swords. Hands, arms and legs lay scattered apart from their bodies, exaggerating the gruesome aftermath of the slaughter. It made no sense. And why were there no signs of Vercetian casualties?

They approached Hallot, who was still receiving treatment for his extensive, though superficial, injuries.

'What happened here, Commander?' Zander asked.

The medic gave them both a curious look, as he was still tending to the wounds. Hallot shrugged him off and answered the Supreme Commander.

'We were investigating an anomaly in the shield as per our mission plan. Engineer Cobb accidentally triggered a sensor, so we thought that Vercetians coming to investigate was possible.' He leant forward holding his head, dizzy for a moment. The medic tried to attend to him but was waved off again. 'I'm all right. We called it in to headquarters, and to be honest, my men and women were looking forward to a skirmish with the enemy. They turned up late afternoon and positioned themselves on the beach landing.'

Hallot got to his feet unsteadily, and moved slowly into the centre of the cave. 'My troops took up positions around the cave. We could see them through the shield, about ten of them, moving into attack positions. At that stage they shouldn't have been aware of us due to the pitch black and the shield. We thought to have the advantage.'

He seemed to be moving remarkably well now, Zander observed and gave Mancer a sideways glance—one eyebrow raised. Mancer's face was unreadable.

'They deactivated the shield,' continued Hallot, 'and sent in a flare. The battle started then. We had superior numbers and better cover. Their shields should have given out long before ours. They should have been turning tails and running, but they didn't. Their shields showed no sign of weakening, especially the forward three Vercetian soldiers—they seemed invincible. They must have been the cyborg super-soldiers that Premier Gor mentioned. We had no answer for them.'

Hallot stopped and leant forward, hands on knees. A mixture of fatigue and emotional despair? Zander wondered. Or a damn fine performance? He had no trust for this man.

'Our shields gave out, and my troops started taking full-on laser fire, many of them were killed. Then the super-soldiers stopped and took out swords, of all things. They took on my men and women in hand-to-hand combat. We didn't stand a chance, and they seemed to be enjoying it. I was manhandled by one of them and was knocked out.' He pointed to his head wound. 'I don't know why I wasn't killed; perhaps I was just overlooked.' He sat down again, head in hands.

Zander and Mancer moved back into the cave. Mancer leant towards him. 'This doesn't feel right. In all my years in the military, I've never seen anything like this. We need to put a lid it while we investigate further.'

'Too late,' Zander replied. 'The images of this are already back in the capital. The news corps were surprisingly close. We weren't the first here.'

'Deity knows what Gor will do at this news,' said a deflated Mancer.

CHAPTER 16

The Mole
Earth - The Republic of Ireland - 2005

THE WALLS around him were slowly shifting and warping. Nothing would stay in focus. He drunkenly tried to head for the door, but when he reached it, it folded into the wall like a strawberry sinking into custard.

The voices appeared again. Bodiless heads surrounding him, facial features always just out of focus.

"You are no Trun. The KBS is ashamed of you. You are a failure!"

"I've tried my hardest. You don't know what it's like."

"A failure, you should be ashamed."

"No. I've tried and tried."

"You aren't a failure—we are all the same. Trun and Vercetian, we are no different."

"I know that now. I think I've always known it."

The voices from unknown faces bombarded him from both sides. He tried to cover his ears, but his hands didn't reach.

"Leave me, leave me alone! Leave me!'

He woke with a start, the memory of his dream staying with him for a few seconds before fading away. He didn't need to remember it, though, it just reflected how he'd felt for a long time now.

* * *

BEING deep undercover wasn't easy. Not having family or other members of the Knowledge Base Society helping you wasn't easy. He was isolated. He'd trained from birth for this, it was his vocation, but it was hard to distinguish between enemies and friends when they were one and the same. Back on Preenasette, he had regular contact with his Trun friends and family, and they would remind him of what the Vercetians had done to them. How they had betrayed them in an unimaginable way.

But that was nearly three hundred years ago. A memory that was fading into the archives of time, becoming a scary children's story rather than a rallying cry for vengeance against your archenemy. The Vercetians he now lived with rarely mentioned it. They had archived it. Moved on. On the rare occasions it came up, they appeared ashamed of that part in their history but felt they had atoned for it by introducing the current ruling system, which wouldn't allow those mistakes to happen again. A fact he was all too aware of after having lived with them for so many years on Verceti and Earth.

He'd done his job. He would have been expected to take the action he had. His original mandate had been specific. When he had secured selection on the Life Team seventeen years earlier it was clear. His primary role was information gathering. The Vercetians must never discover his identity and purpose; this was the strength of the KBS on Verceti. "If the war turns for the worse, you will need to keep your options open, even if that means killing the Princess. You must make that call as you see it. But they must never discover you."

He'd made an attempt on the princess's life. They had gone to extremes to hide her, protect her from the Trun. It had been the right call, but he was glad he had failed. He was fond of her. Who wouldn't be? He'd been close to her through the magic years of childhood and had watched her blossom into a charming and engaging seventeen-year-old woman. The act he was about to perform would be his final one as a KSB spy—to dispatch a message globe revealing their location and wait to see how the Trun military would respond. Would they even be interested?

This moment had been years in the planning. The failed assassination attempt had made him extremely careful. Everyone watched everyone else. During the escape from Preenasette, Prime and Temper had kept the details of their plan secret. The flight of the Life Teams had caught them all off guard. By the time he had realised they were escaping with the Princess, it was too late for him to send a message without being completely compromised. They were all shuttled onto a Delta Sphere and were only told about the actual nature of the mission once in space.

But careful planning had gotten him this far.

He was well outside of the security dome that protected Harwood Hall, at a spot he that was a favourite place to visit—a clearing in the woods, a natural amphitheater where he could look at the stars at night. Two and a half years of coming here, just to mask this one moment.

He held the small metallic device that would travel across solar systems in his hands and activated the preset guidance system. He thought he heard a noise behind him and turned, listening intently before dismissing it as nothing. He released the globe and watched it disappear into the night sky.

He sat there a while longer, pondering. He had come to love

this hollow in the woods and enjoyed remembering his home and family. He missed his mother and father much more than he ever thought he would. How was the war going? He wanted to see an end to it and wanted to go home to Trun Rizontella. He'd never been there. Neither had his mother, father or grandfather, none of his family. Deep cover in Verceti was nearly a religious calling. The five years on Earth had had a profound effect on how he viewed his world. Preenasette was divided into just two cultures, the Trun and the Vercetians, compared with the multitude of differing cultures on Earth. His planet's differences were minor compared to here.

Trun was the harsher continent, with a severe climate and little arable farmland. Throughout their history life had been tough, but that made them strong and durable. Verceti had a temperate climate, and any crop could grow in the verdant soil. Life was easier for them. They had time to study the arts and philosophy. The Trun had the majority of the planet's metals and precious stones, but they had to mine it from some of the most desolate parts of their world.

Their societies grew up out of drastically differing backgrounds, but the similarities between the two races were also so obvious when viewed from afar, and Earth was far. In appearance there was no difference, apart from variations in the shade of their blue skin, but these changes occurred in both cultures. Their love of music, humour and art were nigh on identical.

He didn't want the two races of his world to be apart now.

He'd seen the conflicts at all levels between the races and religions of Earth: the constant wars, atrocities, the bickering. But somehow they seemed to remain pure in a way he couldn't understand, and shouldn't have been able to comprehend. Amidst the anarchy, there always seemed to be an act of kindness stubbornly pushing its way through.

He was confused, but he knew Preenasette could be a better world. He wanted the war to end.

HE WAS ALSO IN LOVE! And that complicated everything even more.

CHAPTER 17

May Day
Earth - The Republic of Ireland - 2006

AFTER THE VERY MEMORABLE summer of 2002, the children had met up during most of the school holidays for the next few years. Mandy's parents, Prof. and Mrs. Walker, were still crucial to the Vercetian Life Team, carrying out varied and often mundane administration duties for them.

As Grace's skills developed further, she began practising her Extrasensory Perception (ESP) on Mandy and Jon. She helped them try to access a part of their brain that in most humans was almost entirely unused. It wasn't long before she could get into their heads to communicate. Mandy was very receptive and after about a year could string sentences together back to her. Jon, on the other hand, struggled and never really got past the odd word. Mandy and Jon tried to communicate with each other, but without Grace's help, it was a lost cause.

But in general, life was pretty normal. The Vercetians wanted to keep a low profile, but not to the extent that the locals would think of them as reclusive. As they perfected the holo-imaging that created their enhanced facial changes, sharpening their appearance, their confidence in their ability to appear normal grew and they began venturing out and mingling with the community. They enjoyed the local fairs and markets, immersing themselves into the simple life of rural Ireland. The younger Team members, Peter and James in particular, enjoyed visiting the pub, favouring the universally renowned Earth speciality known as Guinness.

* * *

JON, Mandy, Grace and Krankel crossed the boundary of the security shield that surrounded Harewood Hall and headed into the woods towards the small road that led to Kilbal-ligowen. It was May Day, and Jon's small town was celebrating the seasonal transition. Jon had cycled over but was now walking back with his friends, his hands in his pockets.

Grace, as usual, had her arm through his. They strolled along casually, enjoying the warm spring day. The woods were alive with new sights, sounds and smells, Mother Nature well on the way to weaving her magic for yet another year. Mandy was playing with Krankel, though the big dog was more inter-ested in the goings on in the woods that only he could sense. He went racing through the undergrowth after a squirrel and, for now, was gone. Jon could see Mandy pondering. In the past, she would have immediately come to his other arm and slipped hers through, then started some daft conversation on a subject only she could dream up. But she was feeling awkward about doing that, and he could totally understand why.

The Walkers hadn't visited since the Christmas holidays, the longest Amanda had been away from Jon and Grace since they had met five years earlier. Jon and Mandy were young adults now, both at senior school, CSEs done and university beckoning, and both dealing with the psychological and physiological changes that came with that territory. Jon's first meet up with Mandy yesterday had been unnerving. She had changed. Ever since he'd known her he was aware that she was pretty and had an interestingly shaped figure, but now she looked beautiful, and he could only glance covertly at her figure, feeling guilty—afraid she would catch him out. They were both keeping their distance.

'Come and join us, Mandy.' Jon knew exactly what Grace was doing. Nothing much got past her nowadays. She was very astute to the workings of both he and Mandy. He was aware that she operated on two different levels: her Princess Tauriar level and her Earthly Grace level. He knew her Grace level inside out but was only vaguely aware of what she got up to behind Harewood Hall's closed doors. 'Come on,' she repeated.

Mandy moved next to Jon, hesitated, then slipped her arm through his. Jon felt a tingle, even though there were two jumpers and one shirt sleeve between them. The feeling slowly wore off, and Mandy finally broke the ice.

'So, O'Malley. Have they finally managed to teach you joined up writing in the sixth form yet?' Mandy looked across at Grace as she laughed just a bit too loud.

'Oh, I *have* missed your wit, Miss Walker. And you, Gracie Fields, can watch it too,' replied Jon, feeling the tension between them easing.

'Grace Kelly, don't you mind young Jonathan. Princess and all that. And don't forget to curtsy.'

Jon looked sternly at the Princess. 'And it's year five here in Ireland, six is next year. Both make up the Senior Cycle.'

'And it's year twelve and thirteen in England, but my school still calls it lower and upper sixth,' chimed Mandy.

'Why is everything so complicated on this little world?' laughed Grace. 'I struggle to understand how you're not still living in caves.' She laughed again, and was off with Jon and Mandy in hot pursuit, just like when they were younger.

'Krankel. Save me,' Grace wailed pathetically, now in complete hysterics.

* * *

A HALF HOUR later and the little group had arrived in Jon's village.

Jon was explaining about the tradition of decorating bushes in many of the gardens they were passing. 'It's called the May Bush. The children decorate a bush, often a hawthorn, with ribbons and tinsel to celebrate May Day.' He was enjoying a rare occasion of knowing something the girls didn't.

'Why do they do it?' asked Mandy.

'Er... I don't know,' said Jon, deflated.

'The bush is associated with good luck for the house,' Grace offered.

'Are you accessing your super-duper database again, your highness?' asked Jon.

Grace nodded. 'Long life, a pretty wife and a candle for the May Bush.'

Jon looked dejected. 'Even your Irish accent is better than mine.'

After a while, Mandy asked, 'Who are your minders today, Grace?'

'Peter and James. Who would you expect, when the opportunity to sit in the beer garden all day is a distinct possibility.' She looked off to nowhere in particular, her sensing look. 'They're already here. I've asked them to keep a low profile, from us at least.'

Eventually, they reached the village green. The May Day festivities were centred there. The Green was just under an acre of lush green grass at the fork of the three roads into and out of the town centre. The roads, closed for the celebration, were now the route for wandering families and townsfolk. Around the Green were two public houses, the local church, a village hall next to the church, three shops—a post office, a newsagent and grocery store,—and some residential dwellings. Centred splendidly in the largest of the three grassy sections was an inspiring Maypole. Normally only associated with more major towns, Kilballigowen's Maypole was the pride and joy of its three thousand residents. Later in the day the customary dance involving men and women joining hands to form a large circle would commence. An individual dancer would weave through the ring, collecting other dancers on the way, representing a winding serpent.

In every direction something was happening. Cake making and flower arranging competitions. Stalls galore offering games to be played, food to be bought, soft drinks of every colour of the rainbow to be drunk. Tables and chairs outside of each pub were vying for customers. Even the front gardens of the houses facing the fair had tables and chairs, and bunting and May Bushes. It was the one day of the year when their residents could act like landed gentry.

They stood for a while, wondering where to go first. Everything looked so inviting. The moment they stepped onto the grass though, there was a perceptible hush from everyone around them.

Royalty had arrived. A celebrity was amongst them. The quiet was only broken by delighted whispers. Then, two children ran over towards them, shouting excitedly...

'KRANKEL!'

* * *

117

THE CHILDREN PUT their arms around the big dog, then stepped back and stroked him. Soon there was a throng of folk around Krankel, young and old, all speaking to him and wanting to pat him.

When Grace had first taken the giant dog into the town a couple of years back, he had become a celebrity. A freak of nature, they had all thought, but a fabulous one. His friendly disposition, to humans and other animals alike, had endeared him to everyone. Grace and Peter had taken him to the primary school a while back at the request of the teachers. There had nearly been a riot in the secondary school when they found out Krankel was visiting the younger children. A hastily arranged visit was made to the high school the following day. He had even made the local newspaper.

The Vercetians didn't mind this attentiveness, in fact, they welcomed it. It diverted attention from them. To the locals, Harewood Hall was the home of Krankel. And some other people lived there too.

Grace spent the next half hour touring the fair so that everyone could meet Krankel. Jon and Mandy tagged along behind.

'Can you tell if Grace is communicating with the giant hair-ball?' Jon asked Mandy, making sure Grace could hear.

'I can't tell,' she replied. 'Unless she's directly communicating with me I don't hear her at all.'

'I bet she's telling the hairy beanbag to stop milking the attention from his adoring public.'

Grace didn't respond or even appear to have heard anything, but a moment later Krankel turned to Jon with a hurt look on his face.

Eventually, interest in the big dog waned, allowing them to visit the garden of the Red Lion Public House. Peter and James were at a bench-style table, so they joined them.

James went to the bar to order some soft drinks for them, leaving Jon and Peter to start digging at each other.

'Tough job you pair have today,' was Jon's opening salvo.

'Sure is,' replied Peter. 'Much harder than cycling with you.'

'That's because you're always so far behind me,' said Jon.

'Well, at least James and I aren't playing second fiddle to a dog today,' Peter laughed.

'Well some things don't change,' said Mandy in mock exasperation. 'The biking boys still bickering.'

'Oh, Mandy. They're getting worse. Drives us all crazy.' Grace looked up at the sky.

'Haven't you girls anything better to do than interrupting us? Especially when I'm totally outsmarting bike-boy here,' said Peter.

James returned with a tray full of drinks. 'There we go. Have I missed anything?'

'NO,' the girls replied in unison.

'How are you enjoying lecturing at the University, James? Mandy asked. 'You've been there a while now.'

'Six months,' he agreed, 'and loving it. With Grace at University and no one to tutor, it's an ideal solution.'

'He just can't bear to be away from me,' said Grace.

James gave her a false smile, 'Too true, your Royalness.'

A small Lhasa Apso at the next table was yapping away at everybody and everything pulling on its bright pink leash. Everyone at Jon's table was starting to find it hard to ignore to the noisy little mutt.

Jon and Peter had moved on to cycling and were planning their next bike ride.

'We may get a couple of hours in later if we get back in time.' Peter said.

But Jon was right next to the dog. 'Sorry Peter, what did you say?'

He looked at the dog, somewhat frustrated, then at his owners, an elderly couple. The little canine was obviously their pride and joy, but did appear to be hard work. They were chastising her—Dotty —in the gentlest of manners, smiling apologetically to everyone around them. Jon turned back, feeling sorry for them. For a moment he caught Grace looking straight at Krankel. He'd seen that look before. They were communicating.

* * *

'LOOK AT ME, look at me, I'm their dog, I'm their dog.
   Look at me, I'm their dog, look at me, I'm their dog.
   I'm their dog, look at me, I'm their dog, look at me.'
Dotty, the young Lhasa Apso, turned back to her owners, who smiled at her and told her she was being a clever girl and to carry on. That's what she thought they said, so she did.
   'I'm their dog, look at me, I'm their dog, I'm their dog.
   Aren't I cute, yes I am, aren't I cute, yes I am.
   Look at me, I'm their dog, look at me, I'm their dog.'
There are lots of owners around today, thought Dotty, I must tell them all.
   'I'm their dog, look at me, I'm their dog, I'm their dog.
   Aren't I cute, yes I am, aren't I cute, yes I am.
   What a day, yes it is, what a day, yes it is.'
There's a big dog over there. I must tell him too.
   'Look at me, look at me, I'm their dog, I'm their dog.
   Look at me, I'm their dog, aren't I cute, I'm their dog.
   What a day, look at me, aren't I cute, I'm their dog'
The big dog padded over to her. 'Why shout at everyone, little friend?'
   'That's what owners want, big dog,' Dotty explained.
   'I'm their dog, look at me, I'm their dog, I'm their dog.
   Look at me, look at me, I'm...'
   'QUIET!'

Dotty stopped, her eyes wide and she asked, *'Why, big dog?'*

'Because, little lady, your owners aren't clever. That's not what they want. Instructions bad.'

'What do they want?'

'To stop telling everyone you're their dog, not tell them you're pretty, not make them look at you. They want you to show them.

'Don't shout. Show what a gorgeous lady you are. Show your beautiful fur, long and wavy. Know you're their dog by the broad smiles that light up faces when you're there. Get everyone to look at you, show grace, poise and beauty.'

Krankel leant closer to the little dog and whispered, *'Show, don't tell,'* and padded back to Grace and the others.

THEY WERE all mesmerised by the exchange between Krankel and the little Lhasa, consisting of one giant bark by the big dog that caused everyone in the garden to look around. Jon was desperate to pay a visit, so excused himself and popped indoors to the toilet. When he returned, all was quiet. The little dog was now parading back and forth in front of his owners, as though she was in Cruft's show ring,. Two young children who were earlier admiring Krankel from afar now sat cross legged watching the little dog, while her owners sat back, feeling suddenly very proud of Dotty.

Grace, Mandy and Jon finished their drinks and returned to the fair, with Krankel adopting his lord of the manor persona again.

An hour later, after watching the Maypole dancing, they were walking back to the manor house, discussing the fallout from the discovery of a missing message globe the year before.

'Are you going to move out, Grace? asked Mandy.

'Do you need to move out,' Jon said, 'could be the question.'

'Contingency plans are in place,' Grace replied. 'Another two properties are being viewed. One in Cork and another country residence in the north of County Kerry.' She looked at Mandy. 'Your parents are invaluable, as usual.'

Grace went quiet for a while, contemplating. Jon looked at Mandy. They both knew she had something on her mind and waited until she continued. 'You can imagine how much we talk about our situation here on Earth. Before we left our home, Prime was told by the High Council they would have perfected a way of contacting us after a couple of years. Telepathy spanning the galaxy. Unbelievable, I know, but that is the power of our minds—yours as well as ours. Message globes have too high a risk of interception. We all want to go home. It's been nearly five years, without any contact from Preenasette.' She looked away.

'Have we lost the war?' she said finally.

The shock on Mandy's face was plain to see. 'Surely not.'

Grace turned and stared straight into Mandy's eyes. 'The possibility exists. That's why we were sent off world in the first place. We may not have a home to return to.' She shuddered at the thought of it.

Jon put his arm around her and held her close. 'But the war has lasted for hundreds of years. The status quo between both nations... you said so yourself. Two countries equal in nearly every way. The tables just can't turn against you that fast, Grace. Verceti hasn't lost the war. More likely your High Council hasn't found a way to contact you. Spanning the galaxy is not exactly child's play, is it.'

Grace appeared to lose her composure. 'Maybe they've forgotten us.'

Jon had never seen her like this; she had always seemed so upbeat about everything life had to throw at her. She looked up from Jon to Mandy, and her face blanched. 'Well, maybe just out of sight, out of mind.' She started sobbing. Jon was struggling to decide how to comfort her and looked pleadingly to Mandy for help.

She put her arm around Grace, letting Jon step back. 'Grace. This isn't like you.' She used her other hand to lift the Princess's face towards her and softened her tone. 'What is really troubling you?'

Krankel, sensing his mistress's angst, stood by her side resting his head against her. She stroked his eyes and ears gently.

'I don't know what's wrong with me lately, but I keep doubting myself. I'm being taught to be a future leader of my country. I'm being mentally and physically trained to perfection—or as perfect as a Vercetian can be. But I'm not. I don't even think I'm worthy of the Princess title.' She looked from Mandy to Jon and back again, her holographically altered eyes full of moisture, just as any human eyes would be.

'You're too hard on yourself,' Jon said, a softness to his Irish accent the others had never heard before. 'Think of all the beautiful things you can do.' A gentle smile spread across his face. 'Look, you can talk to a giant walking furball.'

Grace was staring at Jon forlornly, the Earthling that she had come to think of as a brother, seeing his crooked smile and unkempt hair and dazzling eyes. She felt pitiful and wanted to be pathetic, but he wasn't going to let her. Neither of them were going to let her. She forced a smile, weak to start off with, then broadening, until she was trying to avoid beaming from cheek to cheek. She laughed a little, so did Mandy. Jon joined in, and the three of them stood, deep in the woods, holding each other and giggling like children.

Jon and Mandy spent the next half hour reminding Grace of all the great things she was capable of, trying to repair her broken confidence. They were making painfully slow progress through the woods, but then, there was no reason to rush. Peter and James were no doubt close by, and probably moaning that they would never get home at this rate. They entered the grounds of Harewood Hall and were near the lake when Grace surprised them by making her excuses to leave.

'Peter and James have something important to discuss with me. They're three hundred metres to our left. You two make your way back. See you later. Come on Krankel.' And they were off. After about thirty yards Grace turned back and shouted, 'Watch out for that hole in front of you!' And then she was gone.

'Very subtle,' said Mandy.

'What?'

Mandy pointed at the hole that had upended her bicycle, the day they had met.

'Oh, that.' Jon knew exactly what Grace was doing, but thought it safest to pretend he didn't. 'Why would she do that?'

'You can't fool me, O'Malley, just like neither of us can fool Grace.' She smiled wryly at him. 'She's been in our heads since we were children. She knows what we're both thinking before we do. And she's sensed confusion from both of us since my return.'

Jon knew Mandy had sussed him and decided to see where this was going. 'She's sensed we have feelings for each other that we don't understand.'

Mandy wagged a congratulatory finger at him. 'The boy does have a brain.' She smiled at him.

'Well, I don't know what my feelings are for you, Miss Walker.' Jon was still just about holding his nerve.

'And, let's just keep it that way, shall we?' Mandy was close to him and still wagging her finger, but much more gently. The end of her finger was touching his chest each time, which he found very off-putting. 'I don't want to fall for the only boy I've ever cared for. I'd rather we stay mates—for now anyway.'

She moved her hands to his shoulders and looked him straight in the eyes. 'Mates?'

Jon felt a flood of relief wash over him; he felt the same. He smiled meekly back at her. 'Yes, mates.'

'Great,' she said, then slid her hands to the back of his neck and kissed him deeply. Jon was dumbfounded. He tried to say something, but his lips seemed to be totally in synchronisation with Mandy's kiss. He was powerless to resist.

After a few moments, she pulled herself away, giggling. 'But I still wanted to know what that would be like.' She walked backwards away from him. 'And Grace will want some juicy gossip when I report back.' She turned and began to run. 'Try and catch me when you come back to your senses.'

Jon didn't follow. He wasn't capable of running. Then he heard in the distance, 'Not too shabby, O'Malley. Not too shabby, at all.'

CHAPTER 18

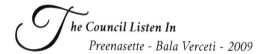

he Council Listen In
Preenasette - Bala Verceti - 2009

THE BALA VERCETI HIGH COUNCIL leaders sat facing each other around the circular table in the meeting chamber. Bakta, Kam Major and Cascan Ofier weren't present. This wasn't a full council meeting, just the four Councillors and the eldest Royal, Domeriette.

Bana Domeriette, the Council Elder, had a deep frown that highlighted her apprehension of the decision they were here to make. At seventy-nine, she was near the end of her tenure on the council. When not frowning she was still an attractive woman, maintaining an ageing beauty that only comes from ignoring the multitude of anti-ageing devices made available to those with a desire to look young at all costs. But she had a big decision to make—probably the most critical of her nine years as Elder—and it showed on her face.

"Quantum Quinary Psychic Vision." Ventar had come up

with that. He'd even given it an acronym and a name: The Q2PV Collective. The council had been working on this for the last sixty years in one way or another. It was the natural next step in their intellectual evolution and involved a process where the combined mental abilities of the four High Councillors and the eldest Royal were used to reach out over vast distances. The process needed five to complete the circle, so accordingly, the past four cycles of the council the eldest Royal had been invited to attend these psychic ability enhancement sessions.

The problem weighing heavy on Domeriette's mind was the ethics of using these combined abilities. The training process, as a mental exercise, was exciting, but using it? It was akin to the mathematical and theoretical physics needed to design and construct a devastating bomb. It presented a fascinating set of problems to solve in the classroom, but using it in the field was a whole different question. Here, their dilemma was that they had created a way to impose themselves on other people's thought processes, and if they started down this path, where would it end?

They had hoped that it would be a method to keep in touch with the three Royals in hiding, but to date, they had been unsuccessful navigating the vast distances involved. With the war going so badly, they were contemplating using it on the Trun Council to try to discover their tactics in advance and respond accordingly and redress the imbalance that now existed. Bakta had officially made this request to the Overseeing & Ethics Committee, a committee chaired by Cascan Ofier who sat just below the High Council and acted as a second conscience on such matters. They had given their approval—'desperate times require desperate measures' was their reply. But the final decision still rested with Domeriette.

The High Council had made the decision weeks ago, but she had delayed ratifying it until now.

'Time for action. We shall do this,' she finally decided. 'Take your positions and prepare for mediation.'

* * *

THEY WENT to a white onyx table located in a curved recess in the southern wall. A large circular glass window and a glazed ceiling made it a magnificent setting, with an incredible view of the city and out to the sea, where the tiny islands were reaching up towards the sky like sharp little needles.

They sat down and held hands, the circle now formed. They closed their eyes and began the process of deep meditation.

Princess Domeriette, or Dom-Bala as she was nicknamed—to avoid being confused with the older Domeriette—was responsible for forming the Conduit. Domeriette acted as a Seeker. Camcietti's expertise was as a Reader of Thoughts. Tauriar would create the Channel home, and finally, Ventar, serving as the Evaluator would complete the circle to Dom-Bala.

The High Council were preparing to listen to the Trun's Quarter Luna War Council meeting, which the Vercetian intelligence agency had established was tonight.

Dom-Bala started proceedings by opening up a conduit to the Trun capital Rizontella, the vicinity of the Council Building. This psychic tube was very short for her. She had, in training, opened them up into deep space. The tube was now ready for Domeriette, Camcietti and Tauriar to transfer their psyches to the War Ministry building.

Domeriette, as the seeker, took control of the far end of the conduit and began sifting through the invisible ether for a dominant voice. They wouldn't be capturing words and sentences, but thoughts—not always the one and the same, especially from politicians. The dominant voice would have the highest density of data packages around it.

Domeriette guided Camcietti to these packages. Acting as the reader, he collected them and passed them onto Tauriar. They appeared to Camcietti as imprints of data surrounding the target. He could sense them, but he didn't have time to process them. It was all he could do to grab them mentally and move them on through the circle.

Tauriar opened a channel back to the Verceti High Council room, following a route parallel to the conduit. He transferred the thought imprints through this channel, to an eagerly waiting Ventar.

Finally, Ventar, as the evaluator, started receiving the thought packages and tried to make sense of them and to get them into some coherent form. This analysis was passed on to Dom-Bala who, in turn, transferred it on to the other three who were operating psychically in Trun. They would hear the commentary as they were carrying out their duties.

The first speaker at the Trun War Ministry meeting began by introducing the principal dignitaries around the table and ran through the topics for the evening's debate.

* * *

IT WAS WORKING WELL. The second and third speakers were picked up and their individual thought monologues captured. They were reporting on basic administrative affairs associated with the war. The Vercetians listened to the commentary from Ventar and at the same time could feel the passion in the Trun thoughts. They had a deep pride in their commitment for this war, still feeling the injustice done to them over three hundred years earlier. Domeriette was appalled that after all this time they still felt so strongly.

Haven't they seen what we've done since those dark times? They knew how we felt and what we did to atone. With no contact and no dialogue, no wonder this war is never ending.

The third speaker finished, and the hall became quiet. Quieter than it had been all evening. Someone important must be readying themselves, thought Domeriette. After an extended pause, for effect perhaps, the next speaker's energy source began to ripple into the ether, and the thoughts imprints started to form. Domeriette sensed the location of this psychic power supply and eased her mind towards it, creating a beacon for Camcietti and Tauriar. Camcietti opened his mind to the imprints, absorbing them as quickly as he could and packaging them up into nice neat bundles ready to pass on to Tauriar. Tauriar had just despatched the first bundle when the imprints started to change. The cohesive flow of the patterns seemed to pause, somehow evaluating its surrounding space. A shadowy entity was aware of them now. They could feel it probing, assessing. Then it went completely quiet. They could all feel something coming.

The attack, an instant later, was brought with such venom and fury it stunned the High Council members. Camcietti took the full brunt of the vicious assault. His mind was wide open and was swamped by evil intent—there was no escape. He began sinking, drowning. His psyche was slipping away. The others looked on helplessly, stunned by their inability to act or help their besieged colleague. Camcietti felt he was falling into a well, his hand stretching out to an ever decreasing circle of light. Deeper, deeper, deeper. All went blank. His psyche had completely disappeared. The others felt it blink out.

Domeriette and Tauriar felt the peripheral effects of the attack on Camcietti; they also felt the evil. Tauriar, in a blind panic, released the channel and with Domeriette flashed back through the conduit that Dom-Bala was now struggling to hold open. A moment later their psyches had rejoined their physical forms back at the council chamber. They sat together at the onyx table, looking at each other. Their eyes were wide with shock and horror.

Ventar, shaken, slowly said, 'Before the attack, I picked up one thought, a thought directed at the Trun Council...'

"Oh, how I am going to enjoy the slow and painful deaths of every single one of you."

The others looked at him, appalled.

Domeriette's senses slowly returned. She looked at each of her devastated friends' faces, and finally, her eyes settled on Camcietti. He had slumped to the table, facing her, eyes glazed over, and he was obviously quite dead.

* * *

'The Vercetians psychic power was most surprising. I was able to neutralise one whose mind was wide open to a neural attack. I'm sure my identity remains unknown.'

'The speed and ferocity of your attack would have caught them by surprise. But the level of skill they have shown is very concerning.'

'Yes, if they try again, they might be much better prepared to defend themselves. And possibly detect our true nature.'

'They were using a psychic corridor technique? They need five, then. They will be a member short and incapable of replicating the psychic bond with only four. It would take years to train a replacement.'

'Perhaps. But the Vercetians method of replacing ruling council members means that one of the exiled Royals has already received most of that training. And, if it *is* one of the older ones, they would be ready to assume the fifth position almost immediately. Detection at this stage would be a great inconvenience to us and might compromise the advantage we hold in the Game.'

'It could cost us this Game. I will not allow that to happen. Our hold on this planet is not by any means secure yet. We mustn't be detected. The prevention of their return is now of utmost importance. We know the locations of two of the three. Arrange visits. I will not accept an interruption to our long-term plans.'

CHAPTER 19

*J*on Leaves University
   Earth - Cork, The Republic of Ireland - 2009

GRACE LOVED Jon every bit as much as any sister loved her brother. She loved Amanda as well, but Jon had always been there for her. When Mandy went back to England after the holidays, Jon still visited most weekends. He would cycle in the morning with Peter and spend time with Grace and Krankel in the afternoon. After a while, he had his own bedroom at Harewood Hall, for Saturday night sleepovers. The Faulkners had invited Jon's parents over a few times and had gotten to know them well. Jon treated Harewood Hall as a second home.

Grace was keenly aware of her future position on the ruling council of Verceti and took her training and responsibilities deadly serious. She was, though, still a child moving into adulthood and she enjoyed the company she could only get with friends of her age.

All of this came to a head when Jon announced that he was

135

considering going to university, should he pass his school exams sufficiently well.

Grace wanted to go too!

PRIME AND TEMPER finally gave in, after two months of relentless pressure from Grace. There were some caveats, though. Firstly, she would need to come back at weekends and "enjoy" a couple of intensive training days. Grace was happy with that; it was what she had expected. She also had to cover some assignments during the week, over and above her university work, easy though it was. Secondly, Peter and Helen were to accompany her there, and she wouldn't be allowed to stay in Halls of Residence. They needed a place that could be made secure. Grace was not so happy with that, but it was non-negotiable. The Walkers were drafted in at very short notice to help find a suitable property.

So, in the autumn of 2008, the two of them began university life in Cork. Grace was studying Astronomy and Jon, Sociology.

Grace and Jon were nearing the end of their first year and were at the University College Cork lecture theatre listening to the middle-aged professor talking about the role of police in modern society. It was Jon's sociology lecture, and Grace, who had left her lessons for the day, was here to shuffle Jon along because she wanted lunch.

'And, if we are to believe Professor M K Gollins in his 1982 paper: The Role of Police in a Changing Society, we could come to a conclusion.' Professor Thorpe droned on.

Grace, who was sitting two rows in front of Jon, could feel his eyes boring into the back of her head.

"*Grace!*"

"*This Professor Gollins hasn't got a clue, Jon-boy. He should be teaching elementary school kids.*"

"Get."

"Come on Jon. I'm bored and I'm hungry."

"Out."

"I don't know why you're persisting with sociology; you'll never be any good at it."

"Of."

"Are there any girls you like in this class? What about the cute blond on your left? I could send her a subliminal message that you're interested in her."

"My."

"I could tell her you're sexy and fun to be with."

"HEAD!"

'So, if you could read chapters seven through ten please, we can review the change of policing methods in the 90s next week. Thank you all,' said Professor Thorpe, winding up.

Grace and Jon met up in the corridor just outside, and she put her arm through his as they strolled in a leisurely way to the Uni bar. 'I find this subject hard enough without you continually wittering in my head,' Jon complained. 'Why couldn't you go to lunch on your own?'

'Then I would had to sit with Peter and Helen, and that looks odd. They look like my minders. Okay, I know they are, but half the university think I'm a bit different as it is. And before you say anything—don't.'

Grace continued without letting him butt in. 'And I need to rescue you from the torment of these lessons. Where would you be without your friendly, neighbourhood alien mate looking after you?' She poked him in the ribs. 'I want to "hang with the gang", but it's still a bit early for them.'

She got the chuckle from Jon that she was after. 'That's why everyone thinks you're a bit different.'

'Jon O'Malley.' She feigned anger. "I have just one word to say to you.'The inside of your brain sucks, and I'm out of it!" She started away up the corridor.

"Sex!" Jon replied in a feeble telepathic attempt... 'Six, I meant six,' he shouted after her. 'That's six words!' but Grace was already halfway to the bar.

* * *

JON CAUGHT up with Grace at the university bar and ordered some soft drinks and a bar snack. Grace's home diet was very low in carbohydrates. On Preenasette all carbs were natural, not manufactured. The standard of food on Earth was not good, driven by corporate businesses questing for huge profits with scant regard for the health of the general population.

Grace was having sautéed fish and steamed vegetables, cooked especially for her by one of the ladies in the cafe of the university bar. She was probably the only person to receive such special treatment. After her first week at uni checking out the food on offer and not taking anything, the ladies had taken pity on her. She had told them she had a food allergy that restricted her diet quite severely. They added a few simple dishes to Grace's specification. Jon had sausage, eggs and chips, piled to overflowing on the plate. Grace didn't know where he put it all.

Eventually, the others turned up. Anna, Nigel and Ken. Greetings exchanged, more drinks and food ordered, and a level of merriment that only seemed to exist on Fridays, when all lessons were over for the week.

'You get away with murder, Grace Faulkner,' exclaimed Anna, smiling. She was studying Astronomy with Grace but had stayed for the entire lecture, Grace having sloped off. 'Professor Taylor turns a blind eye as usual to the star of his class.'

'The teacher's pet,' teased Ken looking up ever so briefly from his deep and meaningful conversation with Jon about the new mountain bike groupset about to be launched by Shimano.

Ken loved cycling every bit as much as Jon, but the sort of terrain Jon cycled on terrified him.

'She left early, so she could come and annoy me at my lecture,' said Jon in an exasperated manner.

'How many times have we told you not to confuse that poor little brain of yours with lectures?' Ken quipped, to the amusement of all.

Nigel piped up as always to defend Grace's honour. 'I'm sure there was a valid reason for Grace leaving early,' and he waited for the said valid reason that never came.

Nigel, the "clever" one of the circle, had had a crush on Grace for most of the year. He fondly imagined his feelings were a secret, but everyone knew, including Grace. Jon had often thought, "If he only knew," and felt quite sorry for him at times. But he was a gentleman and would never make the first move. He was, though, in heaven when debating with Grace. He would raise some obscure subject that went over the top of the others' heads, and she would wickedly question some aspect of it. 'I'm only guessing but...' Or, 'Yes, but what if someone did...' She would lead him through a debate, and he would revel in the intellectual challenges she set him.

Anna continued, 'Professor Thorpe doesn't tolerate any disruptions in his lectures. How does Grace annoy you, Jon?'

'She has her methods,' Jon said guardedly.

'And what are you up to this weekend?' Ken asked Grace. 'On that big country estate of yours.'

'I'll be playing hide and seek with my dog on Saturday, and spending the day doing martial arts on Sunday.' She pretended to do a karate chop on Ken, being very girlie about it.

'That's why we love you, Grace. You're so weird,' Ken laughed.

'And,' Anna jumped in, 'when are we going to get an invite to visit you there? You know we're all dying to look around.'

'Soon, I promise you.'

Their odd dynamic worked well. But there was one subject that they all agreed on, and that was that Jon shouldn't be there.

He had a gift, and it wasn't sociology. It was riding his bike. Ken had been pushing on the subject for some time now.

'Given any more thought to the offer from the Fortune race team, mate?' He was putting Jon on the spot again. 'They're not going to keep asking forever.'

'I'd love to, but that would mean quitting university. You know that, Ken.' Jon said, a certain shortness in his reply.

Ken didn't care. 'You have a duty to use that god given gift of yours, out there against the rest of the world's best downhill cyclists.'

'Seize the moment, Jon,' Anna added. 'Follow your dreams.'

'College will always be here for you, Jon.' A very rare opinion from Nigel, who up until now had thought of bike racing as a superfluous pastime, compared with academic studies. 'Grace has her group of oddballs here to look after her while you're gone.'

'Was that almost a joke, Nigel?' giggled Anna.

Even Grace was smiling. She never got involved in these discussions, as it would break her heart if Jon left. Krankel's too. But even she was starting to see the time had come. She was also aware that she was probably the reason Jon hadn't left already.

While Jon was away from the table, she promised the others she would speak to him over the weekend, 'If I have time between doggie hide and seek, and Kung Fu fighting.'

CHAPTER 20

The Final Test - Cadre 188
Zerot - 190 Years Earlier

BIRJJIKK STRODE into the underground Combat Arena for the final time. The amphitheatre-shaped cave, carved into the granite rock, was a place she knew only too well. The six giant celestial monoliths spread evenly around the arena had borne witness to the butchery she and her fellow academy comrades had carried out here over the last ten years of their training. Six pens stood between the monoliths, holding Birjjikk and her five remaining comrades. The outer gates were still locked. Two hundred elders looked on. She stood there, as she always did, looking up at them defiantly, her gaze sweeping past those who would judge her today. As always, most of them avoided direct eye contact, feigning disinterest. But today, that would be the furthest thing from their minds.

Today the Final Test would decide who would become the leader and Player of Cadre 188, the next team to enter the Zerot Killing Games.

Birjjikk's gaze moved to her comrades.

Opposite her was Graffojj, the one apart from herself to declare his intentions to lead. She would have to kill him if her leadership was to mean anything.

Aligned with her bid were Carffekk on her right, and Denttikk on her left. Carffekk was a very able warrior but had shown the potential skills of a master planner. Birjjikk had seen this ability early in their training and had spent many years cultivating a relationship with him. All of the great Cadres of the past had two common denominators, a brutal and ruthless leader and a master tactician. Denttikk was a beast of a woman and had hero-worshipped Birjjikk ever since her first display in the arena. She had taken instantly to the bear and took on the duty of caring for it. They became inseparable. Kindred spirits. But when Birjjikk was about, the bear only had eyes for her. Denttikk had always thought of herself as the best warrior of the group. One of the strongest she may have been, but she lacked finesse, and she never understood that. But Birjjikk was fond of her—in the same way that she was fond of the bear—and more importantly, trusted her.

Opposite her in Graffojj's camp was Henkk to his left and Cumbajj to his right. Birjjikk would have had Henkk as her fourth team member—he was solid and trustworthy she felt, even though he'd chosen Graffojj today. Cumbajj hardly made it to Birjjikk's consideration. She was vicious, but would never be a good team member. She always seemed to have a different agenda. She only made the final six because of the inferior skills of the remainder of the academy.

The object of this last foray into the gladiatorial arena was to choose a Team Leader. The unwritten protocol was that the adversaries for the position should fight to the death, and their aligned colleagues should play no more part than to ensure none of the other support players interfered. Non-interference was very rare, though, with emotions running high and the emerging feelings of the Brukkah breaking through. Things would often get out of control.

The Brukkah. All Zerot strove to attain it, but it was their curse too. For full sexual arousal, a Zerot needed to reach the Brukkah, and the only way this ancient race could get to that stage now was to kill. For most, frenzied killing was the only way to reach it. The Killing Games were designed to facilitate this.

Swords, daggers and handheld shields were the only weapons allowed today. All technology ordinarily available to them—which was formidable, their last twenty years of training had taught them that—was prohibited.

The outer gates opened, allowing the six young Zerots to enter the arena. They slowly walked to the centre and formed a loose circle. Birjjikk and Graffojj stepped forward until they were face to face. They drew their swords and crossed them formally. A small nod of the head from each of them acknowledging the formalities complete, and they stepped away again, rejoining the circle. They would now await the chief elder to start the proceedings.

Birjjikk studied Graffojj. She had fought him a thousand times. They knew one another inside out. As the two best warriors of the class, they had enjoyed trying to beat each other, no matter the means, laughing at and taunting one another in the process. They knew each other's every move, could read every feint, could predict the other's next move, attuned to the merest physical precursor movement. But now it was for real. To the death. Knowing that this day would eventually come she had held back some of her most daring moves. Fighting sequences she had spent endless hours perfecting alone and in secret, away from any prying eyes. She would be a fool to think he hadn't done the same.

They both had Fangorn swords: a narrow and delicate single edged blade made for speed and accuracy, with a gentle curvature attained by hardening and quenching each layer of steel. The protracted polishing process made the blades gleam, the cutting edge the sharpest known to the Zerot. An elongated, jewel-encrusted hilt allowed single or two handed use.

The elder nodded, and a Grunz struck a huge gong to signal the start of combat.

* * *

BIRJJIKK CROUCHED SLIGHTLY and began circling Graffojj, feeling the others edging back to give them both room. Her opening gambit would be to lead with an advanced practice routine and see how he responded.

She set herself for Galka 9. A light thumb and forefinger grip, letting the weight of her sword create an angulation with her arm. Feeling for solid footing in the gritty sand of the arena, she lunged forward, slashing at Graffojj's right side.

She felt the minuscule shift of his weight as he made a circular parry, deflecting her sword away neatly.

He countered with a straight jab that found only Birjjikk's waiting shield.

She fended off his blow, and watched her short, sharp stab at his midriff easily parried by his shield.

Birjjikk stepped back, discarded her shield and with the same hand withdrew her dagger.

Galka 9 to the letter. Graffojj was happy to play the game for the moment. Did he have a plan, wondered Birjjikk? Or was he hoping she would tire first and make a mistake? She was obliquely aware of the other four, all shouting encouraging support to their would-be leader. Denttikk's thundering voice was drowning out the others.

Galka 9 was finished off as well as a complete cycle of Gargalka 6, all carried out at blinding speed and incredible accuracy. Birjjikk remembered the words of advice from her sponsor Sammanna, of the Rebutti Dynasty. 'Feed the men enough wire to allow them to garrotte themselves.' Over the last ten years or so, she had done just that. And always making her technique appear slightly inferior to his. Always looking more tired and out of breath after training sessions. Millions of little ways to make him feel superior and invincible. At the end of each day, she would repeat the day's training, enacting excellent technique and stamina.

After two more training cycles and little sign of Graffojj taking the initiative, Birjjikk took charge.

Now was the point where she would show her superiority —time to get inside his head. She left the practice routines and went into free play, slowly speeding things up, and sharpening her attacks. Graffojj dealt with this comfortably, but Birjjikk caught the momentary widening of his eyes—surprise at her change of pace. She was pleased with this and continued ramping things up. After another couple of engagements, she backed off, stepping back a couple of paces. They circled each other until Birjjikk reached her shield. She holstered her dagger and picked it up, making sure she kept eye contact with him, displaying supreme confidence. Win the mind game first, and the fight will follow, Sammanna had taught her.

She noticed Cumbajj acknowledge what must have been the faintest of instructions from Graffojj, and she started moving closer to Denttikk.

Is this his play? Is he planning some outside interference to break my rhythm and give him a winning advantage?

Birjjikk edged around to keep Cumbajj in sight. She was planning something now with Denttikk, hands gesticulating followed by the briefest of pushes to her shoulder. Whatever Cumbajj had in mind, Denttikk was taking the bait.

Graffojj launched an attack, which Birjjikk defended easily, and he continued Galka 2. She was disappointed with his lack of initiative, but decided to act out this latest practice routine until she fully understood what was happening in the wings. A few moments later she realised that she had misjudged Graffojj, this routine would have them changing positions halfway through and Denttikk and Cumbajj would be directly behind her. She could revert to free play and maintain her position but decided to stay with the routine and see what played out.

Halfway through the Galka 2 and Graffojj lunged to Birjjikk's left, looking for an inside opening for a blow with his knife. She parried with her shield. He turned away from her swivelling 180 degrees so that could attack her sword hand. She followed his movement and parried again with her shield. Her back was now to Cumbajj.

She slowed the pace slightly to give herself more reaction time.

A brief glance behind her caught Denttikk shoving Cumbajj away. Giving the momentum Cumbajj needed to fall towards her and in the process, take her legs from under her.

She turned back to Graffojj. His eyes were on Cumbajj, and his body was tensing, ready for a death lunge.

Birjjikk was ready though, and as Cumbajj was about to sweep away her legs, she leapt, performing the start of a backwards summersault.

Her mind was set.

Graffojj was diving in for the kill.

Her rising left foot glanced off the flat face of Graffojj's lunging sword.

She twisted, allowing her shield to deflect his sword further and felt his balance falter.

His side was now vulnerable. Birjjikk was still twisting, her sword nearly in position to deliver a death blow.

She couldn't help grinning at how easy this was.

But her grin disappeared as she saw Denttikk dive in after Cumbajj; now aware of the tactics she was employing. An unwitting Henkk, sword drawn, was just about to drive it into Denttikk, thinking her the villain.

Birjjikk had a decision to make. Win the fight or lose a friend.

She thrust her sword downwards, driving it deep into Graffojj's side.

As she rotated further, she lost her grip on her sword, now firmly lodged in his torso and caught sight of Henkk's sword piercing the flailing Denttikk.

As Birjjikk completed her summersault, she found herself facing Henkk, his blade recovered from the dying Denttikk. Her eyes were enraged, and she was pushing him back with her shield, her other hand reaching for her knife. Henkk's demeanour was stoic. His posture suggested he knew he'd acted correctly and wasn't going to raise his sword to the Cadre leader. As she drew her knife, Carffekk stepped between them, facing Birjjikk.

'Kill him, and we only have three in our Cadre. Henkk was acting honourably, he knew nothing of Graffojj's plan to beat you.' He watched as the rage slowly drained from her.

She stepped away from them and turned to her opponent and her friend, both dead on the arena floor. A sheepish Cumbajj had gotten up and was dusting herself down, unwilling to meet her eyes. Birjjikk turned and looked up at the Elders, raised her arms as if ready to scream, but didn't. She bowed, but nothing about the gesture conveyed respect.

She motioned for the three remaining to join her. Carffekk, Henkk and Cumbajj complied. Cadre 188 was now complete. She led them out of the arena as their leader and Player, ready and eager to join the Killing Games.

CHAPTER 21

The Dory Family Trip to Earth
Preenasette - Trun Rizontella - 2009

THE MILITARY APARTMENTS to the south of the Allacrom Central Command Centre in Trun Central Territories were as bleak as the surrounding landscape. Aesthetics were not at the top of the architect's list during this development. Made from dark grey granite slate, they stood in endless rows of six-story blocks. All that broke up this monotonous continuity was the interweaving elevated mono-tram lines, all heading to and from the north: to the Command Centre, the Space Hub and the training barracks.

Kean DeMancer was making his way to his father's house. His mother Lizetter made sure he visited her ex-husband as least every ten days, since joining the Reticent Guard he was apt to find reasons not to go. He approached the ground floor apartment of block 2506H apprehensively and spoke into the voice recognition entry system. A moment later and he was walking into the kitchen where his father was drinking

Comfier tea. The layout of the apartment was identical to his mother's, but it couldn't be any different. One was a home, the other a place to sleep and eat.

'Hello, Father,' he said, helping himself to Cransome juice from the cooler.

His father, nose in some military document, looked up and smiled. A craggy, old wrinkly smile, but one with warmth. 'Good morning, son. The gods of probability have ordained that we both get the same off-world posting. Who would have expected that?'

Kean breathed an inaudible sigh of relief. It appeared he would be spared the ritual admonishment from his father for not joining the Trun Squadrons after completing his military training two years before. He was expected by all and sundry to follow in his father's footsteps, but, to his father's disappointment, he chose a more covert career as an Infiltrator in the Reticent Guard. He hated the pomp and ceremony that was part and parcel of the Squadrons. He also wanted any advancement to be attributed to him, not who his father was. The main reason though, was that he was happier working alone than in a team, and in the RG that was considered a prerequisite.

He answered, 'Yes. Who would have thought?' His father looked very solemn, lacking any of his usual verve. Even when he was chastising him for abandoning family tradition, he did it with a certain charm and dramatic flare. That was missing today. 'You don't look happy about this posting, Father. Aren't you pleased?'

'No. He looked up, and Kean thought with surprise he was looking his age, something he was excellent at hiding. 'I'm not. I'm the second in command of the Trun military, and I'm dragged away at a critical phase of the war with our aggressive neighbours to go and apprehend a teenage princess, for goodness sakes. I have at least two dozen men under me capable of this.' He was getting flustered, his cheeks turning a dark sapphire blue.

Kean was confused. 'Why has the Supreme Commander asked you, then? It seems strange.'

'Zander hasn't asked me. The order came from the Council. He was outvoted.'

Kean knew that politics had become prevalent in the Trun military over the last few years, but knew better than to press his father on the matter. He changed tactics. 'Do you know what my role is? My superiors have told me little.'

'That's because your superiors know little. They're being frozen out of the decision-making process, as are we.' Kean had never seen his father open up like this before and was starting to think that some of the vague rumours whispered by so many might well be true. His father continued, 'I know what your assignment is, but it's not my place to tell you. The Supreme Commander will tell you in a few days time. He considered that. 'What I *can* say is that your RG training will stand you in good stead, and I think you will do very well.'

A rare compliment.

'You will be part of an advance party travelling by TW Sphere,' his father continued. 'And I will follow with a much larger military complement, a TC cruiser most likely. I'll probably arrive a year or so after you.'

Kean knew that two-thirds of the known wormholes were too small for a vessel the size of a Cruiser, whereas a sphere could navigate most of them. His father would have a longer, more convoluted route to wherever their destination was.

* * *

A FEW DAYS LATER, and Kean was in a small anteroom waiting to be briefed by the Supreme Commander.

When summoned to the meeting, he wasn't surprised to see

his father there, next to Zander. They had become friends eleven years ago when Zander had first taken the top job, a surprising appointment from the Northern Trun Military. It had coincided with his parents breakup, so his father diverted all his energy and skill into helping this young man succeed. Mancer was whispering something into Zander's ear, and he was nodding.

There were three others around the table. One was Commander Hallot, the other two, Kean assumed, were his companions for the trip to Earth.

Zander looked up to start the proceedings, his dark eyes giving nothing about his mood away.

'I will go around the table and introduce you all.' He looked to his left, past Mancer, to a small man in his early thirties. His mousy head cap was unusual for a Trun, they mostly had black caps that complimented their blue skin tone. The man scanned the table and nodded in acknowledgement. 'This is Sub Commander Blomquist Tray, the pilot of this expedition. I will brief Tray separately, but for now, he is to get you to Earth.' Zander looked in the direction of Kean and at the woman next to him. 'He will land you in the southern part of this country,' he pointed at a projected image of a map. 'Once he has helped with settling you both in, he will return to a concealed orbit around the planet. We have some other jobs for him to do, but he will be there to relay your reports back to Preenasette, and liaise with Commander Mancer when he eventually arrives.'

He moved his penetrating gaze to Kean, who couldn't help wincing slightly under the scrutiny. 'This is Kean DeMancer of the Reticent Guard. He will make friends with one of the two human juveniles known to be associates of the Princess. A Jon O'Malley.' He was looking at notes. 'He is of a similar age and has a passion for bicycle riding, as do you. That will be the common interest to get you close to the Earth boy.'

Without hesitation, Zander moved his gaze to the woman

on Kean's left. 'This is Amir Sonia.' She was in her late twenties and had a serious expression. Kean was disappointed. He wasn't exactly hoping for romance during the journey, but a bit of flirting on the way would have been fun. 'Sonia will be tasked with seeking out the female, Amanda Walker.'

Finally, he nodded at the military man. 'This is Commander Hallot. He will be coordinating the whole expedition and will report directly to me.' It was evident there was a certain coolness hanging between these two men. From his RG training, Kean was picking this up in abundance.

Zander went on, 'You have, no doubt, read the extensive notes sent by our operative in the Vercetian Life Team on Earth. Firstly, you will make no attempt to contact this agent. You will find all traces of his identity erased from the notes. Secondly, you are to be in a position to direct Commander Mancer's forces straight to the princess's location upon his arrival.' Zander paused for a moment and then continued, 'Be warned. There is extensive security around the Royal after an assassination attempt.'

'You leave in three days time. Read the notes and get yourself prepared.'

* * *

KEAN AND SONIA exited the room, leaving Zander, Mancer and Hallot to brief Tray.

'You are to report directly to Commander Hallot,' said Zander. 'Particularly regarding any unusual activity by Sonia. We know little about her. She comes highly recommended by the office of Premier Gor. But we do not understand their interest in this mission.'

Mancer picked up the thread. 'Log all of her communications and make sure everything goes through Commander

Hallot, who will keep the Supreme Commander abreast of any developments.'

Hallot finished with, 'You are the eyes and ears of this mission. It mustn't fail. Commander Mancer needs to have immediate access to the princess when he arrives on Earth.'

'Any questions?' asked Zander of Tray. 'No? Then you are dismissed. Commander Hallot, please escort the Sub Commander out.'

When they were alone, Zander said, 'Your plan to flush out Hallot is in place. Tray's a good man. He'll monitor them both and hopefully find something to tie him to the subterfuge going on here.' He lightened the conversation somewhat, asking Mancer about the makeup of the task force he would be taking.

'A full ground squadron comprising thirty soldiers, four mechanoids, and a standard support, surveillance and maintenance crew of fifteen,' said Mancer. 'A TW Sphere for the return journey and Four 3W Fighters should ensure enough firepower to overpower the Life Team and fend off any interference from the inhabitants of Earth. They are about three hundred technological years behind us.'

Zander had pulled up a 3D map showing the route between their star system and Sol. 'You will need to cross the waste space between the galaxy's inner and outer spiral arms.' Zander stopped to think. 'That would require an additional two years in cryogenic stasis. Someone is not making this easy for you.'

Mancer's look said it all.

CHAPTER 22

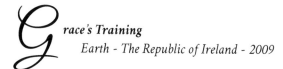

race's Training
Earth - The Republic of Ireland - 2009

MOVING SLOWLY.

Breeze is light. But wrong direction. Fragrance everywhere, little critters, flowers and insects. Forest coming alive after cold time. My fur dances as wind touches it. All normal, though. Can't smell mistress or boy.

Noises fantastically tangled. Wind past my ears, buzzing insects avoid me at last moment, birds in trees are excited and chirping as they chase each other—they see me before I see them. The ground creaks slightly as I pad along, little slimy things croaking and shuffling away. All normal and all filtered out. I hear the sounds a long way away. What is different? What is out of place? Nothing. Can't hear mistress or boy.

I want to play-fight boy. My favourite game. But mistress said today is a different game. Find mistress. Find boy. Can't hear in mistress's head, she has closed it. Will make a big circle, then wind will help.

I see everything now. Scurrying critters, swaying plants and buzzing insects, the sunlight carving its way through the trees and bushes to get to the ground. All normal, all filtered out. I see a long way, past all these things to a patchwork of remaining light. What is different? What is out of place? Nothing. Can't see mistress or boy.

I start to run.

Not as fast as when with boy on his machine. That is fun. No. Fast, but can still see, hear and smell everything. Sensations fly at me from everywhere. I breathe it all in. Fantastic. Then filter it. What is different? What is out of place?

Something...

I stop. A smell. So very brief. The boy?

Nose up high, I find it again. Easy now. Follow the line of smell straight to boy. It's getting stronger. Boy is close.

Smell has gone, find it again. Can't. Mistress is helping boy. They must be close.

I move slowly onwards, filtering, filtering. I stand dead still, waiting, waiting.

Something there. Or, something not there. A space with no smells or sounds coming from it. Get closer. See it now, things are moving differently around it. One of mistress's bubbles. Push my nose through. It is boy. He scratches behind my ears. Lovely, but must find mistress. Boy runs off. I filter him out.

"*Krankel.*"

"*Mistress?*"

"*Find me.*"

I feel her. I know where she is, excited to find her. I arrive, but she's gone.

"*Mistress?*"

"*Find me.*"

She's over there now. I race to her. She's not there.

"Mistress!"

"Find me, Krankel."

She's moved again. I will find her. She's not there again.

"Last chance, find me."

I stop. Ignore mistress. I sniff and listen and look.

"Krankel."

Ignore. Sniff, listen and look.

"Krankel!"

Got mistress. Hiding in bubble. I leap over to her, burst through bubble and she hugs me.

"Good boy Krankel, good boy."

* * *

'You did well yesterday, Tauriar.' Prime was giving the Princess some final instructions as he always liked to do before her quarterly practical skills assessment. 'You masked your bubble location and fooled Krankel. But today is a whole different level of testing. Campazee has worked for weeks on this. When you enter the Blue Room, you are on your own and will be acting in real-life conditions. All of the skills you have learnt so far will be needed to get you through this test. Your training has been thorough. Meditate here, and when you're ready, enter the Blue Room. Impress me, Princess.'

* * *

Grace entered the room, and stood there silently in the centre, legs slightly apart and knees bent. Adopting the Shanjah position: arms out, elbows straight, palms together.

Katie was adjusting some controls in the corner of the room. 'The challenge will start soon.' She left, leaving the door slightly ajar. Grace assumed Douglas and some of the others would be in the viewing area. Krankel was in one corner of the room, curled up and fast asleep, his mind closed to her. Katie's work, probably.

Two figures entered the room via the same door but closed it this time. They were dressed head to foot in blue holo-suits. Grace tried to probe to see who they were, but they were masking their identities. From their body shapes and posture, she suspected that it was William and Katie. They moved silently to opposing corners, squatted and remained perfectly still.

Grace automatically shifted her weight to be able to react to either of them, though doubted they would come into play before the scene was set. She calmed herself. Retreated into her mind to respond from there, rather than relying on her physical senses.

The banks of blue holo screens that covered every surface of what was once the staff dining quarters in the grandeur of the Hall's past, blinked on as the programme began loading. The blue screens resolved into a scene of an Avaska field, right on the edge of a small oasis. Soon there was unfathomable depth to the holo-room. Rippling bright green grass of the Avaska seed could be seen stretching off to the distant horizon.

Grace felt exposed. She was in the open, and the long grass would restrict her movement. On the other hand, the lush foliage of would provide cover, but who knew what surprises Katie might have hidden in there? She probed for Krankel— nothing. His undefined role was destined for later.

The open field of grass would be better, and she looked around to see how she could manipulate the environment to her favour.

She crouched down, obscuring herself, and concentrated on making a cylindrical air pressure node. She increased the pressure from twenty atmospheres to forty, then sixty. Eventually, it was heavy enough for her purpose. She guided it away from herself in an ever widening circle, flattening the grass. Firmer footing for whatever might follow. She was pleased with how quickly she finished the pressure node. It was one of her favoured mental tools and would no doubt be important today.

She waited patiently. After a couple of minutes, her mind wandered back to her early days on Earth with Jon and Mandy. She had tried one of her pressure nodes on Jon, but it ruptured, making a noise that had him in hysterics. She remembered Mandy saying, 'So, to become just one of four members of a ruling council that presides over an advanced, highly enlightened civilisation, you have to know how to make a whoopee cushion?'

Concentrate, Tauriar, she reminded herself and awaited the challenge.

* * *

MOMENTS LATER, a Karinja She warrior stepped brazenly out of the bushes surrounding the oasis, and stared at Grace defiantly. Part of a caste of dynasty warriors from Verceti's history over two millennia earlier, these warriors were famed for their tenacity and fighting skills. Much of Grace's defensive training today was based on the martial arts of this era and mainly these fighters.

She was tall—just like Katie—and was a menacing scarlet colour, the result of intricate red tattooing all over her body. Her head cap was painted bright red, showing her status as a master. She held an ornate fighting staff in her right hand and wore a short Karin blade tucked in her belt.

Grace knew Katie had a passion for this era, it and was certainly the holo-matrix template for this opponent. But she mustn't think of her as Katie. This warrior would have programmed skill levels well above that of her colleague.

A staff appeared on the ground next to Grace. A test of her fighting ability. The longer she could survive without using her modern day powers, the more impressive her performance would be.

The She warrior waded through the grass until she reached the clearing. Now holding the staff in both hands she assumed an aggressive pose. Grace, staff in hand, moved into the centre of the clearing and prepared to defend. The warrior leapt forward, staff swinging high and coming down vertically at Grace. She defended, moving to the side and deflecting the blow. The warrior would be programmed at a level similar to Grace's, so she was confident enough to return the attack, trying to catch her opponent's body. The warrior was too quick and in the space of an instant, opened an offensive, making Grace move decidedly quicker.

The pace of the confrontation evened out. It had a cat and mouse feel about it: each testing the other. Grace was now feeling confident in her ability to keep the She warrior at bay. But this was a test of all her skills, and she was bracing herself for more.

That something more came in the form of a swarm of Gorotti birds flying out of the centre of the oasis and gathering to attack her. In Verceti nature, these small birds would flock to fend off predators wanting to steal their eggs, diving at them with sharp beaks, sacrificial darts that rarely failed to deter their target. Here, though, they were larger and looked mechanical—much more menacing.

Grace was now threatened on two fronts, but as soon as the birds commenced their attack, the warrior began to fade away. She needed time to assess this new threat, twenty or so flying darts would need an ingenious solution. A time acceleration bubble would give her that solution.

She focused on a wafer thin layer of air around herself and accelerated the sine wave magnitude of the protons surrounding the layer atoms. This changed their natural frequency, and being proportional to time, slowed time within the bubble. She would have about thirty to forty seconds before the bubble failed. The psychic power required to hold this state increased exponentially. The Gorotti birds slowed to a near dead stop.

Twenty-two of them, breaking apart into two distinct groups. An attack from two sides.

Think Tauriar, think!

She moved quickly to one side so that when she reappeared in normal time, both flocks would be in the same plane when turning towards her. The mechanical birds started turning slowly, their sensors still picking up Grace's rapid movement. Grace formed a large wedge-shaped air pressure node, ready to deploy the moment she was back in normal time. She burst the bubble and deployed the wedge, deflecting most of the higher birds down towards the lower ones, causing multiple collisions. About half of them were taken out, but the remainder were still making a beeline for her.

Her last resort was to make a shield node to protect herself, but time and her skill were deserting her. The barrier lacked pressure and only managed to stop about eight of them before crumbling away. She braced herself for some holographic pain as the remaining three Gorotti birds hit her.

* * *

THE BIRDS FADED AWAY, and so did the pain. Grace picked herself up and dusted herself off. She nearly cursed, but that wouldn't have gone down well. Princesses of any kind don't curse.

She was struggling to think what else she could have done what she might have missed—but nothing came to mind.

Get with it—the next challenge will be any time now.

* * *

KRANKEL PADDED out of the Oasis, his mind still closed to her. He looked up at her, barked once, and turned, heading back into the shrubs. Grace followed him.

They made their way along tracks through the oasis perimeter—a dense growth of olive green privet with lightly scented white flowers. After about twenty feet, the environment opened up, revealing an array of exotic flowers and small bushes, all indigenous to Grace's home world. She recognised most of them, well aware of the dangers lurking within the radiant beauty. The lush plant life started thinning out as they approached the oasis itself, the density of the foliage now replaced with dark maroon slate shingle. The slate rocks increased in size as they drew closer to the water's edge, strewn with larger rocks, some semi-submerged in the bright blue water. The oasis was about forty feet in diameter with a small geyser that surged intermittently.

Krankel stepped up onto a large, partly submerged rock and lay down—head up and attentive, looking at the other side of the water. During the next eruption, an apparition appeared in the middle of the spray. An eight-legged octopod, an amusing looking sea creature from her home world.

Its strange blue eyes stared directly at Grace as it fanned its tentacles away from its body. From a tentacle tip, a data thought imprint appeared. She knew immediately this was a test of her targeted mental training, for when she became eldest Royal and joined the Ruling Council members in the Q2PV Collective. She was struggling with this. She was able to identify and recognise the thought imprints and get hold of them, but unable to apply sufficient momentum to despatch them forward.

To her right a rift appeared, a small wormhole at treetop level. In the Collective, one member would assume the role of the Channel and transfer data imprints along this conduit, sometimes light years away, even spanning galaxies. But if they didn't receive them with sufficient momentum, their chances of forwarding them on would be minimal.

Now three tentacles blossomed data imprints at their tips, each a different shade of green. The darker the colour, the stronger the impression of the thought. An expert would capture and transfer all of them. Grace needed to concentrate on the darker ones first.

She closed her eyes and focussed. The octopod shimmered a ghostly silver form, as did Krankel and the rock, the bushes and the small lake. The imprints remained shades of green. She grabbed the first one, her mind's eye locking onto to it and propelling it towards the Channel. Slowly at first, but managing a steady acceleration. It popped out of existence as it passed through the small rift.

She grabbed the second one. There were five now.

Moving too slowly. Lock. Extract. Export.

She concentrated on the thoughts the octopod generated. She locked, extracted and transported them along the now familiar route to the Channel. Again and again and again. She was pleased with her progress dealing with all of the darker and medium green imprints. Only the light green ones faded away unsent.

The octopod was relentless. As soon as a thought imprint was removed or disappeared, it was replaced by another. They reappeared faster than Grace could grab them.

She began to panic but reminded herself the test might be unbeatable. She had to stay focused for as long as possible.

This task is easier than expected, she thought as she whipped the little packages off to the rift. But then she saw something in the corner of her eye. At the rift, a large number imprints hadn't entered. There was an almighty jam. A green mosaic of imprints all nudging and bumping one another.

How did that happen?

Grace's ego deflated. She vainly tried to move some of the

ones closest to the rift. Gridlocked. She opened her eyes, and it all disappeared. She put her hands to her face in despair.

I'm never going to be able to do it.

But the holo room wasn't going to let her mope. Stepping dramatically out of the lagoon a mythical Swamp Troll leered at her. It was over ten feet tall, and seeping green puss from most of its body. It carried an axe in one hand and a stunted sword in the other, and voiced a guttural bellow.

Krankel's mind opened up to Grace and he stood, growling at the troll.

Grace knew that she would have to fight this beast with her mind, its strength far too much for her. Again, she needed time.

"Krankel, with me."

She ran around the water's edge away from the troll. She made a pressure node, stood on it and hovered over the lake, keeping clear of the geyser.

"Keep away from the beast, Krankel."

She knew she could avoid the beast indefinitely. But she needed to demonstrate a method of dealing with this situation. She would try and reason with it.

'What do you want Mr. Troll? I am not your enemy.'

'Thudder hungry.'

The troll turned back to the water and stepped in.

'Mr. Troll, there are much tastier things to eat than me. I will give you indigestion. The fruit of the mango bush behind you is sweet and will cure the sores on your body.'

'Thudder want meat.'

He was in up to his waist. His droopy belly seemed to float on top of it. The troll was halfway to her position, so she moved out of lunging range.

'There is no meat on me Mr. Troll. You would still be hungry and would have wasted your time.'

'Thudder has lots of time.'

Grace manoeuvred to the far side of the lake, stepped off

the node and collapsed it. She quickly formed a new one, cone-shaped, and directed it towards the troll, point first.

A change in strategy.

'Mr. Troll. You can't defeat me. I am invincible.'

She started prodding it with the node. It bellowed at this invisible attack. Grace stopped.

'I can destroy you anytime, Mr. Troll, but I won't. I like you, Mr Troll. We can be friends. Is there a Mrs. Troll and baby trolls?'

The troll was out of the water now, still batting the unseen attack. It looked at Grace, menacing and full of evil intent. Krankel was at her side, snarling, aware of the danger. Ready to die for his mistress.

'No Mrs. Troll. Just Thudder.'

It raised the axe and with surprising speed for one so big, charged her.

Krankel reacted immediately, racing towards the troll.

'Krankel!'

He ignored her, the urge to protect her too strong. He leapt onto a rock to give him the height he would need to reach the troll's head. But Grace could see the arc of the trolls axe heading straight to Krankel's stance. She focussed hard and formed a time acceleration bubble. It worked, but it was too soon after the last one. Time hadn't fully reset, she would only have seconds to act.

Everything froze. Krankel was only six feet from the axe.

Another node to deflect the axe, thought Grace. But she was exhausted. No test had ever taxed her this much. She doubted herself. She questioned her right even to be a princess. This cost her valuable seconds. When she pulled herself together, she imagined the wedge shape node she would need, and where to position it for maximum effect. She broke the bubble and set the node in place.

Back in real time, the axe headed inexorably toward the

dog. The wedge worked, but only to a degree. The pure strength of the troll's massive arm overcame the deflective resistance of the wedge. The axe struck Krankel and sent him flying into the bushes.

Grace saw a limp Krankel sprawled under a bush, lifeless, and she cracked.

She glared at the troll, eyes murderous, forming another cone-shaped pressure node—long and thin, a weapon.

'You…'

She could easily accelerate it straight into the troll. A fatal blow.

Then a voice.

"Tauriar!"

She hesitated. Just long enough to come back to her senses. She dropped her guard and calmed herself. The troll bore down on her, its body fading away as it passed through her.

She fell to her knees, exhausted, and the room changed back to the staff dining room full of blue holo screens. She wanted to cry. She had failed on so many levels, but the fact that she was unable to protect Krankel hit her hardest.

She fought back the tears, sat up on her knees and put her arms behind her head. Krankel was first, snuggling his large shaggy muzzle into her. She dropped her arm around the big dog's neck, taking some solace that in reality, he was all right.

William and Katie were next to reach her, holo headwear off, and helped her to her feet.

'Well done,' said William. 'You did great.'

'What do you mean?' said Grace. 'I failed miserably.'

Katie smiled. 'The no-win scenario. You were never going to win. It's a test of how you cope with defeat.'

* * *

THE FOLLOWING DAY was a bank holiday, and Grace and Jon

were strolling through the grounds of Harewood Hall. The sun was shining, but this early in the year was still weak, so they were both wearing warm jumpers, scarfs and woolly hats. Krankel followed closely behind them, though he wasn't his usual exuberant self.

'This hat causes havoc with my holographic hair,' Grace complained.

Jon laughed. 'So switch it off, why don't you. I very much doubt you're even feeling the cold. I don't mind which Grace I walk with.'

'I *am* cold,' she replied, giving him an indignant look. She moved her arm from his and fiddled with the hat again. 'Jon. There's something I want to talk to you about.'

Jon took his hands out of his trouser pockets and rubbed them together to warm them. 'This sounds serious,' he said, smiling.

She turned to face him. 'It's about everything the gang were grilling you about on Friday.' She paused for a moment. 'I agree with them. I think you should go and race professionally. Follow your dream.'

Jon didn't reply. He put his hands back in his pockets and pushed his elbow out slightly, waiting for Grace's arm. She obliged and they carried on strolling.

'I've been thinking seriously about it for a while, but didn't want to leave you. Now, though, I know you have a great bunch of friends to support you, and I don't think I'll be missed too much.'

'Oh you'll be missed all right,' Grace said, snuggling closer to him. 'My sweet alien brother heading off into the big bad world. I'm more worried about you than me.' She looked up at him and smiled. 'It's just a shame your telepathic abilities are so rubbish, I might have been able to keep in touch. We'll have to spend a fortune on mobile phone calls and roaming charges.' She kept smiling, knowing he rarely rose to her insults.

'Okay, I'll contact the team's manager and see if they still want me.'

'Of course they'll want you. And Mandy has already told me that she'll happily donate her handlebar basket to help you go faster.'

Jon laughed loudly. 'That doesn't surprise me.'

'And Krankel will miss you.'

Jon looked back at the dog. 'I'll miss him too.'

Krankel appeared much more interested in chasing a nearby squirrel, but suddenly he perked up, looked at Jon and bounded over, jumping up and draping his front paws over Jon's shoulders.

'You're in his head again, causing trouble,' Jon complained.

It took a mock mini fight to settle Krankel down

They carried on walking, joking about this and that, and throwing sticks for Krankel when Jon asked, 'You haven't said much about yesterday. William told me you did excellently, but that you still doubt yourself.'

'It's not that. When I think of some of the things I did well, I'm pretty pleased with my performance. All Royals have this test at my age and are never told its real purpose until afterwards. After a night of reflection, I'm more at peace with myself, and life in general. It's just...' Grace paused.

Jon waited a few moments then said, 'It's just what, Grace?'

She moved in closer to him, her face turned downwards. 'When the troll killed Krankel, I forgot for a moment that I was in the holo-room and none of it was real. I wanted to kill it. And would have done if I hadn't been distracted by someone calling my name.'

'But you did stop. It was part of the test, and you passed. Don't beat yourself up. I'm sure Douglas thought it right to distract you, to give you that split second you needed.'

'It wasn't Douglas.' She looked up at Jon.

'But none of the others have the ability to do that, do they?' Jon looked confused.

'No, they don't. But it wasn't him. He hasn't mentioned it, and besides, I've had him in my head since I was a little girl. It wasn't him.' Grace continued, 'I thought it might have been a member of the High Council, but if they'd found a way to contact us they'd be updating us on the situation on Preenasette, and whether it was safe to go home. No, it wasn't them either.'

'Well, who the hell was it?

'I wish I knew.'

CHAPTER 23

anders Concerns
Preenasette - Trun Rizontella - 2010

DOMANTRY ZANDER ENTERED the main living area of his apartment. The motion sensor picked him up and set the lighting to a soft, welcoming background level; the heater hub began glowing. As the door closed behind him, he felt relaxed and secure for the first time today.

He removed his cape, unclipped his body armour and stretched, the sensation of muscles and sinew releasing from their cramped confines was exquisite. He sighed, opened the drinks cabinet and poured himself a large Campion whisky.

'That terrible was it?' His wife Roseanne strolled into the room in her dressing gown, carrying their two-year-old baby girl. 'Christiana has been waiting for you. There's no way I can get her to sleep.' On seeing her father, she threw out her arms to him. He sipped his drink, put it down and took his daughter.

'Why aren't you asleep, young lady?' he said sternly. It had no effect. He kept whole squadrons of men and women in perpetual fear, but these two women made him melt. He leant over, kissed Roseanne and whispered, 'We need to talk, my wife.'

She raised an eyebrow. 'Let's get your little girl to sleep and you can tell me what's on your mind.'

A few minutes with her father had done the trick, and Christiana was asleep.

After putting his daughter to bed, Zander took a shower. The red-hot, ice-cold oscillation of the water temperature assaulted the nerve endings of his skin, stimulating his senses and elevating his heart rate and breathing. Only when the drying cycle had finished gently soothing him did he relax entirely, a calmness that had eluded him all day. He slipped on his dressing gown, returned to the sofa in the living room and resumed sipping his whisky. Roseanne had prepared him a snack.

'So, what's concerning you, my darling?'

Zander looked at her, searching for the right words. The reflections from the flickering firelight made him want to dive into the dark blue depths of her eyes and lose himself. Make his problems disappear.

'There's a force at work, an evil force, deep within the core of our society. I can feel it, manipulating our every move. With one aim, to escalate the war.'

Roseanne was startled. 'Tell me more.'

'I don't know. There are lots of little things, undefined but palpable. A war to remove the Vercetian's threat is turning into a war to annihilate them completely.'

'So, what is tangible?'

'Well, take computer led offensives. At this evening's meeting, the Council Inner Circle passed a motion from the new Minister for Technological Strategies to increase the scope of computer driven attacks. That was my responsibility and they've taken it from me. We know from past experience that Artificial Intelligence is a useful tool but should not be left to think for itself. That is where we are now heading. The possibility of more bloodshed will increase substantially. Mistakes will be made, civilians targeted in error. Soldiers' wives and children killed. The whole landscape of the war starts to change.'

Roseanne leant forward and put a soothing hand on his shoulder. She could feel him shaking with anger. 'I'm starting to see, my darling. So they start targeting our civilians.'

'Yes, and I'm worried about you and Christiana.'

They both went quiet, deep in thought.

Eventually, Zander continued, 'This war has always been carried out on a military level. We don't target civilians, and neither do they. There have been some bloody battles in the last two hundred or so years, but it's been soldier fighting soldier. Now the rulebook is being thrown aside.'

'Surely, you still have influence in the Inner Circle, to steer them back on course.'

'My authority as Supreme Commander is being undermined. They're taking Mancer from me, sending him on an off-world mission. He'll be away for years. They're isolating me.'

He watched his wife unconsciously run her nails over the intricate patterns of her head cap, her eyes distant. She stood up and looked straight into his eyes.

'We start planning tomorrow. But for now, let's retire, my darling. Our daughter is asleep, I'm wide awake, and it feels like I haven't seen you for days.'

She leant over and kissed him tenderly, stood up and released her robe, letting it drop to the floor. She smiled at him, holding the moment for a few seconds, then turned and walked towards the bedroom. Zander sat back, studying her sublime silhouetted shape, gliding gracefully across the floor. She had parked this problem for now, and it was time for him to do the same. He finished the last drop of his whisky, stood up and followed her.

CHAPTER 24

*M*andy & Mom
Earth - London, England - 2010

AMANDA WALKER RETURNED with another bottle of the exquisitely fruity Dog Point Sauvignon Blanc. She was with her mother at one of their favourite bars, drinking their favourite tipple. Its odd name first attracted them to the elegant wine. On her budget, it wouldn't have been her first choice, but as her mother would more than likely pick up the bill, she was delighted to partake. They didn't find their diaries matching up these days often enough, so they both treasured these girlie meet ups. They were within spitting distance of the House of Commons, in the Red Lion public house. There was an early evening buzz to the place with all sorts winding down after a hard day working in Westminster. Amanda tried to squeeze through a group of men riveted to the story been told by a colleague. His voice was nearly as loud as his bright red corduroy trousers. A white silk shirt and a brown tweed waistcoat with a flaming red back tamed the trousers to acceptable office apparel—a little eccentric, but this was London. As he revealed the punch line, Amanda almost had the bottle knocked out of her hand by one of the group. He immediately apologised to her and then gave Ann a little nod of apology too. Her mother smiled at him, and he turned back to his friends. Her mother, the Right Honourable Ann Walker MP was now a cabinet minister. Amanda knew this was one of the few places where she could sit with friends or family and blend into the background. Everyone here was leaving the highs and lows of the day behind, and in the most part extended the same courtesy to others, be they a famous politician or the office junior.

'I'd rather be on one of Dad's Amazon treks, I think,' Amanda said, sliding into her seat. 'Though I doubt there would be any wine there.'

She watched her mother top up the glasses 'Oh, I don't know. I've been on treks with your father when he would carry a bottle of wine for the whole day, just to liven up the evening's proceedings. You might have been conceived on one of those trips.' She gave Mandy a knowing naughty smile.

'Oh, Mom. Gross,' moaned Mandy. 'That's not an image I want, thank you very much.'

Mandy finished telling her mum about her last visit to Ireland. 'Jon is excited about his trip to Australia. It's his first time at the World Championships. It's in Canberra, just south of Sydney.'

'Well, he wasn't suited to university life,' Ann observed. 'It's just not his thing.'

'No, he was never going to get on University Challenge.' Mandy replied mischievously.

'How is Grace taking to him going?' asked Ann. 'That's both of you out of the picture now.'

'She's all right. She has her little group at Uni. "Grace's Groupies" Jon calls them.' Mandy smiled. 'Because they follow her everywhere.'

She missed Grace, but both she and Jon had their dreams to pursue. 'I wish I knew where things were going with them. With no news yet from their home world, I think they're all getting twitchy. Grace said one or two of them are talking about risking a return, but Douglas won't consider it. Grace is also aware that some of them are thinking she should be leading them now.'

'He's been chatting with your father about that,' said Ann. 'He thinks so too. It's the natural progression of a Life Team when the Royal Trainee reaches Grace's age.'

'Maybe so,' replied Mandy. 'But Grace isn't ready to assume that position.'

'Hmm…' Her mother was deep thought for a moment. She had a habit of drifting in and out of conversations, she was used to processing a lot of information. Amanda waited for her to drift back in. When she did, she switched the track of the conversation. 'And how do you feel about Jon leaving? Following his dreams.'

It was Mandy's turn to get lost in thought. She knew exactly what her mother was talking about, the enigma that was Jon and Mandy. Just like chalk and cheese. From that first day in the woods, there had been something between them. An attraction she could never understand. When she looked into those incredible blue eyes, there was a connection, one that had never been there with any other man. And that kiss a few years back had had a far greater effect on her than she would ever care to admit. Her mother had always been one of the most switched on people she knew. Nothing got past her. 'Mother, Jon and I are friends. Our lives follow entirely different paths now. If we ever tried to take our friendship to another level, and it didn't work, we might never get back to what we have now. I don't think I want to risk that.'

Ann left it there and changed the subject again. 'So. What have you decided to do with your life?' Mandy looked at her mum, knowing that she wanted to talk about the main reason for their meet up, following her telephone request earlier in the week. 'Can I have some Mommy time to discuss my future?'

* * *

'WELL...' Mandy paused, trying for a little clarity in her now slightly giddy thought processes, '...after much deliberation, I've decided I want to follow you into politics. I want to be a Member of Parliament.'

Her mother's look of horror lasted two or three seconds until Mandy could keep a straight face no longer and burst into laughter. 'Ha ha, got you.' A look of total relief spread across her face and quickly turned to mock anger. Mandy knew that the last thing she wanted was for her only daughter to enter politics.

'Seriously though, Mother, you made me study Business Management at Uni.'

'Suggested,' interrupted Ann.

'And in a couple of months, I'll finish and get a first.'

'Maybe. Big maybe.'

'I speak three foreign languages. French, German and excellent Mandarin from our two years living in Hong Kong when I was younger.'

'Yes, I was there too, and it was nearer three years.'

'And I want to travel.' Mandy stopped, indicating the end of this particular, much interrupted, monologue. She knew how to frustrate her mother.

'So....' She watched her mother roll her hands in the manner that suggested there needed to be more.

'What?' Ann exclaimed, exasperated, causing a couple of the noisy party to look round.

Mandy leant forward. 'Well... I want to join MI6.'

'You can't get me a second time, Amanda.' She watched her

mother look up at the ceiling. When she looked back, Mandy met her with her most determined face. 'You're serious, aren't you? Explain.'

'I want to be a Business Support Manager for MI6, carrying out coordinating work for overseas operations,' Mandy replied.

'What does that exactly involve?' Her mother had a pretty good idea, but wasn't giving up on the interrogation yet.

'MI6 operatives are tasked to gather information for the good of Great Britain. They need to be managed. Accommodation, finances, documentation. A whole load of backup work to enable them to function. That's what I want to do. You work with agents in the UK for the first couple of years; then you can work abroad.'

'So, how did you find out about all this, Miss Moneypenny?' Her mother's face was curious now rather than intense. 'Phone them up and ask?'

'Er, not exactly. It's all on the first page of the MI6 website. How to join the Secret Intelligence Service. What jobs are available. I want to manage data to support intelligence gathering.'

'Have you mentioned this to your father?'

'Yes.'

'And?'

'He said he thought it was a good idea if you did.'

'Typical.'

Her mother's voice softened. 'You're not going to be discouraged, are you? You've got your father's eyes and your mother's determination.' She considered it. 'Could be worse, I suppose. You could want to enter politics.'

Mandy raised her eyebrows.

'There's more?' her mother picked up on the unasked question.

'Well, it appears to be a very competitive position with many applicants. For me to get a favourable reply will be pretty difficult.' She shook her head. 'I was wondering, Mummy dear, in your position and all, whether you could put a word in for me?'

She braced herself herself for the inevitable reply.

'That's not how it works young lady! There is a thing called ethics. The press would have a field day if they found out I was helping my daughter get to the top of the pile for a governmental position.'

It was still loud in the bar, but that didn't stop Mandy leaning forward and whispering, 'They wouldn't find out. That's why it's called the *Secret* Intelligence Service. It's not the same as—let me think— as though you were aware of the existence of aliens on the planet, or something, and had kept quiet about it for many years.' Mandy's face was the picture of innocence.

'You are a despicable daughter, Amanda Walker.' Mandy watched her mother drift away again. 'I do have a meeting with a Home Office civil servant next week. I might just mention in passing that you're thinking of applying, but that will be all. If you get the job, it will be on your own merits.'

Mandy smiled at her mother. 'Thank you.' She picked up the bottle of wine. 'More wine, Mother? After all, you *are* paying.'

CHAPTER 25

*G*rantham's Discovery
   Preenasette - Trun Rizontella - 2011

SUB COMMANDER GRANTHAM LEA looked out of the window of the Mag Train as it flew due west towards the port city of Santraneed. The rolling landscape meant he could focus on some distant scenery, unlike the past hour when the Forest of Plenary had been a blur through the windows. As usual, his sister was asleep. She could sleep anytime, anywhere and on anything, and would only wake up as they reached their destination, invariably complaining of being hungry. He had already bought her a muffin in readiness.

They had been sent by Supreme Commander Zander to meet with a member of the Reticent Guard and receive information too sensitive for standard forms of communication, which, over the last year, had become insecure. Their uncle, Anton Pilz, was overseeing the arrangements for their mission. Pilz had become close to Zander since the off world despatch of Commander Mancer two years earlier. He was one of the few faithful members of his inner circle. Zander had even promoted him back to the rank of officer. Grantham knew Zander did not trust Commander Hallot, promoted to his number two by the War Ministry.

His uncle had welcomed the closer ties with his boss. Strange things were occurring throughout Trun and in its leadership. And the tone of the war had hardened significantly following the Vercetian atrocities and their increased aggression. The creation of a Secret State Police—Sestapol—under the auspices of the Reticent Guard, was a worry and a mystery to all of them and the subject of some wild speculation.

They, or more precisely he, was to meet Captain Karter of the Reticent Guard on reaching Santraneed and would be handed the communication. He was to return the sealed Envogram directly into Zander's hands. Bess was his backup, in case anything went wrong. She had certain skillsets that made her good to have in a fight, and their excellent telepathic rapport, a commonality in twins, was also a big plus when dealing with someone from the RG.

Grantham had little trust for the Reticent Guard. A secret organisation, that dealt in secrets, and were autonomous of the military or council. Although working directly with both groups, they tended to remain at arm's length. Their current leader, General Kirk-am, was part of the Council's Inner Circle. She held an official position equal to Gor and Zander, ensuring the RG's complete independence. Uncle Anton would dismiss Grantham's mistrust though, citing that the Trun Rizontella society needed a reliable RG. "It's vital the Reticent Guard remain apart, and enforces the standards we all adhere to. Their integrity is paramount, and any corruption of them would be devastating for us.'

Nevertheless, he still wanted his sister close.

The Mag Train started its long slowdown for its final destination—Santraneed. Bess stirred, slowly waking and completely ignoring him. Strangers on a train sharing a table. She reached for the package he'd pushed across to her and started eating the muffin. She was dressed as a military nurse, the classic extensions to her head cap that denoted her profession also helped to cover her features, masking her resemblance to him.

Grantham loved this old trading port and always enjoyed visiting. It was one of the few Trun cities that retained many of its historic features. The train stopped in the peripheral newer part of the city. All of the commercial, military and political buildings were in this quarter, but his meeting was elsewhere, down at the dockside. He could see advantages and disadvantages to this. His plan was to walk from the station and give Bess time to pick up transport and follow at a discreet distance. Bess was to make contact with Major Tang, an old colleague of Mancer's at the local military HQ, who would give her anything she needed.

As he made his way from the station, the topography began sloping dramatically downwards to the sea, and Grantham tried to imagine the bustling port in its heyday.

The most dramatic part of the view from here were the Needles, the shortest sea stretch between the landmasses of Trun and Verceti. A myriad of trading ships would have weaved their way between the hundreds of tiny sharp-pointed volcanic islands that reached upwards to the sky. The Trun ships with hulls deep in the water, trading their hard gotten ores and minerals mined from the outer reaches of their wild lands, while the Vercetian's majestic clippers would carry the exotic foods and spices grown on their abundantly fertile land. It must have been a sight to behold, with hundreds of cranes loading and offloading the trading ships and a bustling infrastructure of ancillary transport ready to distribute goods throughout the land. But now there were no ships, and the cranes that were left standing hadn't moved in over two hundred years. The only thing to see now was the faint shimmer of the Vercetian force field forming the impenetrable curtain between the two nations.

Grantham continued on. Winding roads surrounded by derelict buildings guided him to the docks where he was to meet Karter at the Windward Tavern, one of the few alehouses still operating.

There was just a sprinkling of people at the dockside, carving out goodness knows what sort of living. He felt he'd gone three hundred years back in time. None of the modern conveniences you would find in an average city. The tavern didn't even show up on his finger tablet; he had to ask for directions.

When he arrived, the inn sign was creaking quietly in the gentle breeze. Between the words Windward and Tavern was a painting of an old sailing vessel, of a kind probably not seen for half a millennia. He needed to duck to get through the front door, and once inside it took a few moments before his vision adjusted to the darkness of the room. Karter was at the bar. They ID checked each other. After getting a beer, he suggested they retire into one of the alcoves. Grantham made a mental note of who was already in the room.

'I hope you're staying for food as well. The situation isn't as straightforward as me giving you the Envogram and you disappearing. There's more to it.' Karter leant forward and whispered, 'I think your superior is on to something.'

Grantham was quiet for a moment. Not what Zander had asked. He would have to tread carefully here. 'How secure are we here? If the conversation is going off the beaten track.'

Karter's smile was warm and appeared sincere. 'You're dealing with my organisation now, Commander. We have electronically swept the whole building and put surveillance blockers in place. We are secure.'

He hoped Bess was in position. *"This might take longer."*

"Acknowledged."

He decided he would need to tread carefully. 'I better order some food, then. Where's the menu?'

* * *

THEY ORDERED food and another beer. Grantham waited until his spicy game dish turned up before carrying on the discussion. 'So why should I disregard my boss's instructions just to pick up the Envogram and go?'

Karter leant forward again, which for someone with complete confidence in his security, seemed odd. 'Because I don't believe the contents are what you were sent for. I think they've been switched for something possibly... well, less contentious. And by someone with more influence in the RG than my boss.'

'Have you proof of this?' Grantham found himself leaning forward.

'Not conclusive proof. We very rarely work in indisputable facts.' Karter was pensive. 'This is the shadow world. Everything here is hearsay, secondhand, overheard. The only way we're going to prove our suspicions is to open the Envogram and read its contents.'

"Possible problems. Stay alert."

"Will do. There are three RG's out here. I'll visit them."

'You're suspicious. So you expect me to hand over a document that is for my boss's eyes only, based upon here-say, and secondhand or overheard comments from your shadow world?' The look on Grantham's face implied this wasn't going to happen. He was also seriously considering the possibility that this was a setup.

Karter smiled. 'You put it that way, and I would agree with you.' He was quiet for a moment. 'Look. Let's put our cards on

185

the table. The Envogram was given to me yesterday by my superior, known to your boss. While travelling here, I placed the Envogram in the deposit car—standard protocol. Before doing this I marked it—my private insurance. I'm an old fashioned soul; it's just how I am. Someone tampered with it.' He handed it to Grantham and produced a micro scanner from his satchel. 'Look there. And this is the image taken earlier.' We're talking about a seriously difficult thing—breaking into an Envogram. Sonic locks, tracer seams, etc., and doing it in the deposit car of a Mag train. It would need some serious clout to get that done.'

Grantham studied the data. It appeared to bear out Karter's suspicions. 'Say we open it and read the contents. Neither you nor I know what the message *should* say, so we aren't going to know if it's been modified.'

"Get as close as possible."

'Agreed. But we do know the contents should be revealing, to say the least. My boss wouldn't be going to all this trouble to inform the Supreme Commander of the military something that didn't have far-reaching implications. And to do it clandestinely rather than through some committee suggests some parties need keeping in the dark.'

Grantham was surprised Karter knew that Zander was the intended recipient. He had never mentioned it. Would Karter have been told? Could he trust this man? 'So, if we do open it, read it and decide someone has tampered with it, what's our course of action? You have to go back to your superior and tell him you suspected outside interference and opened it. It would alert whoever tampered with the Envogram that we're on to them. And, we'd be no further forward in obtaining the correct information.'

Karter shrugged.

"Coming out hot, any time now."

Grantham reached into his pocket while pushing the

scanner further on the table with his other hand. 'What is this mark here?' he asked.

Karter leant forward, allowing Grantham to touch his stun taser on the back of Karter's hand. The barely audible hum immobilised him instantly. Grantham caught his head and rested it gently on the table, picked up the Envogram and carried on talking. 'Do you see that small mark there? Yes, that one? I won't be a moment. Nature calls.'

* * *

GRANTHAM STEPPED out of the alcove and stretched casually, looking around for the toilet, aware of at least two in the room paying him far more attention than when he'd entered. He paused, checking his tablet before deftly ducking out of the front door. There was confusion behind him; he wouldn't have much time.

'Jump on, quick!' Bess skidded to a halt on a Quadbike, 'I've disabled two of the three scouts out here, but the third will see us soon enough.'

'Is this the best transport you could come up with?' asked Grantham, tension in his voice.

'Relax, brother. The quad is just the quick little runaround that will get us to our Skyjet. Unless, of course, you expected me to fly it straight down the street here.' Bess was shouting now as she accelerated forward and turned sharply, up a tight alleyway. 'They won't have anything like this.'

'How long?' He could hardly hear himself.

'Five minutes. We have to get in the air before they do.'

* * *

ONE OF KARTER'S colleagues from the bar was attending him. In a daze, he asked, 'Where's the boy?'

'He dashed out about thirty seconds ago. Jamba went after him.'

'Find out what's happening outside. Contact Samson.'

Jamba quickly relayed the message, while Karter tried to get his fried brain back in gear.

'Two down outside. The boy has assistance we didn't pick up. Samson said he caught a glimpse of a quadbike. They can't get too far.'

'Idiot,' said Karter. 'They must have something else waiting. Get someone in the air. Now!'

* * *

BESS SKIDDED to a halt in a small clearing. Major Tang and three soldiers were waiting for them by a CUV. A two person pursuit jet was primed and ready for takeoff.

Tang instructed two of the soldiers to jump on the quadbike, and they left immediately in a cloud of dust, heading back towards the old town in an attempt to draw off any pursuit.

'Get in and go,' Tang barked at Grantham and Bess.

Within moments both the CUV and the jet were blazing away from the clearing.

* * *

GRANTHAM AGONISED over his decision to open the Envogram, even as Bess was carefully attempting to do it without setting off any of the sensors that would destroy the contents. A rare skill without the correct scanning key, but it had been one of the reasons Pilz wanted the twins on this mission. Grantham, not afraid of making a tough call, and Bess able to carry out everything else that came under the heading of tough.

A little click and they both breathed sighs of relief. Bess opened it and handed the small oblong message screen to him.

'Last chance to change your mind,' she warned. 'I wouldn't do this.'

'Thanks for the support, dear Sister. What else can we do?'

They sat in the CUV, about twenty miles outside of the outskirts of Santraneed. They were off the main highway on a remote track and were, for the time being, safe from detection. The Clandestine Utility Vehicle was in stealth mode. Unseeable and undetectable. This particular military vehicle was thought to be entirely superfluous in a country not keeping secrets from itself, or even its enemy. But a handful had been developed and then put into storage many years earlier—for a rainy day. Bess had laughed at Grantham's face when Tang shuffled them into the CUV.

Tang's pursuit jet, although seeming the obvious choice of escape vehicle, would have been tracked easily and eventually picked by the Air Space Police. The ASP would have escorted them to the nearest military or RG base, where the stratagem would make or break, depending on the allegiance of that base. With no message onboard, the risk didn't exist.

'We open it. Read it. Memorise it and destroy it. We become the message and get ourselves back to the Supreme Commander. Simple.' Grantham tried to smile at Bess. He switched on the reader.

He read it three times, then passed it to her. She read it.

'Have you got it?' he asked. Bess nodded. He stepped out of the CUV, placed the reader on a rock and vaporised it with a short blast of his sidearm. He discarded the now inert Envogram container behind some boulders, and got back into the CUV.

'What now,' asked Bess. 'All the way back to Allacrom in this thing? We'll be wasting time that may be precious to the Supreme Commander.'

'I agree. The contents of this message change everything.

The Supreme Commander being in this sort of danger. We need to alert him.'

'Secure communications compromised. The Reticent Guard is turning on us. And the Sestapol closing in on our boss.' Bess paused. 'All the rumours must be true. We're facing a civil war, and for what?' Her country turning in on itself was beyond her comprehension. She reached for her brother's hand; a very rare moment of weakness for the one others had always perceived as the dominant twin.

He put his arm around her. 'Don't worry, Bess. We'll get through this.'

CHAPTER 26

*T*he Watcher
Earth & Space - The Republic of Ireland - 2011

JANET KILKENNY WOKE up slumped in her chair. *Oh crap, I've fallen asleep again*, she thought, rubbing the muscles in the back of her neck. She opened the curtain to reveal a cold white blanket outside. Had nobody told the weather that spring was nearly here? Her mind wandered a little more before remembering what she'd been doing the night before.

She switched on the TV for the local news. There was nothing out of the ordinary. She wasn't expecting anything, but worth checking. She rebooted her computer and started searching some of the more credible websites that watched out for these sorts of things. Nothing. She wondered if her ex-work colleagues had seen anything.

She sat back, recapping the events of the last few weeks. She needed to find out what it was she had been monitoring.

'Janet!'

Oh crap, again. 'Yes, Mother. I'm coming.'

* * *

Up until three months ago, CIA Technical Intelligence Officer Janet Kilkenny was on loan to NASA studying NEOs—Near Earth Objects. She was the lead on the LINEAR project, a NASA and Lincoln University joint venture. The LINEAR (Lincoln Near Earth Asteroid Research) project's goal was to discover and track NEOs to see if their orbits were a threat to Earth.

At thirty-five she was flying high in the Agency and was expected to be the next Assistant to the Deputy Director of CIA for Science & Technology. Then her world had been turned upside down when doctors diagnosed her mother with Acute Myeloid Leukaemia, a particularly aggressive blood cancer. The prognosis was not good. She had made the decision to go back to Ireland to spend what time she could with her parents. The outgoing Assistant to the Deputy Director of CIA for Science & Technology had told her he would hold off on retiring until she was ready to take the helm.

* * *

Janet's parents had moved to the USA a couple of years before she was born, but four years ago they made the decision to retire in Ireland. Although Janet had never lived there, she'd grown up in a small, tight-knit Irish community and had an excellent Irish accent when appropriate. On the whole, her mother was in good spirits, but occasionally her reaction to the chemotherapy left her entirely wasted.

'Hi Mum, how are you feeling today, my darling?'

'Not too bad, thanks.' It her mother's stock reply, however she felt. 'Where's your father?'

'I'm here, sweetheart.' Janet's dad walked in, still in his pyjamas, rubbing his weary eyes. 'Tea anyone?'

An hour later breakfast was finished. Her dad was on his way to the local golf club, and her mum was settled in the lounge watching daytime TV.

Janet returned to her musings over the the events of the last few weeks.

* * *

WHEN THE TRUN SPIES arrived in the solar system, they latched onto a small asteroid about fifty million miles from Earth.

For Kean, it had been an arduous twenty-month journey. His two travelling companions were, to say the least, uninspiring company.

Tray was a very insular man. When not piloting the ship or carrying out any of his official duties, he would be reading books on early Trun philosophy and literature. Whenever Kean tried to strike up a conversation it would always fizzle out into an embarrassing silence.

Sonia was even worse. She blatantly refused to have any interaction with either of them and would often lock herself in her sleeping quarters for weeks on end, not answering any communications from her shipmates.

The remaining duties required for the operation of this intergalactic space vessel, were done by androids. Most were now deactivated. The only one still functioning was a simple food processing droid—or Gobbler as Kean had nicknamed it. To kill time early in the trip, he had installed a small but sophisticated voice recognition and response program in the droid, and the tiniest of mini-brains. He had found a great little domestic worker program that he'd integrated into the software, but the combined result of this mishmash amalgamation was something much more akin to a sarcastic vending machine. He had at least created a travel companion that was infinitely more interesting than the other two.

But now they had reached Earth, he had plenty to occupy him.

Kean's first task was to find the probe the Vercetians would most likely have used to access the Earth's information sources. It was highly likely it would have been abandoned in space, and its contents would save him considerable time. And it would be far more comprehensive than anything he would be able to put together.

'Gobbler. Where are you?' Kean muttered, busily trying to upload a scanning algorithm into his search probe that was now in orbit around the Earth.

'Here, Captain DeMancer. Where else would I be?'

'Cut the crap and promote me to admiral, please. I'm hungry. How are you getting on with the Earth food project?' He decided he would need to redesign its outer casing if he was going to take it with him.

'Scan inconclusive, Admiral Captain DeMancer, Sir. Need superior data uplink connection.'

'I'm working on it. You must have *something*.' He completed the upload and initiated the scan. 'This shouldn't take long.'

'Expensive menu or inexpensive—also known as junk food.'

'Junk.' Kean watched the screen impatiently.

'A hamburger? Should be right up your street, Admiral.' The little machine beeped twice, then a red light activated and it chanted, *'Warning! Warning!'* It beeped twice more. *'Only joking Admiral, excessive amounts of chemical additives detected. Shall I reduce to safe levels?'*

'Yes, yes, whatever you think.' Kean was more interested in the results popping up on the screen. 'Got you.'

Gobbler hovered to the food dispenser and extracted all of the ingredients it needed, then set to work. A couple of minutes later, it presented Kean with a hamburger on a small tray held by it's tiny mechanical arms. *'Your hamburger, Admiral.*

Enjoy.' It waited a moment, then added, *'Shall I prepare something for stomach cramps?'*

He grabbed the burger, ignoring the droid's wittering and began downloading the data and transferring it onto tiny knowledge disks. These would provide everything they would need for integration into Earth society. He bit into the hamburger, chewing ravenously. 'This is good,' he told the droid.

'Oh joy,' Gobbler replied.

* * *

KEAN SET to work on the appearances they would be adopting. The standard holographic program reproduced a human based upon Trun characteristics. Kean, a handsome young Trun, was pleased with his new human form. But he wasn't able to get the level of definition he needed. Sonia could assist with that; he'd been told before they had left.

'Finish what you're doing then leave the rest to me,' she said. 'I'll work on something for myself, so start on holo-graphics for Tray.'

Kean thought that was strange but didn't dwell on it. Before Sonia carried out the facial colour refinements, he had to choose hairstyles for them. Hair was a strange concept to him, requiring much consideration. He had a head cap - a much simpler head adornment - a raised thick layer of skin running from the forehead around the side of his head and running down through the nape of his neck. Within the depth of the skin surface were intricate patterns. No two Trun head cap designs were the same, though some similarities were hereditary.

He accessed his knowledge disk. The choice of hairstyles were overwhelming. He eventually settled for the rather unkempt look that mountain bikers tended to have. That was where he intended to spend most of his time he mused. He chose a mousey blond colour, which he thought looked quite good. For Tray, he went for a crew cut. A bland hair choice for a dull companion.

He let Sonia know that he'd finished and left her to access the files and add the definition they still needed.

* * *

JANET KILKENNY HAD SET up a casual ongoing search program to find and track NEOs from her parents' house. She would eventually be back to work in an entirely different role. This was her last chance for stargazing. Besides, this research was her passion.

NEOs consisted of NEAs (Near-Earth Asteroids), NECs (Near-Earth Comets), other meteorites, and human-made satellites, all with orbits that brought them in the proximity of Earth. Satellite surveillance was the primary interest from the CIAs viewpoint. The majority of natural foreign objects came from the Asteroid Belt, ejected into the solar system by interaction with Jupiter's gravitational pull. There were thousands of these in the vicinity of Earth, many well over 1 kilometre in diameter. The largest so far discovered was 1036 Ganymed, which, at 32km, was due to flyby Earth in 2024.

Janet did her own tracking now, looking for an asteroid or meteor that could be the next threat to Earth. If she found any satellites that weren't supposed to be where they were, then that would be a bonus. Her set up in the attic of her parents' home in the village of Carhoonahone, County Kerry, was pretty nifty. She had a very respectable wide field telescope and could take time lapse photos for downloading onto her home computer—a computer augmented with a powerful RAM, and processors obtained using her network of friends "in the know." Being on the foothills of Carrauntoohil, the highest peak in Ireland, meant that the clarity of the night sky was pretty good.

About four weeks earlier, she had been tracking an asteroid, and as usual was recording notes on her dictaphone.

'Feb 26th. Day three tracking 'Daisybell.' Asteroid measures approximately 0.25 km in diameter. You're a bit of a lump, Daisybell, but there are much bigger boys and girls flying around up there. I'm pretty sure now that I'm the first one to be following you. And, young lady, in today's photo 26/2-16.30, you've developed a blemish. A big black spot. You need to wash more. Your orbit is becoming clearer. A few more days and I'll know where you're heading.'

If it appeared it would to pass within five million miles of Earth, she would give it her full attention and study it in more depth.

'March first. Day six tracking Daisybell. Well, young lady, it looks like you may get as close to me as 500,000 miles. I'll need to have a more detailed look at you.'

The asteroid might still be twice the distance of the Moon away, but in astronomical terms, that was quite close. A call to her old colleagues in the USA might be in order.

THE SHADOW WAS STILL THERE. It had only been mildly interesting at first, but once the NEA flyby distance was established, she decided to zoom in as close as her "amateur" equipment would allow. The resolution was far from perfect, but the shadow was there to be seen, cast across the side of the asteroid, blanketing the small hills and valleys. It was definitely circular. The question was: what was casting the shadow? She was now a little more than mildly interested.

* * *

WITH THEIR TRANSFORMATION NOW COMPLETE, nothing was stopping Kean and Tray from heading down to the planet. A missing message globe would have been more than enough to guarantee the Vercetians departure from Harewood Hall. The Trun spies hoped they were still in The Republic of Ireland but were more confident of locating the Princess's two friends.

They waited for a new moon before leaving the relative safety of the asteroid. A direct route straight down to Ireland afforded them the best chance of remaining undetected. The sphere possessed some masking devices, but if anyone were looking for them particularly, they would see them. Their arrival would be at high speed, so any exposure would be brief and hopefully they would be assumed to be a small asteroid.

Their target was a lake by Macroom. It stretched over a large area, and by targeting the farthest point from the town, they would be in a quiet and desolate area. The ships rapid decelerated, and entry into the water was anything but quiet, with a sizeable wave radiating in all directions. Soon, all was calm.

Now the sphere rested on the bottom of the lake gently vibrating, about half of the ship still above water. The water appeared to shake as the sphere sank slowly into the mud and silt that made up the lake bed. A minute later, it had disappeared, and all was silent again.

They monitored the surrounding area for any signs of life or anyone taking an immediate interest. There was nothing.

Now their thoughts turned to becoming human.

Kean ran both his hands through his holographic hair. He liked it. Sonia had made a good job of their facial colour refinements. He suspected he looked a real human specimen, but that needed proving.

'What do you think?' he had asked Gobbler.

'I would have said fantastic if I had any optical equipment with which to view you, Admiral.'

Over the next week, with Tray's assistance, they worked on their language converter, playing about with all sorts of English dialects. They decided not to use an Irish accent, afraid the locals would see through them and chose a neutral English one instead.

After eight days they decided their first proper taste of Earth could start. Two single rooms were booked at the Mayfield Hotel, where they hoped to eat and socialise with the locals. Sonia, who still hadn't finished her own holographic disguise, would stay with the ship.

They exited the submerged sphere via an air bubble, stepping out of it onto dry land and looking a little more dapper than their situation warranted. A trip to the London office would have been more in keeping with the sharp suits they were wearing. They thought nothing of the six mile walk to the town, even though it almost ruined the mock leather lounge shoes they had replicated.

Tray was verging on sociable during the stroll. This adventure was obviously exciting him.

'I can't believe we're about to enter a town on Earth and converse with the locals. How do I look?' he asked, not for the first time.

'You're asking me? We'll soon find out when we talk to the locals. If we're that bad the local police will probably beat us up, take us to jail and throw away the key,' said Kean.

'Really? But the voice translator seems to be working correctly, and we're wearing regular clothing. Why would they want to arrest us?'

Kean sighed deeply. 'Your disk has Earth humour, yes? That was supposed to represent irony, a form of humour. It *is* working, isn't it?'

Tray looked blank for a moment while he accessed his knowledge disk. 'Yes, I see. Becoming human isn't going to be as easy as I thought.'

'It isn't,' Kean agreed. 'But that's why we're here. Don't forget to refer to me as Rob. Okay, Tom? We're here now and here's hoping.'

* * *

'AND THERE ARE your room keys, numbers four and six,' Mrs Farrelly smiled broadly at the two men, big rosy cheeks making her appear warm and welcoming. 'Are you gentlemen on a business trip? You're quite well dressed.'

Rob replied, 'Well dressed? We, er, well we've been to Cork. On business, yes, but we didn't want to stay in a big city.'

'You'll be fine here, Luv. Get yourself sorted and come down for some dinner at about six o clock.'

They were down well before that, ready to practice their conversation techniques. Rob didn't have to work too hard or wait too long, as there was a group of girls in the bar, keen to talk to this handsome new boy. Rob enjoyed being the centre of their attention and very quickly got into character. Unfortunately, Tom took a bit of a backseat, being well above the girls' target age range.

Rob was invited to visit the pub over the road with the girls, where the music was a little more upbeat than the hotel bar, leaving Tom to go to dinner on his own. He was seated next to a table with a blond woman eating by herself, just finishing her meal. Tom decided to try and start a conversation.

'The weather is quite beautiful this evening,' he began.

'Yes, it is,' she replied.

'Are you staying at the hotel?' Tom was feeling a little awkward now.

'Oh no. I work over the road. I've had a tough day, what with my boss away ill,' she said. 'I'd be too tired to cook for myself, so I'm having some of Mrs Farrelly's gorgeous hotpot.' He liked the way her hair moved as she turned her head.

He quickly accessed his knowledge disk, checking what hotpot was. 'Braising steak, onions, carrots and potatoes. Was it enjoyable?'

She looked at him curiously, then smiled. 'Yes, enjoyable. My name is Samantha, Samantha Smith.' She offered him her hand.

Tom knew all about handshake greetings but was a little overzealous with his grip of her delicate hand. 'My name is Thomas.' He noticed her wincing and immediately let her hand go. 'Pleased to meet you.'

'Well, I must be off, my cat will want to feed and I've still a wee walk to get home.' She stood up and put her coat on, trying to button it up, still wincing at her hand. 'Goodbye, Thomas. Enjoy your meal.'

Tom ordered the hotpot off Mrs.Farrelly, and couldn't help thinking he was having a successful first outing.

* * *

FOR THE NEXT stage of the tracking process, Janet Kilkenny set up an algorithm to lock on to the NEA and take photos when it had traversed a defined distance, helping determine its speed more accurately. She left the program running, returning to it after a trip she'd planned for a long weekend in London with some old friends.

After four days of sightseeing, plenty of banter, much shopping and even more Guinness, she was home again. She spent the afternoon fussing and storytelling with her mother, then made her way to the attic to see what was happening. She booted up her computer and downloaded the images captured in the external data drive. The first image appeared, then the second. She set it to slideshow and popped downstairs to get a coffee. When she returned, it had finished. *Impossible* she thought, it should be at least a half hour longer. She grabbed her dictaphone.

'My lousy equipment appears to be on the blink. It looks like I've wasted a few days.' She started the slideshow again. 'March 8th. Reviewing the distance-lapsed photos of Daisybell. Series commenced on March 4th/ First photo 14.30. Second photo 16.18.' She turned the dictaphone off, considering the next twenty photos spaced at similar time differences. The image changed. 'March, 6th, 02.24. Daisybell has disappeared, just a picture of the stars. Seven more photos of the stars in rapid succession and finish. Total waste of space.'

Annoyed, Janet spent the next two hours finding Daisybell again and resetting the equipment. She left it in tracking mode and went to bed cursing all things technological.

Four days later Janet reviewed the next set of results. The tracking had worked perfectly. The results confirmed her first predictions, so she sent the file back to her friend and colleague Emily, at NASA, with a note suggesting they might want to keep an eye on this asteroid.

The results from last week were niggling at her, though. She viewed the slides again, talking out loud as usual, but without the dictaphone. 'An asteroid, then no asteroid. Star system on the slide, then more of the star system on the slide, continuing thusly, then ending.'

She returned to the latest photos. 'Daisybell, you don't look the same.' She flicked between the old and the new pictures and it dawned on her. Where has the shadow gone?

It wasn't on the latest images. Where did it go?

Janet began sifting through the images much more intently now. She was viewing the ones taken around the time the shadow had appeared, particularly the before and after pictures when the bombshell struck.

'It's the background stars! Two background stars have disappeared.' She looked from one to the other. The stars were there, then gone. 'Exactly in the position that an object would need to be to cast a shadow onto the asteroid. An invisible object that doesn't allow light to pass through it? What is going on?'

Her mind was racing. 'What if my tracking software was working correctly and was tracking the mystery object itself? It would mean the object headed towards Earth. At great speed.'

She sat back in her seat and closed her eyes.

* * *

JANET KILKENNY HAD NOT MOVED from her chair for about two hours.

She had decided to try and track its trajectory, and was pretty sure it would have landed somewhere in Ireland. The fact that the night sky had stayed constant suggested it had travelled straight down towards her, give or take a few hundred miles.

She needed a lot more computer power to analyse the data, though, and needed some help from a friend. Her initial thought was it was best to keep this low key. Using NASA's facilities could result in too many questions being asked—for the moment anyway. She spent the next couple of hours getting all the relevant information ready to email to her friend. There was a lot of data, and it needed four separate emails to get it to him.

* * *

SONIA NOW HAD the chance to attend to her transformation.

Kean and Tray were spending their first night out of the sphere. She would have until morning to find a suitable host.

She'd had enough of the Trun host and was looking forward to a change. No further modifications to her anatomy were required, as humans were stockier than the Trun. Her forehead horns and the protruding bones from the upper vertebrae of her spine were still phase shifted away. They were there, but moved forward in time a fraction of a second, thus not visible in normal time.

She had selected a park three miles away, near Macroom, close to a thoroughfare used by locals. The park had an abandoned building once used as a tearoom that would be perfect for her needs. With all research completed, she exited the ship via the air bubble, wearing a tracksuit with hood, dark glasses, and a scarf covering her mouth. A half hour later, she arrived. She set up a scanner on the thoroughfare, moved down the path, hid in some bushes and waited.

Anyone who passed by the scanner would have their age, sex and dimensional suitability transmitted to Sonia. She wanted a woman on her own, between twenty-five and forty years old.

Over the next hour, a steady stream of people passed. Finally, a woman who fitted all criteria crossed through. She was on her way home after a hard day in the local pharmacy and was looking forward to curling up on the sofa with her cat. Sonia let her pass, checked carefully for passersby, then stunned her from behind. She retrieved her scanner before heading on to the abandoned tearoom, her potential host over her shoulder.

Inside the building, she stripped the clothes from the woman and laid her face down down. She had no time to play with her victim this evening. She positioned the scanner directly above the woman's body, set the hover function and locked it in place. She activated it, and it began carrying out a series of sweeps, assessing the work to be done. When it finished, a small green laser beam appeared and started cutting from the top of the skull to the base of the spine. It cut down the rear of each leg and then each arm. The whole of the corpse was opened out, ready for the technological taxidermist to do its work.

Sonia began discarding the Trun epidermis that she had worn for the majority of the last sixteen years. All neural and physical interfaces were severed, and Trun skin crumpled to the floor. She folded it up and placed it a portable storage unit. She would need her Trun host later. Sonia stood in front of the scanner. The physical attributes that had been time shifted reappeared—her short back, shoulder and head horns and extended horns flowing gracefully down to the middle of her back.

She exulted in the comfort of being in her own form, savouring this briefest of moments while the scanner carried out its work.

All of the internal organs, the skeleton, muscles, blood and lymph circulatory systems were phase shifted out of this existence. All that remained was the exterior of the woman that would soon be her new host.

The scanning machine stopped and emitted a short message in her native tongue, 'Time Shift.' She stood there while it moved her horns into the future, and then, 'Enter Host.' Sonia moved toward her new epidermis and climbed inside.

The skin slowly started wrapping itself around her legs and arms. Finally, she was enclosed entirely. The Zerot, in her new outer skin, was lifted from the ground and floated, long blond hair flowing in all directions. The machine rotated her, emitting a plethora of green beams at the body, connecting and activating every nerve ending, every neural and physical interface. Soon, it was complete. Sonia was returned to her feet as the machine turned itself off. She dressed.

The lady lived, though her cat would not be fed tonight.

* * *

PROFESSOR BRAD FOLEY was Janet's Astrology lecturer at Florida International University. They had stayed friends after her graduation, and he had taken a keen interest in her career after acting as one of her references on her application to join NASA—on loan from the CIA.

A man who survived on little sleep, Brad had picked up Janet's email within minutes of her sending it, even though it was still only 4.30 in the morning.

HEY BRAD,

How are Kate and Emily? I hope you are all well.

I'm still in Ireland. Mom's not faring very well at the moment. She has her good days, but the bad days are hitting her harder now. I dread where this is going.

Anyway, as you know, my little set up here is keeping me out of mischief. And I've got something I'd like you to look at with the university computers.

I won't say anything at this stage. Study the pictures and see if your conclusions are the same as mine. I know you like a mystery.

Watch for three more emails.

Love, Janet

BRAD FOLEY WAS FEELING like a boy on Christmas morning as he looked through the emails and began piecing together the timeline of the pictures.

'She's studying a stationary asteroid with an unusual shadow on it. She's on time lapse—no, distance travelled—frame shots. Not a lot happening until these last few. What's going on now?'

He flicked through the pictures again, and a third time. Closed his eyes for a minute, scratched his chin, then jumped up and ran upstairs.

He leant over his sleeping wife, who was stirring from the noise he was making.

'Janet's sent me a riddle. I'm just going over to use the university's computers for a couple of hours.' He kissed her.

'Brad, it's Saturday. What time is it? For god's sake. Be back by eleven, we're having brunch with Ted and Sally.'

'I will.' And he was off.

* * *

BRAD FOLEY LEANED BACK in chair seat in the study lab, with a wry smile on his face. The evidence was conclusive. Janet, on her home computer, had tracked something from a fixed location behind a big rock in space—that could be deemed as hiding—to somewhere in Ireland.

The data was the data, and his computers could do no more than confirm what Janet had suspected, albeit with more speed and a lot more accuracy.

Was it a UFO? Brad thought it might well be. Although he had tracked many objects that displayed typical UFO characteristics and weren't. Was it worth making a fuss over this information? He didn't think so. Janet's data was just too sketchy. Anyone could have reproduced what she'd sent him. Nobody would be interested in this except Janet and himself. He emailed her back and told her as much.

...AND *the landing coordinates are 51deg 54'16" N 8deg 57'25" W, give or take a mile or two. That's the best I can do with what you've sent me.*

Let me know how it goes with any more investigating you decide to do. I'm interested, though as I've said, I don't think anyone else will be.

Love to you and your folks. We're all wishing your mum the very best with her treatment and praying for her.

Keep in touch.

Brad x.

* * *

KEAN AND TRAY made their way back to the hidden TW Sphere the following morning with a spring in their steps. Kean was happy that his popularity with Trun girls carried over to his Earthly persona, and Tray was still delighted with his perceived successful encounter with Samantha Smith. They both had moments where their naiveté had shown, Kean especially. One of the three girls had whispered in his ear to a Rod Stewart record playing *Do Ya Think I'm Sexy?* Kean quickly accessed the lyrics to the song, saw where the couple in the song ended up and panicked. 'No, I don't,' he blurted. She left in a huff.

At the edge of the water, they summoned up a transport bubble, stepped inside and transferred into the sphere. Sonia was still in her room and unresponsive. Kean replicated some clothes more in keeping with the younger men's attire in the public house. The new look was denim jeans, trainers, tee shirt and a short black leather jacket. He went straight back out to meet the girls from last night, for a liquid lunch as they described it. Standard Saturday behaviour in the village, apparently.

Once Kean had gone, Tray sorted himself out some casual wear. He was admiring a holographic image of himself in brown corduroy trousers, brown brogue shoes, and a checked shirt when Sonia stepped out of her room.

But it wasn't Sonia. It was Samantha Smith.

Momentarily confused, Tray said, 'Samantha?'

'No it's me, Sonia. I've completed my transformation.'

'But you're identical to Samantha Smith. A lady at the next table to me at dinner, last night. How has that happened?'

Sonia didn't answer that question, she asked one instead. 'Where is Kean?'

'He's gone to meet some girls from the town. I'll ask again. Why are you imitating a woman from the village?'

It was the last question he would ever ask. Sonia moved with lightning speed. In a moment she was behind him, one arm holding him and the other twisting his head, breaking his neck. She held him for a moment and then sneered as she let him drop to the floor.

'Turdgutter,' she muttered. 'What do I do with him now?'

* * *

JANET FINISHED READING Brad's findings and sent a reply thanking him, and agreeing that it would be pointless to share the data with anyone else at this juncture.

Then she plotted the coordinates on her dad's ordinance survey map.

The Gearagh, near Macroom.

Janet knew of the place but had never been there. A submerged glacial woodland formed during the building of two hydroelectric dams. She remembered seeing photographs of the remains of old trees, eerily visible through the surface of the lake, giving a ghostly appearance. She'd thought at the time that she would like to see this nature reserve.

Perhaps now was the time to go and pay a visit.

* * *

JANET ARRIVED in Macroom on the Saturday lunchtime. She had booked into the Mayfield Hotel for just one night but was early—her room not ready until 2.00 pm. The Plowman's Inn over the road looked a good place to kill an hour or so. She ordered a Plowman's lunch—it seemed rude not to—a half of Guinness, and sat herself down. The pub wasn't crowded by any stretch of the imagination, but still quite lively.

She finished her meal and popped to the loo. While she was washing her hands, she spoke to a girl next to her touching up her makeup. 'I've only just arrived, but I like this little town. I bet you don't get many visitors.'

'Few come at this time of year, though things will start picking up when the spring arrives. Visiting the nature reserve, mostly.' She smiled. 'Why are you here?'

'To see the reserve,' Janet said. 'Mostly, I was hoping to bump into some friends, but the arrangement was never made firm and I'm sure I've got their phone number wrong. Have you seen any strangers in town?'

'Only the lad we're talking with. He came with his friend, last night,' she said.

'Doesn't sound like the people I'm looking for,' Janet sighed.

'He's English, and a bit strange.'

'In what way?'

'Oh, how he dresses—or did last night—and speaks. Can't put my finger on it, but Rob there is killing us. We're having a real good time.' The girl finished touching up her lips and was gone.

Janet went back to her seat and watched the boy with the three girls for a while. He was certainly a natural entertainer. Maybe a bit too natural?

Just after two, she checked into the hotel. She changed into her walking clothes, then made a point of bumping into Mrs. Farrelly again, using the same story she'd used earlier: hoping to bump into some old friends, and had she seen any strangers about. 'Some businessmen from Cork was all,' she had said. A little more questioning and she found out it was the boy Rob and his friend.

She bought a map of the area from a shop and stood reading it in the weak spring sun. She realised she hadn't thought this through and didn't have any plan. After some consideration, she decided to walk out to the nature reserve. It was there on the map, but the road she was on was doing a good job of hiding from her. A sign reading "Gearagh Nature Reserve" over the road saved any embarrassment, and off she strolled out of the charming little town.

Halfway there, she was overtaken by a young man. She called to him, 'Is this the way to the Gearagh, please?'

The lad turned. It was the boy Rob from the public house. 'About another half mile and you'll be there,' he said and smiled broadly.

Janet tried to keep up with him, but his pace, though appearing casual, was relentlessly fast.

He had gained a lead of a couple of hundred feet before the road veered left and she lost him for a short time. When she turned the corner, there was no sign of him. She spoke into her imaginary dictaphone. 'Now, where has he gone?' The road ahead was straight for about a quarter of a mile. The reservoir was on her left, the wood was on the right, with no visible tracks into it. She checked behind. Nothing. *Strange*, she thought.

This part of the road was close to the water's edge, and Janet was captivated by the strange beauty of the lake. Ageless oak sentries broke the surface of the mirror smooth water, guarding any treasures that might lie beneath. One of the few remaining European oak forests had been partially cut down sixty years ago when the valley was flooded to supply hydro-electricity to the city of Cork. The remaining trees still stood, defiantly shouting out against this ecological disaster.

Janet's enjoyment of the view was interrupted by a rustling in the bushes behind her. A woman emerged, fully dressed in apparel more suited to an office than the woods. She stopped and stared at Janet, eyes piercing straight through her. 'Good afternoon,' Janet offered.

The woman ignored her and walked straight to the water's edge, pondering for a moment before turning and walking back around the bend in the road.

What a strange woman. She gave her a minute, then followed her around the bend. Gone. Again. 'Strange. People keep disappearing.' There was another rustle in the bushes on her right, near the way back to the lake, followed by a gentle splash of water.

Janet waited. Then she walked up and down the road looking at the spring flowers sprouting under the bushes, but all was quiet—no further sign of life.

Janet returned to the hotel, showered and got ready for dinner. Downstairs, the reception was deserted, and that gave her opportunity to flick through the guest book and note the details of the guests from the previous day.

CHAPTER 27

ander's Family Escape
Preenasette - Trun Rizontella - 2011

THE TWINS MOVED ON, putting more distance between themselves and Santraneed. Both were deep in thought.

Eventually, Grantham broke the silence. 'We need to risk contacting the Supreme Commander or uncle Anton. We cannot afford this delay.'

'I've been thinking. I could contact Uncle Anton though our FamilyChat. Attach a data message, with an embedded surprise fun type icon. It would seem very innocuous, even if anyone were monitoring it, and I could integrate the message into the image. He'd be sure to scour for something under the circumstances. Easy.' Bess smiled and added, 'And we need to tell them about the CUV. That may be useful to the Supreme Commander. Providing he heeds the advice in the message, he needs to vanish, and they will be watching him carefully.' She was on a roll now. 'And we should join him—unite with the Resistance. That's where the real fight is going to be. We—well mostly you

—are marked now. Our loyalty is known and that may not bode well for us. And the resistance sounds like it could be fun.' She beamed. The girl that earlier needed comfort had disappeared.

Grantham looked up towards the sky, bemused. Only Bess could compare this predicament to fun. He looked back at her, knowing she would comment about his sombre face, then broke into a smile himself. 'Start preparing the message, and I'll put together some commentary to go with it. And for the record, I think it's a good idea. Especially coming from you, *little* sister.'

'Two minutes, big brother. Just two minutes.' And she pulled out her tablet and began composing.

* * *

PILZ HEARD, rather than saw, the message pop up on his hand tablet. From his niece. Hopefully, a hint as to why they weren't on the scheduled Mag train.

UNCLE ANTON.

The girls and I are having a lovely time down on the coast. The pre-wed girly celebrations are going swimmingly. Windsurfing today and a visit to Cliffhanger Caves tomorrow (and the tiniest amount of eating and drinking).

I'll let you know what train I'll be getting back the day after tomorrow when I know. In the meantime, press on the icon below to see what I think of my favourite uncle.

Bessendra.

HE PRESSED the icon and a cartoon image of Bess popped up shouting, 'I love you!' on a three-second loop.

He smiled to himself. The message was there. Hidden in the Ether had been one of their favourite games when she was younger. Concealing data, photos, anything—in the gaps between the binary digits of computer software. They had stopped playing it after Bess had gotten too good for him and it became completely one sided. He hoped she hadn't made this too hard.

Three hours later, and he'd found it. He thought at one stage that he wouldn't, that there wasn't anything to find, but he persisted, knowing it must be there. He opened it and began reading.

A few minutes later he was on to Zander, requesting an audience. He had an update from Major Tang regarding manning levels in Western Trun. Manning Levels was the phrase that triggered the urgency, and they hastily arranged a meeting.

* * *

MEETING WITH RG COMPROMISED. *They reported someone might have tampered with the message. We thought to differ, and with Major Tang's help, we escaped with the Envogram.*

To avoid capture of the message we opened it, memorised and destroyed it. Sorry if this was an incorrect action. I accept any reprimand.

MESSAGE READS:

'ZANDER MY FRIEND. *I fear for your safety.*

It has come to my attention that Sestapol is going to discredit you. Financial irregularities, all cleverly fabricated, of course.

Somebody wants you gone. The worst case scenario, as we

*discussed, and I fully expect that I will be next. They will lock us up
and throw away the key, or worse.*

*You must get out, your family too. Go to Ferenger and see my
cousin Benja Jacob. He is setting up a Headquarters for our Resistance Movement. You need to become its leader, and I'll follow.*

*We hoped it would not come to this, but it has, and you must move
quickly. I've no time frame to give you, but it could be mere days.*

Hurry, Zander.'

WE ARE HEADING BACK *to Allacrom Central Command at full speed
in a stealth CUV, which is at your disposal. We fear we have been
compromised and would request consideration for the Resistance
Movement, should you opt for that course of action.*

UNCLE, *B hopes you didn't find the game too hard.*

SUPREME COMMANDER DOMANTRY ZANDER put the message
down and looked at Pilz. He put his hand on his chin and
thought carefully. This course of action had always been a
possibility, but he still wasn't ready for what he had to do next.

Pilz waited a moment then said, 'They'll be watching you, of
that you can be sure. The Sestapol are getting more audacious
by the day. The CUV might be very useful, and the twins can
help. Maybe send them to get your family. They're a very
resourceful duo.'

'I agree. They're chalk and cheese but dovetail very effectively. Anton, we need to find somewhere we can plan in peace.
We've got to be quick and very resourceful. There are many
things to consider over and above mine and my family's safety.
The future of Trun is at stake.'

Pilz only half caught the latter part of his boss's statement, he was still dumbstruck by the fact he had called him by his first name.

* * *

GRANTHAM AND BESS parked the CUV a half mile from the military apartments of the Allacrom Central Command Centre, still in full stealth mode. They disembarked via the rear door into the evening darkness. The first of Preenasette's moons—Little Stanfort—would appear soon, adding a small amount of light to that of the distant stars. It would be two hours before Big Stanfort appeared. In its full quarterly phase it lit up the sky. They would want to be done well before that happened.

Grantham wore his Sub Commander uniform and Bess her nurse's outfit. Underneath her uniform, Bess was dressed in a black skin suit from neck to toe. A balaclava with only a slit for her eyes would complete the costume later. Only up close could the array of weapons strapped to her be seen. Grantham, not for the first time, was pleased she was on his side. Sometimes she frightened him. Today, her weapons were for incapacitation only, civil war hadn't started yet. Very soon they would disappear into the throng of military personnel swarming around the apartment buildings at this time of the evening.

They slipped into the periphery of the massive apartment compound and started making their way to the Supreme Commander's apartment, deep in the heart of the facility. Commander Block 250 H. Twenty minutes later, they arrived.

Grantham stood by as Bess peeled off down a side street and stripped out of her uniform, putting it in a small bag attached to her waist. Pulling on her balaclava, she began climbing into the darkness like a jet black Tambo lizard.

Grantham would give her ten minutes to assess the level of surveillance around Zander's apartment.

He waited impatiently.

"Sorry, Brother. It's taken me longer—interest is intense, to say the least."

"What are we up against, Sister?"

"Two rooftop guards and three pairs of men at each of the street intersections. One up here is guarding a camka sensor. Everything happening in or around the building is being monitored elsewhere in real time."

"You must take him out last. We will also need a diversion."

"I've something in mind."

"Are you going to tell me?"

"Ha, ha, you'll know. In the meantime, you need to get near the pair watching the south exit. I'll remove a bit of the debris up here. If they don't respond to the diversion, you'll have to take them out. No chatting for a bit, I need to concentrate. Bye, Brother."

He hated it when he wasn't in charge of planning, but he needed time to evaluate strategies. He liked to consider every detail. Off the cuff stuff like this was right up his sister's street, though. He just had to go with the flow, stay alert and hope for the best.

* * *

BESS WAS IN HER ELEMENT.

She slipped back down to street level, put her nurse's uniform on and strolled casually to the busy restaurant on the corner of the southern intersection. Grantham just approaching the men positioned there, but she could tell he hadn't seen her. She walked the length of the restaurant window on the east face waving frantically to a fictitious person inside. Families seated by the window turned inwards, trying to see who responded to the crazy woman outside.

Bess's sleight of hand hid her real intent: the setting of some tiny canisters attached magnetically to the window frame.

Moments later, with her uniform back in her bag, she was scaling the building again, this time counting the windows. Up, then across. When she found the window she wanted, she produced a small laser stitch cutter and made a large circle on the glass pane. It remained in place—just. She continued up three more floors to the roof and secured a drop line back down.

The second of the guards was on this side of the roof. She was an unseen ripple in the darkness of night and was soon behind him. An arm around his head and her thumb deftly pressed into his neck caused him to go limp almost instantly. She held him up and dragged him into the shadows and laid him down.

Timing was critical.

On the other side of the roof, she downed the second guard with her laser, changed settings and destroyed the camka sensor. She pressed a button on a small keypad and discarded it. The canisters on the restaurant window started billowing smoke—hopefully, the diversion Grantham needed. Going back to the drop line, she abseiled down to the window, gave it a sharp blow with the flat of her hand and caught the circular glass with the other before it dropped into the room. Moments later she was in the bedroom and face-to-face with a shocked Roseanne putting Christiana to bed.

Bess removed her balaclava and nodded formally to Roseanne. 'Junior Sub Commander Bessendra Lea here on the orders of Supreme Commander Zander. We must leave immediately.' She removed the nurse's uniform from her bag, 'Put this on, please.'

Roseanne looked at the uniform then back at Bess. 'My husband told me to expect something today. But I didn't think it would involve dressing up.'

'Please put it on quickly,' Bess repeated, her voice emphasising the urgency.

'What is the plan?' Roseanne asked she began putting on the uniform.

'Go downstairs and straight out of the door. Cross the road and my brother—Sub Commander Lea—will be waiting for you. You've met him before; you know him. He will take you out of the compound to a waiting vehicle.'

'What about Christiana?' Roseanne demanded, looking at a now wide awake two-year-old.

'They'll be on the lookout for a woman with a child. Your daughter will come with me.' Bess produced a black cloth and started wrapping it around the little girl. 'Do you like rides?' Bess asked Christiana in a friendly manner.

She smiled and nodded excitedly.

'But where are you going?' Roseanne was aghast, she stopped dressing and watched Bess spin the black cloth around and around her daughter.

'Your little girl and I are taking the scenic route.' She swung what now looked like a black caterpillar with girl's head onto her back and attached two pairs of straps. Opening the window with the hole in it, she turned back to Roseanne and promised, 'Don't worry. She'll be all right.'

She perched on the window ledge. 'Finish getting dressed and go, please. Now!' and she was gone.

Roseanne stared at the open window for a couple of seconds before the reality of the situation sunk in. She finished dressing, and ran down the stairs.

* * *

WHAT HAD BESS DONE?

For the entire journey to the southernmost edge of the

apartments, Grantham had been receiving a severe grilling off the Supreme Commander's wife about of his sister's actions.

'Is she some secret weapon the military created? Was my husband party to this plan? Did he know our daughter was going to be whisked away into the night by a madwoman?'

They were outside the compound, heading into the darkness towards the CUV, conscious that Big Stanfort would rise very soon. He prayed Bess arrived safely with the Supreme Commander's daughter soon.

His CUV signature detector led them to the stealth vehicle and he opened the rear door.

They stepped in to find Zander on one side of the van and Bess and Christiana on the other.

'Get in quickly and shut the door,' Pilz said from the driver's seat, and put the CUV into drive.

Christiana reached for her mother. They hugged. The little girl turned back to Bess and said, 'Auntie Bess.'

'My sincere apologies,' Bess said before Roseanne could react. 'We needed to move extremely quickly. It was the only solution I could come up with, and I didn't have time to debate it with you.'

Roseanne took a deep breath. Looked at her husband, then back at Bess. 'Should I be asking exactly how you *did* get here?'

'Probably not,' Bess replied, 'but your daughter loved it.'

CHAPTER 28

he Day Trip

Earth - Cork, The Republic of Ireland - 2011

ANNA, Nigel and Ken were in the university bar putting the final touches on plans for their day out the coming Saturday. They were going to Fota Wildlife Park, just a few miles to the east of Cork. Anna, a total animal lover, had been badgering them for some time to arrange a visit.

'I've booked the tickets, and the weather should be perfect,' Anna exclaimed.

'And have you got some bread to feed the ducks?' Ken asked. 'And a spare arm to feed the tigers?' As usual, Ken couldn't resist playing Anna up. It was how he treated everyone, but with Anna, it was becoming an increasingly important part of his daily life.

'That's why I've invited you, Ken, the Lions need feeding as well,' Anna replied without missing a beat. 'And Grace has finally confirmed she can come, she managed to get out of whatever she does back at her dad's house every weekend.'

'What about Jon?' asked Nigel. 'Is he still racing this weekend?'

'Yes,' said Ken, 'he's over in Kent. His sponsor wants him there, so that's where he has to be. Good news though, Mandy may be able to make it. Her dad's considering a visit to Cork this weekend, and she's hoping tag along on a freebie.'

'Well, that's good news,' Anna said happily. 'Look, Grace is here.'

They turned in the direction Anna was facing to see Grace coming from the far side of the room, weaving her way through the tables in the crowded bar. To a man, they all marvelled at the effortless way she moved. It was more like gliding than walking. She was looking at them but navigating tables and other students as if some inner radar was at work. Anna envied her hair that seemed, as usual, to move about as if was a windy day. Was the air conditioning system following her? She wished her own hair moved like that.

'Hi, hi, hi.' Grace sat down, appearing flustered. 'How is everyone?'

'We're fine, Grace,' Nigel said. 'Well I am, and the other two are bickering, so they must be fine as well.' Nigel's straight-faced commentary always made the others grin.

'Here's your drink.' Ken slid a lemon and lime to Grace. 'Anna has been finalising plans for our safari on Saturday. She's not the least bit excited about it. You're still coming, Grace?'

'Of course. Wouldn't miss it for the world.'

* * *

GRACE HAD, in fact, spent weeks negotiating this day out with Douglas.

Losing a day of Life Team training was one thing, but being out for the day without Peter and Helen close by was another.

'We'll be in a small safari park, just a few miles from Cork.

What can happen?' Grace was exasperated. 'Just one day without my minders.'

It had taken a full blown meeting of Douglas, Gwyneth, William, Peter and Helen, to decide the risks involved were minimal.

'She has to be given some freedom now and again, Prime,' said Temper. 'She's an adult now.'

So it was that Grace left with Amanda and the other three that Saturday morning, for the first time in her life free of the Life Team.

The bus ride from Cork city centre to the park took about forty-five minutes. As Anna had predicted, it was an overcast, but warm day.

After entering the park at the main entrance, they took stock and studied the maps they had purchased.

'It's a one-way system,' said Anna, knowing the park off by heart. 'We head off through that open grassy range called the Cheetah Run until we get to the Asian Sanctuary, which is a new development still under construction.'

They set off, chatting excitedly. There was a group of American tourists in front of them with cameras pointing and clicking in every direction.

'Why is called the Cheetah Run?' asked Mandy.

'You'll find that out at three-o-clock this afternoon,' Anna informed them. 'That's when they feed the cheetahs, making them work—or in this case run— for their dinner. Chances of seeing them up close this morning are slim.'

Right behind them was a party of very excited school-children aged seven or eight, with teachers and parents making up about a third of the party. After a few minutes, one of the children spotted four cheetahs about fifty metres away, loping slowly towards them.

All three parties stopped to watch and photograph this very

unusual sight. Ten metres from the fence they slowed to a walk, but continued forward.

Everyone was enthralled at the sight of the majestic animals up close. The Americans' cameras went into near meltdown, and the children's excitement was evident. Anna was ecstatic. 'We are *so* lucky, I've never seen the cheetahs act like this before.'

Eventually, the crowd had to go on. Mainly because the people behind wanted a closer look at the cheetahs. But, as they began moving, so did the cats—tranquilly matching the pace of the visitors. But the pace was painfully slow. The people in front of the Americans were slowing right down to wait for the cats, and those behind the children were squeezing forward or trying to move around them.

'We're getting well boxed in here, people,' said Nigel. 'Shall we step away from the fence and try and get ahead of this crowd?'

'Good idea,' Ken agreed. 'Let others get a better view.'

Anna nodded reluctantly, not wanting to, but understanding Ken's viewpoint. Grace, with an uncharacteristic frown on her face, nodded as well. They manoeuvred to the left-hand fence and started walking past everyone trying to get a better view of the cats. As the crowds eased and they found more space, they sped up and chatted excitedly about the strange goings-on. They were interrupted after a minute or so by Ken.

'Guys?' He pointed at the paddock fence which had become visible again. 'We've still got company.'

The cheetahs were still with them. And behind them, the very strange sight of Americans hanging on to bags and large cameras, squealing children trying to get by them with mothers desperately trying to keep up, and a sprinkling of casual visitors, all trying to keep up with the cats.

They had reached the end of the cheetah paddock. As they

carried on down the path, the crowd remained at the fence where the Cheetahs had all sat down facing them.

* * *

As they walked Grace was acutely aware of more strange animal behaviour in the pastures either side of them. This behaviour continued to prompt animated conversation between the other three. But Mandy suspected other goings on and tried to catch Grace's attention.

"Is it you?" The concentration on her face was clear to Grace.

"Yes, it is. But what can I do?"

Without meaning to, she had made a psychic connection with the cheetahs. There wasn't any conversation or communication involved, more a kindred spirit connection. The cats could feel Grace's intelligence and virtue and were just happy to be nearby. She had on occasion experienced this with dogs, though when one appeared glad to see you its reaction just seemed normal. Of course, her connection to Krankel was on an entirely different level.

'Will it keep happening?' Mandy asked, getting close enough to whisper. 'What about the other animals?'

'Yes. Probably to different degrees.'

Grace realised that this would be the case for the whole tour and she had no idea how to handle it. She made a snap decision to try and deflect attention from herself.

'Oh Anna, look how the animals follow you. They must be able to feel how much you care for them.'

'It can't be me Grace,' Anna laughed. 'I've been here enough times. They've never shown this level of interest.'

'It's Nigel's aftershave,' Ken teased, nudging him as he said it.

'They're attracted to my superior intellect,' snapped Nigel, never happy to be the butt of Ken's jokes.

* * *

THEY MOVED on to a small playground and an open enclosure with ring-tailed lemurs in, or out, depending on their mood. It was one of the places where interaction with the animals was encouraged. The fence was tiny—just a three foot high rustic wooden slip board fence, with only two cross members.

'Oh look,' squealed Anna. 'Lemurs. Come on let's get a look.'

They went towards the lemurs, waiting patiently for those in front to move on. Mandy whispered to Grace, 'Will you be okay with these?'

Looking relieved, Grace nodded. 'I'm not feeling much,'

'We should make some excuse and leave the park, don't you think?' Mandy said. 'Better safe than sorry.'

Grace nodded.

They were close to the Lemurs, standing near the fence, watching their antics on the other side. The primates from Madagascar played with each other or just strolled about, long ringed tails reaching for the sky and big eyes full of mischief. Now and then one would come to or through the fence and to the great amusement of the watching crowd. One came and sat on the fence next to Grace, who looked at her friends wearing a nervous smile, secretly hoping it would move on to someone else. In the blink of an eye, it reached for Grace's brooch, snatching it off her before jumping off the fence.

Grace was horrified. 'My brooch!'

If the Lemur went more than fifteen feet away from her and managed to operate it inadvertently, or just broke it, she would revert to her Vercetian shape—in front of everyone.

Mandy knew the chances of Grace changing were significant and looked around, assessing the options open to them.

Even on this warm day, they were still all carrying light rain-coats. She put hers over Grace's head and said, 'You have something in your eye? Come with me quickly, and we'll sort it.' She bundled Grace around and led her to the centre of a nearby children's playground, heading for a pagoda-like struc-ture at the end of a rope walkway. There was a section just below the landing platform that was enclosed on three sides and mostly in shadow. Halfway there, she could feel Grace's holographic enhancements disappearing under her coat. Mandy guided her into the enclosure and stood her up against the rear panelling. The other three were immediately behind, crowding into the confined space, the boys ducking down for lack of headroom.

'What's going on?' exclaimed Anna. 'What are you doing in here?'

Grace was panicking. 'Don't look at me!' she cried and put her hand up to stop anyone removing the coat. Unfortunately, she did that using a much more slender, and bluer, hand.

Her friends were dumbstruck. All three were staring at the thin, and rather beautiful, alien hand.

'Grace,' said Mandy gently. 'Your hand.'

None of them needed to look under the coat to see Grace realising her error. The small movements of her head and the rather too late attempt at hiding her hand said it all. Grace paused, aware of the cat being out of the proverbial bag.

She pulled both of her hands back into the coat and lifted it slightly, revealing part of her face. 'Oops,' was all she could think to say.

'Okay you three, don't freak out.' Mandy was taking control. 'Ken, Nigel. You need to go back out there and get Grace's brooch back from that Lemur.' They didn't move. 'Now!' she half shouted. 'And don't come back without it.'

They left, making their way back to the Lemur enclosure, leaving Mandy to try and smooth the situation over. 'Grace.

Don't worry. These are your best friends, and friends will accept anything about you—even that you're an alien princess,'

'A princess!' exclaimed Anna. 'Oh Grace, why didn't you tell us?' She was enraptured. 'We're friends with a princess.'

'I... am sorry.' Grace looked straight at Anna, revealing most of her face. Without her brooch and its inbuilt translator, she was speaking in broken English, with an accent Anna couldn't place.

They could hear the sound of children's feet tapping about above them as they arrived at the platform from the rope walkway and went squealing down the slide. Two girls of about seven years old ran from the bottom of the slide straight into the covered enclosure, coming face to face with Grace. They stopped and went quiet, then one of them asked, 'Who are you?'

Mandy replied, 'This is Grace. She's off to a fancy dress party.' She leant toward the little girls and said excitedly, 'She's going as an alien princess.'

The girls looked at Grace, then at each other, 'Cool,' they said in unison, and ran off to their next adventure.

A few moments later the boys returned, Nigel proudly holding the brooch aloft and handing it to Grace.

'I thought the park keeper was going to come after us.' Ken's beaming smile radiated around the small enclosure. 'Catching Nigel inside the paddock, chasing lemurs.'

Grace took off the coat and handed it back to Mandy. 'Now you can see...'

She clipped on the brooch and activated it. The solid holographic image appeared, her hair fluttering a bit. 'And now I'm Grace,' she smiled.

'I've wondered why you always wore that brooch,' Anna mused.

'Does this mean we get an invite to your home now, Grace?' Ken asked.

'I always knew you were toying with me, whenever we discussed some far fetched subject,' Nigel gloated.

'Come on, let's go,' said Mandy. 'I'm sure you have a billion and one questions for Princess Tauriar, here. You've got all afternoon to ask.'

So they did.

PART III
EARTH'S END GAME

CHAPTER 29

ob and Sonia
Earth - The Republic of Ireland - 2011

IT HAD TAKEN Kean and Sonia two months working from their TW Sphere to sort out passports, identification documents, bank accounts. Basically, everything they would need to pass as British Citizens. Luckily for Kean, Sonia appeared to have a particular knack for this sort of thing, giving the impression she had done it all before.

They moved into a three bedroom semi-detached house in a respectable suburb of Cork. The rented property was fully furnished, so all they had to do was move in and stock up the larder.

Since the strange disappearance of Tray, the two of them had come to an arrangement that unless they had official business to attend to, they would keep entirely clear of each other. Kean felt a loathing emanate from Sonia towards him, it intensified after they landed in Ireland. As the weeks passed, he began to feel the same towards her.

235

It hadn't taken them long to locate Jon O'Malley and Amanda Walker. Jon had already become a professional cyclist, so it was easy for Kean to slot into his chosen role. He just needed a way to impress the local pro team. Amanda was working for MI6, and though it was only at an administrative level, they both agreed that trying to befriend her wasn't a safe option. Keeping a handle on Jon O'Malley would have to be enough.

Although the use of advanced technology was forbidden outside of the sphere, Kean had brought Gobbler with him. Sonia had a box of unidentified items, so what the heck, he thought. He wanted easy food—and a companion.

He'd fitted Gobbler into a ghetto blaster. One speaker became the ingredients entry point, and the other, the delivery point for finished food. Headphones meant he could chat with the little food processor when they were out and about, and listen to music. He had even fitted a small wide angled camera lens, to compliment the little droids sensors. The ghetto blaster had disappeared after the mid nineteen eighties, but Kean's research suggested its use was still acceptable as retro in some oddball situations—the mountain bike scene happened to be one of them.

Gobbler hovered to Kean, with the speaker open and a beef burger extended out on a small tray.

'Your beef burger is ready, Admiral Roly-poly.'

'Thank you Gobble blaster,' Kean said, not looking up.

'Would sir require any further sustenance? Fish and Chips? A breakfast fry up? A Sunday roast? All three? Or, will your fourth beef burger of the day suffice?'

The ghetto blaster hovered drunkenly towards the waste bin, then opening one of its speakers and imitating a retching sound.

'Oh Gobbler, you are so funny. I may have to modify your programming.'

'Touch me, and I'll electrocute you,' it said defiantly, and hovered up and landed out of reach on top of the wardrobe.

Sonia entered Kean's room—without knocking as usual. 'I've entered you in two local races. You will need to win, and by some margin, to get noticed.'

'I will,' he replied without making eye contact.

* * *

THE FORTUNE FACTORY DOWNHILL TEAM, based out of Cork in Ireland, boasted four potential world ranking downhill riders.

At the team manager Jack Donnelley's cycle store in Cork, the first full meeting of the team before the start of the 2012 season had just finished. Excited apprehension was the order of the day, as would be expected at the start of a new and exciting venture. New boy on the team, Rob Smith, had invited Jon O'Malley back to his for a beer and to look at their spare room advertised for a miserly monthly rent. Jon jumped at the chance to have a look, having struggled to find something he could afford since leaving university.

He liked Rob and the room, well the price at least, so confirmed the deal over a couple of beers, while excitedly discussing the up and coming training camp in Scotland. Rob's Aunt Sonia seemed a strange one. In her mid-thirties and pretty, with lovely long blond hair, but she appeared to have a complete lack of communication skills. Rob said she would be coming with him on tour because she couldn't be trusted with her own welfare, but assured Jon she would be no trouble and that he would hardly know she was there.

Jon thought, what the heck, and co-habitation with Rob and his strange Aunt began.

he *Killing Games*
    Zerot/Gemini 7 - 1992

THE OPPRESSIVE HEAT in the underground cavern would be intolerable for most species, but after nearly ten thousand years of enforced subterranean life, the Zerot had long ago adapted to it. The Gathering Hall was gloomy, the effect of the constant heat haze, but closer inspection revealed an assortment of treasured art stolen from many of the worlds they had conquered. The room was buzzing with discussions and arguments going on simultaneously around three huge circular tables set in a perfect triangle. In the centre, a giant holographic world rotated slowly. The Zerot were about to embark on a planetary violation expedition, and the final details of the Cadre's performance were being measured and evaluated—the Killing Games were in full flow.

The first table was probably the most orderly of the three, with twenty clerics analysing the performance of Cadre 176's twenty years on Gemini 7, in the Pulcherrim system.

They had one hour to complete this task, with the chief cleric coordinating the previously unseen data and the remaining scholars analysing against the preset rules of the game. The results when calculated displayed around the holograph, for the other players in the Game to absorb and digest. The Zerot at the other two tables were getting animated as more and more information appeared.

During their twenty years, Cadre 176—led by the infamous Hammaraffi—had infiltrated the dominant society and had increased the size of its army, tenfold. They declared war on all of its immediate neighbours. Hammaraffi's tried and trusted mixture of subjugation, genocide and ruthless hit squads, had sent evil tentacles squirming around Gemini 7, destabilising the whole of the world's society. He needed a strong performance here. A particularly tenacious species had foiled his last attempt at a planetary violation sixty years earlier, and he and his team had made a rather hurried departure from the planet. The Zerot elders would not tolerate a second failure.

The total population of the planet appeared—2.2 billion. A roar from the second table, representing the Cammaggama Dynasty—sponsors of Hammaraffi—accompanied the announcement of 34 million dead to date. Well above the required minimum. The planet lit up, landmasses now coloured red, shades of pink, or white. Red indicated countries under the direct control of the Cadre, pink partially subjugated—the shade showing the degree of occupation—and white represented unconquered counties. The ferocity and tenacity rating of the inhabitants of the planet were announced next as below average, bringing mocking jeers from the other two Dynasties, undermining the "dead so far" figure. Scuffles between Dynasty military personnel broke out at the second table, but were quickly subdued by their superiors who wanted to plan attack strategies on the different parts of the planet. The more daring and demanding the approach, the higher the tariff would be when the betting commenced.

In total, the equation revealed the percentage of the world under occupation, its technology level, the standard of technology assistance permitted to the Zerot attack forces and finally, the big one, the Brukkah weighing.

The three Dynasty invasion forces would be made up of male and female Zerot soldiers in their prime. The higher the Brukkah weighing, the greater the killing frenzy would be. The better the frenzy, the greater the chances of arousal and mating. The more mating, the better the chances of offspring to keep the Zerot numbers from dwindling further. And this, the ancient race needed badly. Poor breeding had already led to an underclass of Zerot, known as the Grunz, who were now only capable of carrying out the menial duties—only just up from slave caste.

The Brukkah weighing finally appeared and was at best disappointing.

Table two was the focal point of the second hour of the Killing Games.

The three Dynasty military leaders each chose the points of the planet where their planetary violation forces would land and commence execution. They would have eight weeks to gouge a trail of death across the globe to the spot where Cadre 176 was based. In the case of Gemini 7, that was Bortherville in the country of Germaint. The dynasty military clerics at table two were now busy plotting and analysing the difficulty of the route—measured through colour density—and predicting how many millions of the population would be killed. Each of these would be crucial elements later in the game.

* * *

THE DETAILS of the military strategies became apparent by the end of the second hour, with full plans and predictions displayed on the panels. At the third table, the Dynasty leaders took charge, and betting would commence.

Lord High Elder Cajjaabb of Cammaggama Dynasty—who had replaced the ailing Carrakk sixty years ago, following the failed planetary violation—had the opening gambit.

'An excellent twenty years of preparation on Gemini 7 by my Cadre, I'm sure you will all agree. I will open with a three hundred Token bet on the Cammaggama military fully achieving their target at odds two to one.'

Lord High Elder Sammanna of the Rebutti Dynasty jumped straight in.

'Hammaraffi and his Cadre have lost the plot! A planet of Somarian seals would have offered more resistance than this planet.' She paused as more data was given to her by her team, via secure telepathic communication. 'Four hundred Tokens on my force to complete its target at the far more credible odds of four to one.' Her laugh was loud as she banged her delicate hands on the table, only just managing to hide the pain of her overly exuberant demonstration.

Cajjaabb responded in a vicious tone, 'You may be riding high, Sammanna, on the wave of your precious Birjjikk, but that won't last forever. And when it does end, I'll be there standing over you and laughing the loudest.'

Sammanna was quick to react to Cajjaabb, but Lord High Elder Robbijj was faster still, cutting her off before she could snarl back at her adversary. Robbijj was the oldest of the Elders at eight hundred and fifty odd years.

'Children. Let us at least get a few bets on the table before the bickering starts.' His short brown teeth were fully drawn as he smiled at the other two. 'You don't complete over two hundred planetary violations without having the occasional dud. And this is a dud. Cajjaabb. The numbers up there,' he pointed to the revolving world, 'prove that. But the game is the game, and the skill of the winner will be a testament to that, as it would with any other game. My team has three to one odds, which I find very challenging, but the Accett Dynasty will still open with a bid of three hundred Tokens.'

Next, each Dynasty bid on the success, or otherwise, of the others in their quests, using up the remainder of the one thousand allotted to each of them. Here, the rhetoric would get nasty, but it was also where the overall game would be won or lost. Confidence, or lack of, in your opponents, was vital, and your own military's poor performance might not stop you winning the game.

Sammanna's disdain for her rivals, especially Cajjaabb, was apparent, but all of the advice flowing to her from her analysis team suggested a large wager on the Cammaggama Dynasty's military was the key to winning.

'One hundred Tokens on Accett to finish their task and a desperate five hundred on Cammaggama, in the hope that Hammaraffi's recently failed tactics bear some fruit this time.'

* * *

WEEK four of eight on Gemini 7 and the Rebutti Dynasty, led by General Installitti, stopped and looked back at the trail of death she and her troops had left in their wake that morning while heading north towards Germaint.

Two hundred of them were advancing in a line, slaughtering all of the Geminians in front of them. For miles to either side of them, Grunz were flushing out the population of this land and using blanket teleportation to send them to a half-mile wide corral fenced with force fields. The two hundred troops spread across the length of the corral, killing everything in their path.

But it had been two weeks since any of them had experienced the Brukkah. She had yet to get anywhere close. The evening camps were desperate, and no one was copulating.

She looked at the Geminians in front of her. Male, female and their offspring, looking doleful, no aggression, no anger. They accepted their fate. This passive behaviour was no good for the Zerot. They needed to face a pugnacious foe, see the fire and hate in their eyes, and take their lives as they resisted with their last breaths.

Nothing here would ever raise them to Brukkah. The Accett Dynasty military had already left. Time for them to go as well. She gave the order, and the slaughter ceased.

The population of Gemini 7 had saved themselves and their planet. A very rare occurrence when visited by a Zerot planetary violation squad. They were a lucky species. Or, perhaps, an ingenious and an incredibly brave one. Either way, Cadre 176's days were over, and the Zerot had suffered two major setbacks in quick succession.

CHAPTER 31

he Reporter
    Earth - Leogang-Saalfelden, Austria- 2012

SAM GOSLING WAS A FREELANCE JOURNALIST.

He primarily reported on bike races, particularly mountain bike racing. He was on a retainer with Tread Magazine, a South African based mountain bike magazine, but at international meetings would try and sell to anyone willing to flip open their cheque book.

It wasn't glamorous or well paid, but he got to travel, and that's what he loved.

He kept up to date with all the news of the world and copiously read all the local press when on tour. He had always wanted to be a world affairs reporter for one of the broadsheets, but the chances of that happening had probably now passed. Still, he was happy where he was. He loved mountain bike riding and lived in the hope that it would, one day, become a mainstream sport.

He always wore a suit. They were never shabby, but an

unusual fashion sense meant they were always a little too baggy. A telephoto lens camera around his neck and a laptop bag strapped over his one shoulder emphasised the strange look by dragging the jacket halfway off him. But his enthusiasm and ever-present smile endeared him to all of the cyclists, who were happy to give him some time for an interview or just share a beer.

His extensive study of the local news over the last year was showing a disturbing pattern of gruesome killings in parts of the world he visited. Noteworthy of high local media coverage, but not the mass murders that spanned the international press.

It wasn't long before he noticed that these random killings weren't so random. They always occurred around major off-road cycle events—particularly the world championship Grand Prix—the type of events he covered. A man who loved spreadsheets, Sam started one to keep to track of this information. After a while, he'd put together a pretty comprehensive list of locations, dates and times. When he was sure of the connection to the mountain bike racing scene, he started noting which teams and riders were present.

He was now making some tentative connections. The only single common denominator his spreadsheet threw up was one particular race team always in attendance, but of that team, only two riders were always there. The team was The Fortune Factory Downhill Team, and the riders were Jon O'Malley and Rob Smith.

He had made a point of befriending them. A reporter after a story and a couple of beers afterwards.

He was in Leogang-Saalfenden for the downhill world championships, and had arranged to have a beer with them after the race.

* * *

JON O'MALLEY WAS MAKING his way to the starting line. His start was at 11.55am, and he had plenty of time.

He shared the cable car with British legend Guy Ashley, hotly tipped for a podium place. They chatted casually about everything but the next UCI Mountain Bike & Trails World Championships Men's Downhill race, which they would start within the hour and finish in less than three and a half minutes. The race would be won and lost by fractions of a second. Tiny mistakes or successful risks would be all that separated the top ten riders. Whose day would it be? Who had studied every twist and turn of the Leogang-Saalfelden course hardest? The track was dry on Friday's practice day, but there had been torrential rains since, totally changing its character. It wasn't now a case of who had prepared best; it was a case of who had the biggest balls.

Jon's aim was a top ten finish. In his four years as a professional bike rider, he had gained a reputation from his peers as the smoothest and most fluid rider on the circuit.

But unfortunately not the fastest. The more technical the course, the higher up the order Jon would come, having got podiums few times and an occasional big win. In his first year, he had been chatting to a Frenchman and an Aussie at a small meet. The Frenchman had said, 'You are the smoothest rider I 'av ever seen... but you don't race!' After he'd left, Jon remarked to the Aussie, 'That put me in my place.' To which the Aussie replied, 'Well, my dear young Irishman, when you've won seven world downhill championships you'll be able to put anyone in their place. That was one hell of a compliment you just received from the legendary Nico Vouiville.'

The small talk with Guy continued in the cable car. 'How are you getting on with the GT Fury dude?' Jon asked, seamlessly slipping into mountain bike speak. 'One of your techies let me have a peek at it yesterday, it looks awesome, man!'

'It's the dog's, man,' replied Guy. 'Flossed out to the nines.'

'The front end seems so long. Dude, how's that work?'

'Yeah, it looks odd, but when you're on it, it comes alive. You've got to try it sometime man, but not today,' he smiled at Jon.

When Jon had finished his run, he was in fourth place, with a time of 3.24.6 seconds He eventually ended in eighth place after the remaining riders finished. Guy had filled his expectations by getting the silver medal, running the eventual winner, South African Grant Mittaar, right to the wire. Jon dumped his bike with the race crew, showered, changed and went to find some of his mates. It was time for a beer.

* * *

ON A CORNER TABLE in one of the hospitality tents, Sam Gosling sat with Jon, Rob, Guy Ashley and Guy's sister Rhian. With the pressure off, they could all relax and enjoy a beer. As usual, Guy was wading his way through a mountain of food. Sam had regularly mentioned in his reports, his daily four thousand, five hundred calorie food intake, and not an ounce of fat on him. What people outside of the sport didn't appreciate about downhill racers was that, despite having gravity on their side, they needed to be super fit. Bursts of power combined with endurance was a prerequisite, and standing up out of the saddle for anything from two to six minutes took a tremendous toll on their bodies. To stay top of the game, a downhill cyclist trained twice a day and would be no stranger to the gym. Nobody in the sport subscribed to this work ethic more than Guy's sister Rhian. She had come into the championships as the favourite, but a niggling injury had meant she had had to settle for fifth.

'How's the back holding up, Rhian?' Jon asked her.

'Sore. But it is what it is,' replied the tenacious young lady.

'Tough, today. But you'll nail it next year.' Jon tried to make light of her disappointment. Everyone on the circuit liked the laid-back Irishman. He never appeared flustered by anything, and he was always approachable.

Guy and Rhian disappeared, leaving just Jon and Rob with Guy.

Sam decided to probe a little about Rob's aunt Sonia, who was never around. 'So, what's your aunt up to this weekend? Not much to see around here, unless you're into the leisure activities on offer.'

Sam noted that, as usual, Rob, who hadn't raced this weekend, having narrowly missing qualification, was guarded in his reply. 'She's deep into her latest book, a trilogy I think.'

'No desire to come and watch you?' Sam asked.

'Are you kidding?' Jon interrupted, a broad grin on his face. 'The fruitcake wouldn't be seen dead watching downhill.'

'Then why do you drag her around the circuit, to races like this?' Sam persisted.

'Well, I feel responsible for her. She needs looking after, she's unable to cope on her own.' Rob was looking straight at Sam now. 'Why the interest? She has her money. I don't support her, in fact, she subsidies me.'

Sam raised his hands defensively, 'Hey, just asking, mate, not a big deal,' trying to diffuse the situation with his bright smile.

Sam noted that he seemed to have hit a nerve there.

CHAPTER 32

he Lost Prince
   Gorgonea Tertia, Fandom Space - 2000

THE FANDOM SALVAGE ship came to a stop at the small asteroid cluster.

'Damn!' shouted Captain Grunter. 'I want that ship, Burp! If you don't catch it, you'll all be going home with empty pockets.'

'Not to worry, Captain, the fools made a fatal mistake going in there. It's too small, Gurk! We'll have a tractor beam on the vessel in a few minutes and will drag it out,' said Brockko, the first engineer, burping loudly in excitement.

Navigator Basib eventually manoeuvred the massive ship into the perfect position. 'All yours Brockko, Ha. Gaburp!'

Brockko aimed, and zap. The tractor beam snagged the sphere at the first attempt and started slowly pulling it in.

A crescendo of burbs erupted as the three stout Fandom shipmates belly slammed each other in celebration, burping continually.

251

'Ha. They've led us a merry chase, but they're no match for Grunter the great Fandom salvage king! Burp.'

'Where shall we kick out the Vercetians? Or whatever they said they call themselves, Gaburp,' bellowed Basib, 'Relgan 5's the nearest suitable planet.'

'No,' shouted Grunter. 'We'll be passing Doth in a week's time. A pleasure planet will compensate them for the kind donation of their beautiful vessel. They may well get put to work, mind.'

They all laughed and burped, and belly slammed again.

* * *

PRINCE CAMCIETTI WAITED the full three hours that Bala Karach, his Team Leader, had ordered him to. He'd taken over the Life Team a couple of years earlier, but with the evacuation of the Royals, she had wrested the majority of the control back from him. 'Twenty is a good age to take control on Verceti,' Karach had told him in her characteristically blunt manner. 'But being on the run from the Trun is a whole different situation altogether.'

He powered up the one-man escape pod that had been dormant except for life support since the delta sphere had deposited it in a crevasse on a small asteroid. Only now was he able to see who, if anyone, was still loitering close by. Nothing. That was promising. *At least it looks like they're still running from the salvage vessel,* he thought. *Or, Captain Grunter and his merry band of belching men had captured them.*

* * *

CAMCIETTI'S LIFE TEAM had been on the run for three months since escaping from Preenasette with the other Royals and decoys. They had followed their escape route to the Gorgonea

Tertia system, but soon became aware of a ship matching their every move. Seca Constapal, his pilot, was convinced it was a Trun sphere. Both ships so evenly matched they couldn't escape, and the Trun couldn't catch up. After three weeks the supposed Trun ship disappeared, and its place was taken by a large cargo type vessel. This ship slowly caught them up, which they had thought surprising, and then immediately made contact with them.

'Hello, burp. I'm Captain Grunter of Fandom. Welcome to our little bit of space, burp. We rarely have visitors, and we would love you to come and eat and talk with us. We're great hosts, and our food is magnificent. Burp.'

After a lengthy discussion, it was agreed to send Bala Vondra and Dom Billa, the Life Team's second in command and security chief respectively. Karach had finally given in—against her better judgment—to the notion that they needed to get some local help; something that would give them the edge if and when the Trun turned up. They took a two person NavPod and headed off to Grunter's ship. Within forty minutes Grunter was back on the viacomm.

'Hello again. Burp, Grunter is back. I'm afraid the food isn't agreeing with your shipmates...'

Camcietti, out of frame, slid over to Seca Constapal at the helm and whispered in his ear. 'Slowly power up and be ready to move laterally instantly on my mark.'

'What's going on?' he whispered back.

'They're powering something up. Just get ready to move.' Camcietti stayed right on Constapal's shoulder, concentrating hard.

Gunter's ship was surreptitiously edging around sideways to the sphere. Camcietti could see that this was no ordinary cargo vessel. There was a mishmash of upgraded parts that were clearly from other, faster ships. The original two star drive motors ran down each side of the hull. Two-thirds of the way down the intake louvres, new silver drive sections had been fitted. Above and below were additional add ons. These didn't have intake louvres; Camcietti had never seen the like. Maybe these booster units were the secret to the cumbersome vessel's speed.

Grunter had been waffling. 'I don't think it's anything serious. Just a reaction to the spices we use. But they do have an excellent shuttle pod. We do like it. So much so, we want its mother ship, which means you all need to come and visit us as well. Burp.'

Karach said, 'Are you threatening us? We have more firepower than you. I won't let you harm my officers.'

'You wouldn't shoot your own people, would you?' Grunter replied with a belching laugh. 'They are safe, as will you be. All we want is your ship. We are, after all, salvage collectors, burp, and we have the perfect buyer waiting for a vessel like yours. Burp.' More laughing and belching out of frame—his crew joining in.

'Now,' whispered Camcietti to Constapal. 'Go now!'

The sphere moved laterally just as the tractor beam from the salvage ship shot out towards them.

Karach, almost toppling over, shouted belatedly, 'Get us out of here!'

Camcietti's intuition and the subsequent unexpected acceleration of the sphere meant that, for the moment, they had stolen some valuable time on Grunter.

'What about our people?' asked Constapal, busily trying to get as much distance as possible between them and the salvage vessel.

'Our capture is no good to them,' said the Prince.

'Head for that asteroid belt,' said Karach. 'There is cover to hide the Prince in a shuttle pod.'

'Er, I *am* here,' Camcietti sounded wounded. 'Do I get a say in this plan?'

'No,' was Karach's blunt reply. 'I'm responsible for you, and I'll not risk capture. Now, get in.'

Camcietti got into the pod, while Constapal calculated a route into the asteroids. The remaining members of the Prince's Life Team looked on, their particular skills being of little help here. Karach held the door open, giving him final instructions. 'Go to the fourth planet in this system—it's inhabited—and wait for us. We will find you. Power down and stay silent for three hours before you go. Quick. That large one there, head for it.' She closed the pod and then the airlock door. A minute later he was drifting towards an asteroid. Camcietti landed it with a bump, then powered down and checked the time.

* * *

PRINCE CAMCIETTI WENT to the fourth planet. He put the pod into geosynchronous orbit, powered down pretending to be some space debris, and let the mini AI take a few readings of what was below him.

The AI's report back to him suggested that the planet had no indigenous population, but had a scattering of outposts that appeared to be trading ports and a place for long-haul cargo vessels to lay up or get spare parts. It seemed a suitable place for anyone not wanting to draw attention to themselves. He picked an outpost and settled for a landing site about four miles away in a small wooded copse. He hit the go button and leant back in his seat, ready for the ride.

Eight hours later he was strolling into the port. He was wearing his grey robe, not having had time for a change of clothing, but with his hood in place, he would maintain some level of disguise even though he would look a little eccentric.

The port had a small main street with the typical amenities: shops, restaurants, a couple of small hotels. To either side were warehouses, little ones for storage up to large hangers for vessel repairs and maintenance. The top end of the main street led to a large open expanse where all of the visiting ships were parked. An impressive array of machinery from all corners of this part of the galaxy. This picture of technological diversity was Camcietti's first real experience of the width and breadth of intelligent life that existed.

He needed to eat and drink so entered an establishment that appeared to advertise both. His found his senses smacked by a variety of exotic smells as he walked in. Food made up part of it, but another odour unknown him was also present. He looked for a quiet table and chose a corner and positioned himself with his back against the wall.

A grubby looking waiter took his order; water and a vegetable looking dish, sorted without getting into translator territory.

Camcietti looked around the room. The clientele, although a diverse variety of species, were mostly unremarkable. He wondered why he would think that? After all, he should be feeling the wonder in this diversity. Maybe it was the seedy surroundings or the fact that everyone appeared to want to keep themselves to themselves. Two groups of aliens did stand out, though.

The odour that he couldn't identify earlier appeared to be coming from a group of four rough looking traders who were the same species as the waiter. They were taking turns inhaling smoke from a pot in the centre of their table. As each of them took their turn, they momentarily paused and shuddered slightly, apparently receiving some mental stimulation. Rounded shoulders and large hook noses added to the impression that they were slumped over the table. When they looked around, only the slits of their eyes were visible, carved deeply into the ruddy coloured skin. It was as if even the dull light in the saloon was too bright for them. Between the four of them, they appeared to be watching everyone in the room, displaying a high level of paranoia. The one that faced him was certainly taking a keen interest.

The other group that interested him did so because of their outstanding visibility. The only word he could think to describe them was beautiful. In many ways, they were near identical to him with small ears and noses. But they had hair, rather than a head cap. It was the clash of their snow white skin and shockingly purple hair that made them stunning. There were five of them, deep in discussion with what he realised was a Fandom. They were obviously negotiating and had reached an impasse. The Fandom was getting irritated and passing wind excessively.

His meal turned up, and the waiter threw a note onto the table. The bill. Camcietti reached for the pouch containing his emergency survival funds and carefully selected one of the smallest diamonds in it. He handed it tentatively to the waiter with a questioning stare. The beaming look on the waiter's face told him it was obviously a sufficient amount, and more likely very excessive. He pulled his hood back to allow himself to eat, took a mouthful of food and looked up to see one of the beautiful people staring straight at him. It was a girl. Young, maybe his age, eyes locked on his. She broke contact and turned back to join the negotiations. Her eyes were stunning, but Camcietti couldn't help but feel there was a great sadness there as well. A haunting sadness. In that briefest of moments, he had felt an empathy with her race, as though a great tragedy had befallen them.

His meal finished, Camcietti got up to leave. The waiter indicated to him to use the rear exit as someone was clearing up a spill by the front. He exited the rear door, turned right into what was a blind alley, and turned back, only to be faced by the four smoking aliens, taking up an aggressive posture.

The largest of them pointed at the pouch on Camcietti's

waist, his other hand pointing to his own, so there would be no misunderstanding of their intentions, a crooked smile on his face. Camcietti was fairly sure he could overcome them and set his posture, readying himself for a fight. The larger alien pulled out a weapon, pointed it at him and fired, stunning him. As he staggered, the aliens relieved him of his purse, and the large one smashed him over the back of his skull with the butt of his weapon. Camcietti collapsed on the ground.

* * *

CAMCIETTI AWOKE, and his surroundings slowly came into focus.

He was in a room, and he could feel the motion that only came with space travel. He was on a ship. It was some kind of recovery room, everything seemed to be blanched white and sterile. *What has happened to me?* he thought.

An alien entered. It was a girl, and she was beautiful, pale skin and striking purple hair, and those eyes. He'd seen those eyes before, they were so stunning and oh so sorrowful. She spoke to him.

'Carsaress et mundross knanasee vontrupp.'

Camcietti knew his translation implant would now be hard at work.

'Good morning, if it is morning, I am,' he paused and tried again, 'Where am I?' He saw her touch her temple. She spoke again.

'Carsaress of earlydross young vontrupp. Dimmistrag 've fi estravon cradietek aire vet 'oder fauxit plondraxi mouit. Bbrosk swazzik formundredred in ps'drithlre...'

She was giving him ammunition for his translator. He would do the same. 'The captain of the ship commanded his soldiers to adopt a defensive posture,' he continued with the universal translation monologue.

They both waited a few moments, then repeated three more sets of dialogue.

She said, 'Good afternoon, my name is Hadra. I'm a Rammorian, and you are on our ship. What is your name?'

'Daviss,' replied Camcietti, totally unaware of the fact he had given his birth name.

'Where do you come from?' she asked.

Camcietti paused, a strange look on his face. He was wrestling with something. 'I don't know,' he replied, staring into those sad eyes.

CHAPTER 33

entar's Choice
Sadalmelik System - 2012

VENTAR'S DELTA sphere appeared out of nowhere next to a fluo-rescent purple gas giant in Sadalmelik system. The light from the wormhole closed inwards upon itself and blinked out of existence. All traces of their route here were now gone. The vastness of space temporarily tamed by the momentarily linking of separate places and times. Placid wormholes had opened up the galaxy to any race that had achieved quantum drive space travel and had discovered how to find the starting points and predict their destinations.

'Have we lost them?' said Ventar's father Jake anxiously.

A very frustrated Dom Kobios let go of the ship's two joysticks, slipped her feet out of the stabilising pedals and slumped back into her seat. 'Yes, I think so.'

Dom Kobios, Chief of Security, was the only one in what remained of the Life Team that could pilot a sphere. But her skills were limited, and it was one bumpy ride through this latest wormhole.

'You did very well,' said young Prince Ventar, placing a reassuring hand on Kobios's shoulder. She looked at the prince, and as always, was amazed by the calmness he displayed for one so young. 'It's much more fun bouncing off the walls of a wormhole than going straight through it.'

The young prince tried to ease the tension that was thick in the air. They had been on the run in space for the last fifteen days, following their dramatic escape from Thorrid, the planet they had been inhabiting.

* * *

AN UNEVENTFUL ESCAPE from Preenasette had seen Ventar's Life Team arrive at Thorrid, after a thirty month journey. They suspected they had been detected not long after landing, but a week in stealth mode revealed nothing. Engineer Seca Watsin's theory was possible echoes in the already overly sensitive sensing equipment and a false alarm declared. They landed on a small deserted island in this pre-industrial world, where they would stay while searching for a permanent place to live.

They needed a remote location, as the indigenous population were so different to them. No amount of holographic manipulation would allow them to blend in. What appeared to be an old abandoned monastery, high in the foothills of a mountain range, seemed perfect.

They needn't have worried, though. The Humbs—as their translator would eventually declare them—soon found them, and were not the slightest bit bothered about these strange beings in their midst.

At first, they appeared comical to the Vercetians, but it soon became apparent that these creatures were masters at appearing to be busy, but never actually achieving anything.

By age three, a young Prince Ventar was a favourite of the local Humbs.

These hexapods spent most of their time on all six legs, only rising to use the claws on the front pair to carry out menial tasks. The prince was now tall enough to look straight into their faces. The Humbs' huge eyes were on either side of their head, at the ends of their jawbones and supported by copious folds of tissue. Ventar would stare into one of the eyes and listen intently to the clicking that constituted their speech. The Vercetian translator had only ever managed to decipher basic broken sentences.

The young prince, however, seemed to be in continuous communication.

Over the years, the Life Team concluded that the Humbs were stuck in time, and had not developed nor degraded from their current level of technology. They had found evidence that they had been at this same stage for tens of thousands of years. Seca Rase, the team's scientist, studied this aspect of the Humbs over an extended period, convinced that this stagnated development flew in the face of all understanding of every species internal drive for advancement.

Hardly a day would go by without the prince interacting with the Humbs. Stevos thought it charming at first, but over time suspected it was turning into an obsession and would like to have stopped it. But Ventar was growing into a lovely boy and was devouring all the teaching they could throw at him. So, she eventually stopped worrying. His mother and father couldn't stop though, and always felt a particular stress at Ventar's closeness to the strange beings.

Life carried on uneventfully for ten years on Thorrid, with the members of the Life Team filling their days as best they could, waiting for the High Council to make contact, as they had promised.

Then the visitors arrived.

* * *

A TRUN BATTLE cruiser appeared in orbit out of nowhere, barely giving the Life Team time to get under cover of their protective shield. If it hadn't been for Ventar telling Stevos to call all members back immediately, some would have been stranded and readily detectable. They were safe for now, but the Trun had dispatched two fighters to sweep the planet's surface systematically. Sooner or later, they would pass the shielded monastery, and in this technology free environment, would detect them easily, and the game would be up. They needed to escape, but the delta sphere was six miles away, in the nearest lake.

Kobios gathered everyone together around a large old and knotted wooden table. Most of the team were now seated. 'We need a plan. A distraction, to allow the prince to get to the ship. Thoughts, please?' She sat down, so as not to distract them, allowing everyone to think.

Stevos, the team leader, spoke first, desperately aware that this scenario should have been anticipated and thought through years ago. 'What if we split the team? Half will escort the Prince to the ship, while the other half distracts the Trun.'

'It's a certainty the diversionary group will get caught,' said Hondry. 'The ultimate sacrifice.'

'The Trun Commander has no interest in killing anyone,' said Ventar. 'He just wants me.'

'I wouldn't be so sure about the killing part,' replied Kobios.

'Oh, I'm sure,' Ventar said, not even looking up, his hand on the table, his finger circling an enormous ringed knot.

Kobios glanced at Stevos. The "he's at it again" look.

Ventar smiled. 'But it's a good idea; the diversion, that is. The time has come for us to leave this planet.'

'Okay then,' said Kobios. 'If you agree with me Stevos, I suggest we split thusly: Yourself, Hondry, Zeck, Jake, Maot and the Prince go. The rest of us remain.' Her manner indicated she wanted a fight.

Immediately, Seca Zeck, Kobios's second in command, rose from her seat opposite and leant forward, hands spread out on the table in front of her, apparently not happy and staring at Kobios head on. 'Your primary responsibility is to the prince. I should be in charge of the diversion.'

Kobios adopted an almost identical posture from the other side of the table, the two females faces almost touching. 'And what do we do for a pilot?'

Zeck held her ground. 'Okay, so you're all over the place in a wormhole conduit,' There was a glint in her eye and the hint of a smile as she emphasised the one thing she was better at than Kobios, 'but in normal space, you're every bit as good as me. And in everything else you *are* better than me—that's why you should be with the Prince.'

Kobios backed down slightly as Zeck continued, 'Boss, I know you're up for the fight, but this isn't one,' She softened her voice. 'It's a diversionary tactic, first and foremost. You need to be with the Prince.'

'That's settled,' said Ventar, putting an end to the argument. 'We'll go via Watsin's Pass and leave within the hour.' He looked at Stevos for approval.

She nodded her head. 'It's the plan on the table, Vercetians, so let's get to it. Kobios, kiss and make up with your number two and come up with some ideas for diversionary tactics. Preferably, not based on blowing the Trun into the back of beyond.'

Kobios scowled at Stevos, then back at Zeck, who was now sporting a beaming smile, happy to have, for once, got one over her boss.

* * *

WATSIN'S PASS was a topographical marvel.

A thin pass traversing the circumference of the foothills around the monastery, it was only about fifteen feet wide, but its perfectly vertical sides were four hundred feet high. It looked as though a higher being had used a hacksaw to cut a perfect groove into the rock. Every so often a similar groove, at right angles to the pass, headed out towards the plains, eventually losing all the majestic height. The furthest Seca Watsin, the team's engineer and a natural explorer, had travelled the pass was four hundred miles to the north, and its beginning (or end) and five hundred and fifty miles to the south where it swung east and appeared to follow the mountain range a good way further. This natural—or God made—pass also provided a hiding place from any form of low or high-tech detection devices. They would remain unseen for most of their southward journey.

Kobios and Zeck had eventually come up with a smart little two stage diversionary plan—once they had stopped squabbling—which they hoped would give them time firstly to get into the sphere, and secondly get into orbit with a fighting chance of getting a march on the Trun.

With the plan in place, Kobios and Ventar's group left the monastery.

A quarter mile from the lake, a tributary leading from the pass had dropped in height to thirty feet, and Kobios was able to signal the others to initiate phase one. Two of Zeck's team, Stefan and Dall, left the monastery on a land speeder and set off in the opposite direction, heading north at maximum speed. Within five minutes one of the fighters was above the speeder, closely tracking it. The speeder turned in to one of the pass's tributaries. The fighter couldn't enter but could stay above the ever-deepening groove. Soon the speeder signal was lost to the fighter, and when it reached the tee junction with the main pass, it was unable to choose a direction to follow—north or south. Zeck hoped this would cause confusion and momentarily focus the attention of the battle cruiser away from other parts of the planet.

Thirty miles south, Kobios' party was making slow progress. The dash to the lake wasn't quite the rush she was hoping. Stevos and Hondry, after a quick fifty feet or so dash, slowed to a crawl as the low oxygen level took its toll on them. Prince Ventar wasn't helping either, laughing and giggling with them at the back; totally oblivious to the predicament in which they found themselves. *What does he know that the rest of us don't?* Kobios thought before sending Jake and Maot on towards the sphere, then physically dragging the Prince along with her, in the vain hope that each pair would arrive when the ones in front had boarded.

Stevos and Hondry finally exited the transfer bubble and boarded the ship. Kobios was ready to go and fired up the sphere. Back at the monastery, Zeck got the call to go to phase two and contacted Dall, who with Stefan, had doubled back close to the monastery via the pass and were back in telepathic contact. They immediately charged back out and headed north again, hotly pursued by Zeck. Watsin and Rase were driving their overland transporter, also heading north, but via an alternative route. Zeck was hoping it would become clear to the Trun within minutes they were both heading to a northern lake, and that they would naturally conclude they were dashing to their submerged ship.

Meanwhile, Kobios was heading south. She stayed a few feet off the ground, hugging the mountain range. After they had swung east, they began their ascent out of Thorrid's atmosphere and into space. They would soon be detected by the cruiser but should be able to make the nearest wormhole unmolested. The question for the Trun cruiser commander was whether to wait for his two fighters to return or go straight after the sphere.

They made their choice. Kobios could see the battle cruiser heading straight after them. *This chase to the wormhole will be close*, she thought.

* * *

NOW THERE WAS a decision to be made.

Bal Stevos, leader of Ventar's Life Team—or what was left of it—looked around the small table on the flight deck of the delta sphere. They had escaped, for now, from the Trun battle cruiser that had been pursuing them. The question that she had asked of everyone sitting around the table was, 'Where do we go now?'

With her around the table was everyone who was aboard the vessel.

Bal Hondry was the Prince's cultural instructor. He was the other senior member of the Life Team and Stevos's second in command. He was a timid man, but very smart, and great at organising all aspects of the Team.

Dom Kobios was Chief of Security, though she was now acutely aware that she didn't have any security team left to be chief over. They had all made the sacrifice so they could escape. She was a tall and quite stunning Vercetian woman, and was famed as an excellent military strategist. Rumour had it that she'd advised Kam Major and was highly instrumental in the planning of the escape of the three Royals.

Camerra Maot and Camerra Jake were Ventar's mother and father.

That just left Prince Ventar, who at fourteen years old was the youngest of the refugee Royals, though they all assumed there would be another four-year-old princess now on Verceti. Even at his young age, Ventar was central to all decision-making. He was an extraordinary Prince. Bal Stevos, widely recognised as one of the great team leaders, now wondered what else she could teach this young man. He had frustrated all of his tutors over the last few years on Thorrid by deciding what he wanted them to teach him, rather than the other way around. This method of education was particularly problematic for his physical instructor Bal Dall, as Ventar refused to do any physical or martial arts training, claiming that he would never need it.

Stevos repeated herself, 'Where do we go now? Do we look for another temporary home?' She sighed. 'It would be tough. We've lost half of our team and are lacking in so many specialist sectors.'

'What about returning home?' said Jake. 'It might be safe.'

'How will we ever know that?' countered Maot.

'The High Council told us they would let us know when it was safe to return,' Stevos replied. 'How? I don't know.'

'They have ways and will contact us when the time is right,' said Ventar.

How on Preenacette does he know that, thought Stevos.

Ventar continued, 'We should locate to another planet until they do let us know. One more wormhole and the odds of the Trun ship finding us will become minuscule. If we take Rofaxi 12 we can get to here—the Sol System—in four months. We can find sanctuary there, with Tauriar's Life Team.'

'Tauriar's team?' echoed Kobios, to no one in particular.

The others stared at Ventar. In the blink of an eye he had sorted their dilemma out, and none of them could think of any reason to oppose his idea, never mind question his rationale. He smiled at them, stretched his arms, and said that he was tired and would go to his sleeping quarters for a while.

Bal Stevos looked at Hondry, then Kobios, then Jake and Maot. 'Sol it is then,' she said.

* * *

JAKE AND MAOT CAMERRA sat opposite each other at the tiny table in their sleeping quarters, both lost in thought. Their son had amazed them again.

'How does Kalter know what he knows?' his mother asked. A question she had asked so many times before. 'Is he in contact with the Princess? It was those Humbs. They did something to him.'

'This was never how things were supposed to be,' Jake said. 'Whisked away days after selection, and here we are fourteen years later, stuck in the middle of nowhere, not knowing if we've helped or hindered the cause.'

'We should have already told him,' said Maot. 'He's old enough.'

'He knows,' Jake replied. 'He always has. He reads our minds. I'm certain,' He looked knowingly at Maot.

'You've always said that.' Her glance back at him showed a certain disbelief.

'You know as well. Our son is not interested in the past, or that he is a Trun, not Vercetian. He wants to reunite Preenasette.'

'So. What do we do? Amdorma would have told everyone. We still have a job to do.'

Jake looked into his wife's eyes. 'I don't know. I just don't know.'

CHAPTER 34

$\mathcal{T}$he Battle Cruiser
   The Outer Regions of the Solar System - 2013

THE TRUN TC cruiser eased forward away from the rapidly closing placid wormhole. They had arrived at about two-thirds of the way in from the heliopause—the outer rim of the solar system—and the sun. All was static in the silent vacuum of space.

From the outside, the only movement to be seen was remaining sub-atomic particles of exotic matter blinking out of existence, unable to exists outside of the wormhole. A light show that no one would ever see.

Inside the cruiser, preparations were being made to activate the quantum star-drive. Two large propulsion units dominated the sides and rear of the vessel, comprising nearly half of the total ship. They began near the front as wide, flat, rails, their size increasing as they ranged towards the rear. They finished by wrapping around the entire back of the ship where two massive exhaust funnels discharged the ion particles from the quantum drive engines. The central part of the cruiser was cone shaped and smooth with a domed front. That portion housed the bridge, navigation and tactical stations. The upper central part of the cone contained the cargo bays, crew quarters, medical facilities and recreation areas, while the bottom housed the hanger bays for four 3W fighters and a TW Sphere. At the rear of the cone were engineering, the space garden, and manufacturing; making this the perfect long range self-sufficient spacecraft. The only imperfections on the smooth hull of the craft were the three rows of fifteen cannon turrets, two positioned either side of the base of the ship and one along the top.

INSIDE, Mancer was talking to Captain Rapha, 'How long before we reach Earth?' He was anxious to get this job done and get back to Preenasette. He would be taking the TW Sphere back with the captured princess.

'Twenty days, based on travelling at one hundredth light speed—standard interplanetary safe travel mode. You will need to instruct me to proceed faster than that Sir, and we will need to instigate some additional safety protocols,' the Captain replied matter of factly.

'No, no,' Mancer said. 'Just desperate to get this all over and done with.' Captain Rapha was facing a smiling Mancer now. 'Unless we have a squadron of Vercetians on our tail and you want my help, the helm is completely yours, Captain.' He continued, 'Still no sight of Sub Commander Tray's sphere?'

'Nothing, Sir. Right now I can only assume is that he's on the planet, if anywhere at all.'

'This is worrying.'

* * *

FOUR DAYS OUT FROM EARTH, the battle cruiser was a frenzy of intense activity; final checks and adjustments to the sphere, the fighters and all manner of equipment that hadn't seen any action for the duration of their journey.

Captain Rapha was standing over the surveillance technician's console, making sure Sub Command Brawn was entirely focused. They were now in prime territory for a Vercetian advance monitoring satellite to pick them up. Their search droids were scouting the way ahead. Rapha and Mancer were not overly concerned about being detected early—it was just luck as to whose technology would discover the others' first. It would be good to reduce the Vercetians warning, though—less warning and hopefully a mistake made.

A report came in as he was watching.

'A Vercetian satellite has been found and destroyed. An eighty percent chance of our detection, Sir,' Brawn said in a dejected voice.

'Not to worry,' Rapha said, 'carry on and let's assume we haven't.'

Mancer joined them. 'Any news or contact from our scouting party yet?'

'Nothing,' Rapha said. 'It's as if they didn't arrive.'

'Let me know when we do make contact,' Mancer said, a quizzical look on his old battle-weary face.

CHAPTER 35

An Interpreter Required
Earth. South Africa - 2013, Friday

JANET KILKENNY, CIA's Assistant Deputy Director for Science & Technology, paced the hotel corridor in Pietermaritzburg, South Africa, hands on hips, her whole demeanour shouting frustration. A delayed flight the evening before and now her interpreter Malcolm having come down with some mystery bug and a doctor who seemed to be taking an age. All this and a meeting with her Chinese counterpart only a few hours away.

'He has Salmonella food poisoning. I'm afraid he's going to be laid up for between two and seven days,' the doctor finally informed her.

'He's not in any grave danger then?' asked Janet.

'No, not at all, though he will probably feel awful for at least the next twenty-four hours. He needs plenty of liquids to stay hydrated.'

'Thank you, Doctor.'

'Not at all. I can get someone to get this medicine from the drugstore. Instructions for use will be clearly labelled. I'll be on my way now.' His polite nod was missed by Janet as she turned away.

Damn it. I'll have to cancel, she thought. But that would appear weak. The image of the sneaky Chinese negotiator smiling as his interpreter told her something entirely different would goad her. She needed a good translator.

She popped into see Malcolm, and it was clear from the poor man's face he was suffering. Back at her room, she called Henry at the American Embassy.

'Henry, my translator has food poisoning. I need someone fluent in Mandarin for this afternoon's meeting. Can you help?'

'Good morning to you too, Miss Kilkenny,' replied Henry J Jones, a chief attaché at the American Embassy. 'Give me an hour, madam, and I'll see what I can pull out of the hat.'

'Sorry, JJ,' Janet said in a thick Irish accent trying to atone for her curtness. 'Do your best, buddy.'

Breakfast was delicious. Not eating on the plane to Durban had left her famished, and decidedly healthier than Malcolm at the moment. The full English helped her demeanour no end. Her phone rang while she was savouring her second cup of coffee.

'Speak to me, Henry!' Janet was now giving it her full Bronx. He was one of her favourite colleagues.

'As you wish, Madame,' he said, continuing his best English butler impression, happy to play along with Janet's little game. 'Unfortunately, Mandarin interpreters are a little thin on the ground here in South Africa. But, Gertrude at The British Embassy has got an MI6 support officer who she says is quite good. Not interpreter standard, but the best I can offer.'

'Okay, Henry,' Janet said after a few seconds. 'I've come too far not to see them.'

'I'll arrange for her to come to your hotel at lunchtime. Her name is Amanda Walker.'

'Great, thanks, Henry. I owe you,' Janet said, signing off.

'I'll add it to madame's long list,' Henry said.

* * *

THE MEETING WENT WELL. Amanda had missed a few bits of the conversation and misinterpreted a few gestures, but on the whole, she thought Janet was pleased. It was 5.45pm, and Janet had no more engagements for the day. 'Fancy some dinner, Amanda? You've got me out of a hole today. I'll pick up the tab. Well, the Agency will.' She smiled warmly at Amanda.

'Yes, that would be great,' Mandy replied.

'A colleague recommended an Italian restaurant on Mayflower Street. Fancy that?'

'Yes, Janet.'

'Let's go then.'

The meal was good. Both ladies chose the spaghetti bolognese and a great bottle of Chardonnay. They chatted about the meeting and general life in the CIA and MI6, and about Anglo-American relations. The waiter cleared the table and Janet ordered cognacs to complement their coffees.

'So, how does the daughter of a British cabinet minister become a member of MI6?' Janet asked, seemingly happy to chat on a more intimate level.

Mandy was feeling a little tipsy now, but was enjoying Janet's company. She felt she could be slightly more open with her than she would normally be. This woman was, after all, nearly at the very top of the CIA and certainly not a security risk. 'The thrill and the adventure I suppose,' she said. 'Not that it's all that. Most of the time it's quite mundane, but it does have its moments. I was also part of an adventure when I was a teenager, and that's spoilt me for accepting mediocrity.'

'An adventure? Is it one you can talk about?'

'Well, not really.' Mandy knew she'd slipped up and tried to change the subject. 'How old were you when you joined the CIA?'

'I was twenty-four with a passion for technology,' Janet said and carried on telling her what she had hoped for from joining the CIA.

Mandy sensed that Janet backed off somewhat, aware of her awkward response. Knowing she had touched on something that should have stayed off limits.

Janet continued, 'Though my real passion is astronomy. Before my current promotion, I was attached to NASA, tracking NEO's.'

'NEO's?' Mandy asked, trying to recover her composure.

'Sorry. Near Earth Objects. They include asteroids, comets and any of the thousands of satellites that now orbit Earth. We were tracking—they still are—objects that might collide with Earth, and in my official capacity, what other countries were sending up there. Your father would know all about it. He's well known in this field.'

'My father has his grubby fingers in many things astronomical. Sounds interesting,' Mandy said. 'I see the connection with the meeting today now. I must admit, I was a little confused as to what it was all about. Concentrating too hard on the translating didn't help.'

'Which you did well, my dear,' Janet smiled. 'When are you heading back to England?'

'My work here is finished,' said Mandy. 'But I plan to stay on for a few days. An Irish friend of mine is riding in the downhill mountain bike world championships the day after tomorrow. It's only an hour's drive from here. I'm going to support him.'

'Not Jon O'Malley?' Janet had a puzzled look on her face.

'Yes, do you know him?' Mandy could feel the tone of her voice noticeably cooling.

Janet seemed to lack confidence for the first time today. 'Of him. He's Irish after all. And I have dual USA/Irish citizenship.'

Mandy changed the subject, talking fashion for professional women. But she was desperately trying to fit together all of the pieces of a small jigsaw puzzle. She was convinced that Janet knew more about Jon than she was willing to admit. It's wasn't as though he was a famous mainstream athlete. And her position, the NEO's and all that entailed. Did she know about Grace and her Life Team? Her head was spinning.

Janet paid the bill and suggested they walk back to her hotel. 'I'll get you a cab from there.'

As they approached the hotel, Amanda was at a fever pitch. She had to say something. 'How do you know Jon? Do you have a professional interest in him? Is he in danger?'

Janet looked into her face, clearly seeing her anxiety. She grabbed her arm lightly but firmly. 'Let's go to my room. We need to talk.'

* * *

WHEN THEY ARRIVED in Janet's room, she sat Amanda down on the sofa and went to the drinks cabinet and poured herself a scotch. Amanda declined.

Janet sat down across from her. 'We both have an interest in Jon O'Malley. I'm intrigued to know what you know, and you're desperate to know what I do. We can skirt around the subject, or we can cut straight to the chase. I'm willing to go first and tell you what I know. You can decide then what, if anything, you want to tell me.'

Amanda thought for a moment. This was getting out of her comfort zone. She needed help. 'Can I phone my mother? Can she listen to what you have to say?'

Janet's look was surprised, but she composed herself. 'Fine,' she replied.

Amanda phoned her mother.

'Hi, darling. I was just dropping off. Can this wait until tomorrow?'

'No mother, it can't. I'm with Janet Kilkenny, CIA's Assistant Deputy Director for Science & Technology. I've helped her out today, here in South Africa, with some Mandarin translations. Over dinner tonight we have, somehow, touched on to the fact we both have an interest in Jon, and it is obvious something is amiss. Janet was just about to tell me what she knows, and I asked if you could listen in. I'm worried about him.'

Ann was now, of course, wide awake. 'Yes, Mandy. Are we on speakerphone?'

'We are now.' Amanda touched a couple of buttons.

'Hello, Janet. We've never met, but my husband mentions you often. He is certainly an admirer of your work. I'm intrigued. What is this all about?'

'Hi Ann,' Janet replied. 'Thank you for those kind words. I'm happy to talk freely, as long as we all agree that what is said here doesn't leave these four walls, so to speak.'

'Agreed,' Ann confirmed.

'Several years ago I was on a sabbatical from work, looking after my terminally ill mother in Ireland. I had plenty of time on my hands, so I set up a mini observation station in my parents' attic. Being on the foothills of Carrauntoohil, night-time clarity was pretty good. I'd previously been on loan to NASA studying NEO's.' Janet paused to assess Ann's knowledge.

'I'm aware of NEO's,' Ann said.

Janet continued, happy that Ann, probably through her husband, had some basic knowledge. 'Anyway, I won't go into too much detail, but I came across a shadow on an asteroid that I later discovered could have been a UFO.'

'What year are we talking about?' asked Mandy.

'It was about two years ago, 2011,' Janet said. 'Whatever it was, I tracked it to Ireland. It was right there on my doorstep, so off I went to do some amateur sleuthing. I've never had any definitive proof, but I'm sure I've identified at least one, possibly two of the occupants of the vessel, and I'm nigh on positive they are now travelling with Jon O'Malley.'

'Oh Mother, they've found him!' Amanda was trying to hold it together but was feeling the strain.

'Steady, darling. Let me think a moment. Ann paused for a good thirty seconds, before replying, 'Thank you, Janet. Thank you for your honesty.' She paused again, then decided. 'I think we need to tell you our story.'

'Back in 2000, my husband and I were selected by a group of aliens who were on the run from their war-torn planet in the Alpheratz system.'

Janet's eyes lit up in amazement. She looked up at Mandy, who silently acknowledged the statement with a nod.

'They were looking for a sanctuary, somewhere to hide their princess until such time that it would be safe to return home. They are technologically more advanced than we are, but are a peaceful race that has been trying to broker peace with their neighbours for many years. We helped them settle on a remote estate in Ireland. There were, or should I say are, eleven of them. The Princess, who we named Grace, is the same age as Amanda. One of the final selection criteria was that they wanted Grace to have a friend. They befriended a local boy—Jon. Unfortunately, one of the Vercetians—that's how they refer to themselves—was an undercover spy for the Trun—their enemy—who made an early attempt on Grace's life. The attempt was thwarted, but Mandy and Jon discovered Grace's true identity. They've been friends ever since.'

Janet whispered to Mandy, 'I was never one hundred percent sure, but I always hoped I was right.'

Ann continued, 'They never identified the mole, but about

eight years ago a message orb went missing, and the Vercetians knew their location had been compromised. They set up this second residence here in Cork, to relocate to upon detection of an enemy vessel.'

Ann chuckled softly. 'You, Janet Kilkenny, in your attic in Ireland, managed to find a space ship that their advanced technology couldn't.'

'They have an escape plan. Having become fond of our world and its inhabitants, they don't want to be the cause of Earth becoming a battleground. If the Trun come for Grace, they'll send a battle cruiser. I think we can assume they will be coming by the advance party already here. I just hope the surveillance system in our solar system gives them us early warning of its arrival. They plan to leave the planet so that the cruiser follows them. If they leave now, the Trun ship will still search Earth, which wouldn't be a good thing. This way they will draw it away. Jon is in danger. They are obviously using him to find Grace, and may have already succeeded.' Ann stopped to give Janet time to digest everything.

Amanda, who had refrained from interrupting her mother's monologue, spoke up. 'You need to help us, Janet. You need to help them and Jon. They're good people.'

'Would you like to meet them, Janet?' Ann asked, taking the initiative. 'Can you fly to Cork tomorrow? I can meet you there and introduce you to Douglas, their leader.'

CHAPTER 36

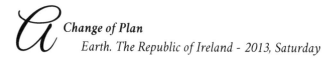

Change of Plan
Earth. The Republic of Ireland - 2013, Saturday

JANET AND AMANDA arrived at Cork Airport the next evening. She had used Henry again to arrange the charter of a private jet from Durban directly to Cork. Henry duly obliged, but not without a little poke at her. 'Is Madame off to check out the quality of the Guinness again?'

The drive from Pietermaritzburg to Durban was a quick one hour trip along the N3 in a borrowed embassy car. The flight made one refuelling stop at Casablanca in Morocco. As they landed, Janet raised her glass of orange juice to Mandy and said, 'Here's looking at you, kid.' Mandy gave her a blank stare. 'No?' She continued, 'How about "Of all the airports, in all the towns, in all the world, we had to land here." Yes?' Mandy wondered what she was on about and smiled meekly back at a forlorn looking Janet.

Her mother had told Mandy to return to Cork with Janet. 'We need to sit down and decide how we respond to this development. We must assess any danger to Jon. They've been with him for two years, so I doubt a couple of days will make a difference.'

Mandy had strongly disagreed with her mother. 'I should be with him. If they know about Jon, they know about me. It would be quite natural for me to visit him, and I can assess the situation myself, and maybe even warn him.'

She had made a compelling case, but Ann was insistent. Janet had chimed in with her agreement of her mother's assessment. 'Let's discuss it. If sending you back in there is the right thing to do then fine, but let's have some backup with you. I'll keep the jet on standby when we get to Cork.'

Her mother was concerned about her. 'I know you're worried darling, but we must have a coordinated plan of action.'

Mandy reluctantly agreed. She had seen little of Jon the past few years, as their lives had moved in different directions, but the danger he was now in had cemented the fact that she couldn't imagine a life without him being some part of it.

It was a long journey back to Cork, but Amanda had no shortage of stories to tell Janet about the Vercetians. She told her in detail about their escape from Preenasette, the two princes who were despatched to other destinations in the Milky Way, and the attempt on Grace's life when they had first met. Janet was engrossed and couldn't get enough information about them. She was awestruck at the thought of other races out there travelling between the stars. They had so much to learn. She kept asking Amanda about every little detail. The appearance modifying brooch was something she would love to have.

Janet was also fascinated with the history of the war between the two nations. Mandy tried her best to explain it. 'Grace did tell Jon and me all about it one rainy afternoon.'

She told Janet about the physiology of the Trun and the

Vercetians being practically identical, but that their cultures and philosophies had followed very different paths. 'The Vercetians, Grace's people, had the more fertile and temperate land. Life was easier, giving a lot more time to develop in the sciences and arts. Whereas the Trun had a hard and bleak existence and were a tough, but also a resourceful people.'

'During the pre-industrial period, a healthy balanced trading relationship existed between the two nations. The Verceti traded in exotic foods, spices and fabrics, and the Trun traded in precious stones, minerals and coal from their extensive mining industries. Technological advancement proceeded through the industrial era into the computer age with little more than minor military skirmishes and trade embargoes coming between the two nations.

'The serious troubles started after the advent of space travel. The Vercetians had the technology for this next phase of their evolutionary development but only limited natural resources. On the other hand, the Trun had an abundance of natural resources but lacked the technology. The planet's early ventures into space proceeded with an unstable alliance between them, but the distrust was increasing. The Vercetians were becoming more secretive with their technological advances and the Trun with their development of precious metals. When the Trun developed a material that would significantly revolutionise space travel— Boron Metal Matrix Composite—the advantage shifted to them. Boron MMC used a continuous fibre reinforcement that made it strong. But its advantage in space travel was its thermal properties. With hardly any linear thermal expansion over a 900degC range it was capable of handling all of the stresses that ultra high acceleration could throw at it.

'The first war saw the Vercetians attacking Trun Rizontella and commandeering one of their major mining and development facilities. For four years they used the Trun miners to extract the raw materials they needed and stole the MMC manufacturing secrets. Only when the Vercetians discovered the same raw materials in a remote part of their own country did they leave the Trun manufacturing facility. A state of war continued between the two nations for the next ten years.

'During this time, there was a major rebellion within the Vercetian population, most of whom were abhorred by and ashamed of those actions. The government, previously administered by corporate-affiliated greedy politicians, was replaced with the leader of the rebellion, Almola Camcietti, as the first head of a ruling council. In the next few years, a plan was crafted to form a council that would keep this situation from ever happening again. They would elect a new member every ten years, and every time as councillor was elected, the eldest sitting member would retire. A system was put in place to train replacements for the outgoing elder. Selected at birth, they would spend forty years being trained by a Life Team. A calling, to ensure their leader's number one priority was the well being of the Vercetian people. This system of ruling continues, with some further refinements, to this day.

* * *

JANET AND AMANDA made their way into the terminal where Ann was waiting for them. With her was a short, stocky man with spiky hair. He gave Amanda a bear hug, then held out his hand to Janet. He introduced himself as Douglas Faulkener.

Mandy and her mother smiled at each other as they watched Janet trying to study him without appearing obvious.

'Come on, let's go. We've got a taxi waiting outside,' Ann said.

A fifteen-minute taxi ride got them to a large detached residence that would have once housed an affluent family and now acted as Grace's Cork home, and where the full Life Team would evacuate to on detection of a Trun ship.

Gwyneth, Katie, and Mr. and Mrs. Shaw welcomed them into the large dining room and suggested they sit down at the table. Mr. Shaw brought in tea and two plates of superb looking cupcakes.

Everyone chatted for a couple of minutes before Grace strolled into the room, totally unmodified and looking serene in her blue splendour. Janet's face was a picture, exactly the dramatic entrance that Ann had planned with Douglas and Gwyneth.

Grace and Amanda made a beeline for each other. They hugged and kissed and started talking excitedly about each other's appearance. Grace released Amanda and turned to Janet, her tone now quite formal. 'Welcome Janet Kilkenny, CIA's Assistant Deputy Director for Science and Technology. Please accept my sincere apologies for this staged introduction. But it's not quite finished yet.' At this prompt, all of the Vercetians touched their brooches, and a crescendo of blue coloured the room. 'Welcome to our little piece of Verceti on Earth.'

* * *

AN HOUR later and things had quietened down.

Douglas, Gwyneth, Princess Tauriar, Amanda, Ann and Janet were sitting around the table. The Vercetians had reset their brooches and assumed human form. The last hour had been spent casually discussing a multitude of different things, ranging from diet and differences in physiology between the two species to general security and—to Janet's delight—some of their advanced technology. But now it was time to discuss the matter in question.

Ann kicked it off. 'Janet, I told you yesterday about the plans Douglas has regarding their escape from Earth. He has informed me today that those plans need reconsidering. There have been some significant developments over the last forty-eight hours that now need to be factored in. I'll let him explain what's been happening.'

'Thank you, Ann.' Douglas' elbows were on the table with his hands clasped just below his chin. 'Our plight has taken a sudden and very disturbing turn for the worse. We have detected a Trun battle cruiser on the periphery of your solar system. It's just a matter of days before they reach Earth.' He looked apologetically at Ann, conscious she was unaware of this turn of events. 'That's not all. We have also discovered that our Trun mystery friend has sabotaged the guidance system of our sphere.' He went on to explain that it could have been done anytime during the past year, as the artificial intelligence controlling the shield was no longer active, having been relocated to their Cork residence. 'We're still checking, but it is feasible it could have been done remotely.'

'Are you assessing the damage?' asked Janet

'We have Helen, our scientist and Peter, our pilot at the site. I'm expecting a report imminently,' Douglas replied. 'We're desperate to get it working before they arrive.'

No one spoke.

'So, there's nothing further to discuss until that report comes back,' Amanda said, getting restless. 'Can we talk about Jon now?'

'Yes, I think so,' said Ann. Douglas nodded.

'Are we sure that these associates of Jon's are from our world?' Gwyneth asked.

'I'm sure Ann has already told you about my little tracking project that first located their ship,' Janet said. 'With the help of a professor friend with access to one of the USA's prominent university's facilities, we tracked its route to the Gearagh, a submerged glacier woodland and nature reserve just north of here. I never found out where they had landed but was pretty sure I found *them*.'

'What was strange about these people you suspected were the vessel's occupants?' Gwyneth asked.

'Well…' Janet looked around the table, suddenly aware that her story seemed weak. 'The day they arrived, they said they had come from Cork. According to the hotel manageress, they had no car, and the only bus to the town had broken down fifteen miles away on its way to Cork.'

'Their clothing was out of place—big city suits, and they turned up with no luggage.' She looked around the table seeking acknowledgement of her interpretation of the facts. All she got was pleasant smiles. She continued, 'We both saw the boy the following day after they had checked out of the hotel, in a casual outfit. Had he bought new clothes? Where was his suit? They didn't know anyone in the village; it was their first time there.'

Janet pushed on, 'And at the Gearagh, he disappeared by the lake. Then a strange woman appeared, literally out of the bushes, in smart clothing, wandering aimlessly, and then she vanished too—at the same spot. A week later I read about a woman who went missing from the town on her way home from work. The photo in the newspaper was the spitting image of the strange woman by the lake.'

'It does all seem a bit odd,' said Ann. 'Anything else about them, Janet?'

'I got their names. Robert Smith and Thomas Jones.' She threw her hands in the air. 'Who'd choose those names? I never heard anything about Thomas Jones again, but two months later Rob Smith was on the back page of my dad's local paper, having signed for the Fortune Team—Jon's team. Deeper in the article, the reporter stated that he'd won two local races to impress the team principal, but had no cycling track record before that, that anyone knew of.' She shrugged. 'Nothing overly strange about that, but if you put it into the context of an alien trying to get close to Jon, it all makes sense.'

'You've got to agree there's a lot of strange in these facts,' Janet appealed for anyone to show some moral support.

Finally, Douglas said, 'I think you present a very compelling case, Janet. I, for one, believe you came across a Trun spy ship, and that this Rob Smith is cycling with Jon with a secret agenda.'

For the next few hours they tried to thrash out a solution to the two main problems they faced.

First was the arrival of the Trun battle cruiser. Probably only a few days from Earth.

Second, and more pressing, was the situation with Jon in South Africa. Jon's safety concerned them, of course, but also the Trun with him were bound to be the first contact for the battle cruiser. Put them out of commission and Jon is safe and the cruiser is on the back foot.

Eventually, they came to a plan with which they were all happy. Prime summed up the actions as he now saw them.

He looked at Amanda first. 'You will return immediately to Durban in Janet's jet, and join up with Jon. William and Gordon will go with you but will keep their distance for the time being. You need to make Jon aware of our suspicions, and warn him he may be in danger. We need to find out if this friend of his is a Trun. Be very careful Amanda, if he is, then there will be others. You know what they're capable of. They're the same as us: holographic disguises, enhanced mental abilities. But William and Gordon will be close.'

Mandy nodded, looking eager to get going.

He checked his notes and turned to William, their Chief of Security. 'You and Gordon need to flush out all of the Trun. We need them neutralised before the arrival of the battle cruiser. They will have a communication device somewhere. Find it.'

William nodded. He had never heard Douglas speak with

such authority in all the years they had been together. But then he'd never had to.

Next, it was Janet.

'Janet, my friend. Firstly, we are indebted to you for this discovery you made. We now have a fighting chance of a clean escape. But you have agreed to help us more.' He checked his notes. 'You and Ann have already contacted Sir Alister Carmichael and arranged a meeting with some of the leaders of Earth, tomorrow. Grace will travel to London later this evening with you to address them.' He looked at Grace with an odd expression on his face, a mixture of annoyance and pride.

Earlier in the discussions, Grace had asked to go to London to address the leaders of Earth. They would need convincing, but Douglas had flatly refused to let her go. 'Much too dangerous. We can send someone else.'

Grace's reply had shocked everyone around the table, especially Douglas. 'I am the leader of the Vercetians on Earth. I decide. And I have decided I will go!'

It was the first time she had ever overruled him, and after the initial indignation, he felt pride. His little girl had grown up.

Douglas finished, 'And finally, I will contact Peter and Helen and divert them.' He put his pad down and spread his hands expansively. 'Everyone happy?'

There was a chorus of agreement from the table.

CHAPTER 37

𝒜 Plea for Help
         Earth - COBRA, Whitehall, London, England - 2013,
Sunday

SILENCE FELL over the Cabinet Office briefing room.

Chief of Defence Staff, General Sir Alister Carmichael leant back in his seat and took a deep breath. *Why have the CIA brought us this girl with her crazy story of aliens and invading forces, and on a Sunday?* he thought. He looked to his left at the Deputy Prime Minister, Janet Pennant-Davies, who was chairing this extraordinary meeting and was greeted by a perplexed look. To his right, the Secretary of Defence Alec Burrows started to speak, but stopped before a word could form. Only Janet Kilkenny, Assistant to the Deputy Director of CIA for Science & Technology seemed unconcerned. But then, she had instigated this meeting.

The room remained silent.

The other twenty-one members of this very select group looked towards Pennant-Davis to give a response to this unremarkable young lady and her plea for help. But it was Carmichael who eventually replied.

'So, you want our help? You'll need to give us more than that.'

'You need more?' Grace reached to her brooch and touched it lightly...

CHAPTER 38

*T*he Capture
Earth - South Africa - 2013, Monday

AMANDA WALKER, with William and Gordon, arrived at Pieter-maritzburg airport late Sunday morning. They jumped into separate taxis, with Mandy going straight the bike race and William and Gordon heading into to town to find accommodation.

She arrived at the downhill course in plenty of time. Jon wasn't due to start his run until 3.35pm—ninety minutes away. She decided to climb the hill and find a daring section of the descent and watch the riders come flying down. She chose a section just past halfway, where there was a triple jump followed by two tight turns straight after landing, showcasing the riders' skills to the maximum.

She stood next to two American lads who seemed well up for the next couple of hours of thrills and spills.

Before she knew it, there was a buzz going around the

crowd. The blond haired American said, 'Rider on the course,' his mate was whooping loudly.

Mandy looked at the series of jumps, trying to imagine what speed they would be going over each one. It would need to be quite slow, she thought. How wrong she was, for when the first rider came into view he was flying, and hit the takeoff ramp so fast that he cleared all three jumps landing sweetly on the final down ramp. The two Americans were screaming with delight, as was the rest of the crowd. The rider was now firmly applying his brakes but still looked to Mandy to be going far too fast for the upcoming turns. With the banking helping him he zipped through both and was gone, the roar of the crowd following him down the hill.

'Oh my God!' said Mandy to nobody in particular, but the blond haired American replied, 'It's gonna be a great afternoon.'

Very soon she was whooping with the rest of them, amazed at what these guys—and Jon—actually did. She couldn't believe that after all the years being so close to him and knowing his love for this sport, that she had never actually watched him race. She turned to the Americans.

'I never knew they went so fast!'

The second American shouted back to her, 'And the girls, dude. The awesome Rhian has just won the women's race. She's world champion, and she's one of yours—a Brit.'

These guys seemed to have a handle on who was coming next, so she asked them, 'Do you know when Jon O'Malley's turn is?'

They consulted their scruffy notes. 'Yeah, two more then the lucky Irishman is up.' and both added a tremendous whoop, whoop, with Mandy joining in.

Next was a Frenchman. His jump lacked height, and his rear wheel landed perilously close to the up side of the third ramp.

He did well to stay upright. The Americans were mega animated. 'Wow… serious casing, man! How did he stay on?'

Then it was Jon's turn. Amanda couldn't help feeling apprehensive. Before she knew it, though, he was flying through the air right above her. He looked majestic, at least to Mandy, and landed effortlessly on the exit ramp, the wheels kissing the ground simultaneously. He eased forward marginally, slowing for the turns. He banked hard for the left one, flowing gracefully through it, then a wobble. He wasn't taking the line for the right-hand turn that the previous riders had. He hit the bend, flying high over the bank, man and cycle completing a full summersault.

There was a groan from the crowd. The marshals were climbing onto the course to get to the bank Jon had gone over. The Americans looked at each other, silently conveying their dismay.

Amanda raced over to him, but she had crowds of spectators to negotiate, many of whom were heading in the same direction to see the wreck. When she arrived, Jon was already on his feet, talking to two marshals. One was holding his bike, and the other was pointing to his front tyre, which had completely ripped off.

'Are you okay?' Mandy was tapping him on the back.

'Amanda. You managed to get here,' He took his helmet and goggles off and pecked her on the cheek. 'What time did you arrive?'

'Never mind me,' she said, fear having risen to angry tears. 'How are *you*?'

He stopped to assess the damage. 'A bit of road rash here and there, but nothing broken.' He smiled at her. 'You must be my lucky charm. The first time you come and watch me, and I crash.'

'You know I'm your only charm.' She grabbed his arm, pulling him to her.

He winced, and she let go, 'Road rash,' he said, trying to smile.

The two marshals, one carrying his bike, began to help him down the hill, with Mandy right behind. The journey that would have taken just over a minute to finish from here on his bike would now be closer to half an hour.

* * *

AT THE BOTTOM, they arrived at the team van, a monstrous thing with Fortune Factory Downhill Team plastered across both sides.

Mandy was still trying to get Jon on his own. She needed to tell him what they thought might be going on but wasn't sure how to broach the subject. She didn't have to, for the time being anyway, because out of the van stepped Rob.

'What happened, man?' said Rob.

'Tyre ripped out, mate. I didn't stand a chance. Really lucky that I found a soft landing,' Jon replied.

Amanda studied Rob, trying to find clues as to his true nature. Nothing apparent.

'This is my friend Amanda,' Jon said. Mandy shook Rob's hand. It felt normal, but then, so did Grace's.

Rob looked at Amanda warily. He knows who I am, she thought. He's given himself away.

'Have you been riding today?' she asked, smiling. She was looking at his riding outfit, with his number still on. 'Oops, I see you have.'

They then carried on chatting, with Jon grilling Rob about his performance. He was currently in sixth place, but there were quite a few big hitters still to come.

'Well, I'm off to get showered,' Jon said to Rob. 'Amanda is buying me dinner later.'

'I thought you were in the chair, O'Malley,' she said, poking him and finding some more road rash.

* * *

AT DINNER, Mandy explained everything they had deduced about Rob. Jon was utterly astonished.

'Haven't you noticed anything wrong with him?' she asked.

'No, just like I had no idea about anyone at Harewood Hall, before the assassination attempt.' Jon looked a little hurt. 'Though I have caught him talking to his ghetto blaster quite a few times.'

'Nothing?' persisted Mandy.

'Now his aunt? Alien all the way. That's one strange woman.' Jon smiled. 'I'm not convinced, Mandy. We're going to have to dig around a bit. Set a trap.'

'Or look inside the ghetto blaster,' Mandy countered.

* * *

THE FOLLOWING DAY, Jon invited himself and Mandy over to Rob's for a late breakfast.

'Mandy's heard about your legendary fried breakfasts,' Jon told him.

'I'll need to get some stuff in,' Rob said. 'Make yourself at home.'

'Is your aunt in?' Jon asked.

'I haven't seen her all morning. I think you'll be safe.'

As soon as Rob left, Jon set about the ghetto blaster. No conventional way of getting in. No screws, nuts or bolts, rivets. Jon looked in Rob's toolkit and saw what he wanted. A sonic entry device. Peter had shown him one at Harewood Hall, and showed him how to use it. He held it close to the blaster casing and depressed a button. He was rewarded with a click. Four secret entry point catches released, revealing a weird looking machine inside.

Jon looked at Mandy. It all seemed perfectly clear.

Unfortunately, all was perfectly clear elsewhere.

An indignant food processor was reporting to Rob about being violated by aliens. Rob was sitting outside wondering what he should do about Amanda. This was all happening too fast, and still no sign of his father's arrival. He would need to chat with Sonia.

* * *

SONIA WAS MONITORING everything from her room. She was aware of the imminent arrival of Mancer's cruiser, but had her own agenda, and it didn't include Rob.

She entered the room to a startled Jon and Mandy and subjected them to a weird green mist from her wristbands. They collapsed.

When Rob returned, she subjected him to the same treatment, and began planning a variation on a night of 'fun' she'd been planning for the last few days.

Later, when she had loaded the back of the van with her three playmates, the reporter turned up on the pretence of a couple of beers with the other boys. She knew exactly what he was here for, and now would be the right time to sort him as well. The last thing Sam remembered was a strange green mist emanating from Rob's aunt's wristband.

* * *

THE DAY after William and Gordon's arrival in South Africa, they lost contact with Amanda and Jon.

They visited Rob's apartment, but there was no one in sight.

They contacted Grace, informing her that her friends were missing.

'Janet's arranging another jet, so we'll be over there as soon as possible. It will just be me, Janet and Krankel. Janet is arranging for two local South African NIA agents to meet you at the airport prior to our arrival. Bring them up to speed as quickly as possible—especially as to our alien origins—we won't have time for surprises on the day. Janet will have briefed them as much as is possible before you meet up. They'll have transportation for us at the airport.'

'All clear, Gentlemen?'

'Yes, Princess,' William replied.

CHAPTER 39

he Interrogation
Earth - South Africa - 2013, Monday

SONIA PACED UP AND DOWN, waiting in sweet anticipation for her four captives to awaken.

She was in the conference room of a small motel with her four prisoners tied to chairs, in a circle, facing each other. The epidermis that was once Samantha Smith lay in one corner of the room, the scanner hovering above it. No one else in the establishment would disturb them, not now. She had all night.

The situation was a little annoying—having been found out this close to the arrival of the Trun cruiser. Not that she was concerned about the four in front of her. She would kill them and make up a story to gloss over it. She knew where the Vercetian princess was—well approximately—and that would be sufficient for the Trun. No, it would be annoying when Birjjikk found out. Three times now she had been exposed on planetary surveillance postings, and her Player would regard that as extremely sloppy. Some retribution would be forthcoming, of that she was quite sure. *Why am I always the one*, she thought. She had never quite fit in with Birjjikk and the other two. Her antics at the Cadre leadership battle between Birjjikk and Graffojj hadn't helped. She was realistic enough to realise that she had only got into Birjjikk's Cadre because she was the only one left alive. Carffekk, Henkk and, of course, Birjjikk were the nucleus of the team, but rules were rules and the Cadre needed four and all from a single Academy.

Kean was wakening. Years of suffering this Turdgutter. *No wonder I needed to get out and kill.* The humans were exquisite— fear in abundance. *I will kill him last*, she thought, *he'll suffer the longest.* She slapped him hard across the face. He reacted aggressively, but without direction, still being under the influence of the drug.

She stretched, so glad to have shed the human epidermis. She couldn't switch it on and off like the Preenasettians, her physiology was just too different It took her about twenty minutes to change to a human or Trun. Phase shift manipulation and epidermic encasement weren't quick processes, but the result was superior.

Kean was awake now. His eyes were focussing slowly, trying to make out the being in from of him. She smiled at him, her sharp teeth turning it into a sneer. 'You are awake, Kean?' She studied his face.

'Who are you? What are you?' His words formed slowly.

'Don't you remember me? You've been working with me for the last four years.' She was enjoying his look of. 'I'm Sonia.'

"But, you're...'

'Not a Trun? No, I'm a Zerot.' She strolled over to him and slapped him hard again. this time Kean yelped and tried to pull out of his restraints. Sonia enjoyed his defiance. It would change soon enough.

He composed himself. 'So what do you want with us? Why have you kept up this charade for so long?'

'Be patient.' She she leant in, their faces now almost touching. 'For now, all you need to know is that by the morning, you and your friends shall be dead. And your precious planet Preenasette will soon be just a memory. Let's wake your Earth friends. I want to play.'

* * *

AMANDA'S DRUG-INDUCED dream world began dissipating. In its place, unintelligible conversations, cries of anguish and the blurred impression of something moving. As her vision returned she became aware of a strange creature.

It was unlike anything she had ever seen or imagined. The creature's mottled grey skin made it look old. Amanda's first impression was that this being was ancient. Its posture, however, belied the idea of old age, tall with an arrogant strut that oozed confidence. Its face was skeletally thin, with a small mouth housing savage, needle sharp teeth. Its ears were long and thin, pointing sharply, nearly backwards. She couldn't begin to describe its eyes, evil and hate emanated from them. The most striking part of this alien's appearance was the fleshy-looking horns protruding from its body. Six from its hairless scalp, three from each shoulder and a row following the vertebrae of its backbone. Two of the scalp horns were much longer, sweeping back and down to its waist.

It was concentrating on the three men. She could see blood oozing from wounds on Jon and Sam's faces, and Rob, who was now in his true Trun form, was bruised and swollen. Her shins were tightly bound to the legs of a wooden chair, her wrists secured to the arms. They were in a circle, and the creature's back was to her.

Amanda closed her eyes and feigned unconsciousness, wanting more time to understand what was happening here. The creature was apparently bragging to the others.

'...nearly two hundred and fifty years old using your measurements, but I haven't reached halfway into my lifespan. We spend an extended part of our life in estivation—a form of hibernation in the—usually after we have annihilated a planet and its inhabitants, and we're feeling... satiated.'

Amanda heard a loud crunching sound—bone—followed by a scream. 'You ask me questions, hoping to delay the pain, and then you don't listen to me, Kean. Perhaps that will focus your attention.' The creature laughed, a guttural sound from deep in its throat, though it couldn't be remotely related to amusement. 'I'll continue. Please pay attention. In the infancy of our space travel, we stumbled upon a race called the Rammor. A highly advanced civilisation, close to ascendency, so the story goes—that's moving to a higher plane of existence to you, some races seek this—and they took us under their wings. Pets, they thought of us. But after two hundred years of being their little helper pets, we had become indispensable to them, looking after the technology that looked after them. We had stolen, analysed and learnt to use much of their advanced technology. Wait. Is someone pretending here?'

Amanda kept perfectly still until a sudden pain in her shoulder her made her jump— eyes wide open. She was looking straight into the creature's face. She could see from the corner of her eye that the pain she was feeling was its fingernails—no, talons—slowly digging into her skin. The pain was increasing. She grimaced, trying to hold back from screaming.

'Get your filthy fricking hands off her!' Jon was struggling so hard to free himself from his bindings that his chair toppled over.

The creature dropped her and went to Jon. It grabbed him by his hair and effortlessly pulled him upright. Jon was clearly in pain, but his face showed nothing but rage and anger. She sneered at him, 'If you interrupt me again, I shall cut her head off right before your eyes.' She turned back to Amanda.

'The lovely young Earth girl was trying to deceive the beautiful and clever Zerot girl, eh?' She moved behind Mandy and rested three of her fingers high on her cheekbone, talons slowly digging into her skin, little rivulets of blood forming. She was looking straight into Jon's eyes as she slowly moved her hand down Amanda's face, challenging him to utter a word. Jon's eyes were flicking from her to the Zerot creature. Terror and rage in equal measures. As the three bloody tramlines formed on Mandy's cheek, she did everything in her power to keep from screaming. She was on the point of passing out when the Zerot stopped.

'Good,' she said. 'Now where was I? Ah yes. And with their technology, we made a plan that ended with the death of every single Rammorian. We spent the next forty years stripping their planet of everything of value and taking back to Zerot. So, there you have it. Three thousand years later and we're still doing it. But it's a game now, and Preenasette is next.' She walked back to Jon and stroked his cheek, gently this time, then strolled out of the room. 'I won't be long. Don't go anywhere,' she called back casually.

* * *

AMANDA FOUGHT through the pain of her throbbing cheek and focused on Jon. He was staring straight back at her. 'Are you all right, Mandy?' The blood and bruising on his face didn't hide his concern. She nodded at him. 'I'm okay.' His concern immediately changed to anger and he challenged Rob, 'So, was this your great master plan? To befriend *me*, Rob, Kean? Or whatever your name is. Some plan.'

'I'm sorry, Jon, I was just doing my job. We were just supposed to locate the Princess and wait for my father to arrive. He would capture her and take her back to our planet.'

Kean's voice had taken on the broken English accent that Grace had when she wasn't wearing a brooch.

'And you didn't suspect you were partnering Madame Death and Destruction there?' said Jon.

'We need to address our situation here,' Kean said.

'Can anyone move?' Sam joined in. 'I can't even move a muscle.'

'Don't bother trying,' Kean replied. 'Kayson rope. You need a sharp knife to cut through it.'

We're getting nowhere, thought Amanda. *"Grace, where are you? Can you hear me? Please."* A desperate cry for help, but Grace was halfway around the world. The furthest they'd ever managed to communicate this way was about a mile.

"Mandy. I hear you. Are you okay?" Grace was in her head.

"Oh, Grace, the creature is torturing us."

"Who? The Trun?"

"No, another creature. A Zerot. Rob is in his natural form. She's giving him special attention. His arm is broken, and his face is messed up."

"We're not far away. I think I've pinpointed you now. William and a small armed force will be with you in a few minutes."

"Hurry, Grace. Please. And be careful. This creature can get in your head."

"I will."

The men were still bickering. 'Jon, listen to me.' She got their attention. She tried to whisper. 'Grace, William and some others are outside, only minutes away. We've got to keep this creature distracted, to give them chance to get in and surprise her.'

'Are you talking to Grace?' Jon asked.

'I was. Not anymore. The Zerot can hear your thoughts, I think. She knew I was awake, but pretending to be unconscious. Concentrate your minds on each other. Rob, how is your arm?' She could see he was in a bad way.

'Hurts like hell, but thank you for asking.'

Jon looked questioningly at Mandy, but he didn't comment. In the midst of this horror show he was somehow pleased that she could still infuriate him.

'If we ever get out of this I've got one hell of a story for Cycling Weekly.' Sam, the eldest of them, attempted a wry laugh. And for a brief moment the four of them, though bruised and battered, smiled with him.

THEN THE ZEROT walked back in.

CHAPTER 40

entar's Sphere
Earth - Space/South Africa - 2013, Tuesday

VENTAR'S SPHERE was approaching Earth very cautiously, aware of the Trun battle cruiser in orbit around the planet. The cruiser was in geosynchronous orbit above the Republic of Ireland, so Kobios approached from the other side, keeping the Earth between them. Stevos, Hondry, Maot and Jake were around her flight station, discussing the limited range of actions open to them now the Trun were on the scene. Prince Ventar was sitting at the table ignoring them, deep in thought.

'Tauriar's Life Team must be in the country of Ireland,' said Jake. 'Why else would it be there, stationary?'

'But, they don't appear to have found them yet,' Hondry said. 'They are doing nothing,' He waved his arms with animation. 'They haven't released any search or recovery ships.'

'I agree with you.' Kobios was looking at Hondry. 'They appear to still be searching. If the team are under cover of a

311

shield, they may never find them in this technologically dense environment.'

Ventar lifted his head and looked over to the group. 'I think they have people already here, Spies perhaps. They may be trying to contact them. They may be the ones that know the location of the princess's Life Team.'

'Will they be in Ireland?' Kobios asked.

'One would have thought so,' replied the Prince. 'But I'm not sure. We need to keep out of sight for the time being.' He put his head back in his hands and continued concentrating, completely ignoring the others again.

They all went quiet for a while, sifting through their thoughts.

A few minutes later the prince sat bolt upright. 'I've found Tauriar!' he exclaimed, an anxiety in his voice the others had never heard before. 'She is in danger. We must go to her immediately.' He was accessing a holographic map of Earth. 'Here, South Africa. Go. Now.'

'What about the Trun ship?' Stevos asked, while Kobios entered the new course heading into her flight computer.

'Forget about them,' Ventar replied. 'There is something infinitely more dangerous in South Africa.'

* * *

SUB COMMANDER BRAWN double checked the reading on his surveillance screen, then shouted over to Captain Rapha, 'Unidentified vessel—I'm pretty sure it's a sphere—detected in the planet's southern hemisphere. It's on a tangential heading— it appears quite random.'

Rapha and Mancer were immediately behind Brawn, studying the sphere's trajectory.

'It may be a ruse or a decoy to get us away from here,' Rapha stated.

'I agree,' Mancer said. 'Dispatch a fighter,'

'I suggest two.' Rapha looked at Mancer who nodded his agreement. 'Sub Commander, send 3W fighters two and four immediately.'

* * *

KOBIOS ENTERED the Earth's atmosphere at the last possible moment, slowing down considerably. They still had one hundred and fifty miles to go and would arrive in approximately twenty minutes. Soon they would be able to pinpoint their exact position.

Ventar was pacing around, apparently concerned. He approached Kobios. 'Drop me off here, just outside of the city of Durban. I can't do what I need to do on the ship. Now please, Kobios. Lives are at stake.'

Kobios looked at Stevos, who looked back questioningly.

'Leave me, then carry on and rescue Tauriar. Come back for me later.' Ventar could see them both readying themselves to protest and added, 'I'll take my father with me.'

'He's helping me fly the ship,' Kobios protested. 'We're all doing two jobs, as it is,'

'I'll take my mother with me.'

Stevos was still frowning.

'Give her a laser pistol then!'

Stevos could see the desperation in Ventar's eyes. She nodded to Kobios.

The sphere landed, and Ventar and Maot disembarked, moving away quickly as the ship prepared for immediate takeoff.

Two minutes later and all was quiet.

Ventar sat down, cross legged. He looked up at Maot and smiled. 'Please do not disturb me, mother.' He looked back down and was soon in a trance.

Maot, brandishing her pistol, looked in every direction. Seeing nothing, she let it drop to her side. She sat down on a nearby rock, thinking how hot it was and wondering what the heck was going on.

CHAPTER 41

*T*he Rescue Attempt
        Earth - South Africa - 2013, Tuesday

WILLIAM AND KURT approached the front of the motel. A couple of weary travellers wanting a bed for the night. Grace, Janet, Gordon and Oscar skirted around to the rear, looking for an alternate way into the building. Krankel was glued to Grace's side, feeling his mistress's anxiety.

They didn't communicate telepathically, not wanting to alert the Zerot. The CIA agents had short range radios that were low tech and likely to stay off its radar.

Kurt reported in, speaking as quietly as possible. 'No activity at the reception desk. Emergency lighting only, and the no vacancies sign is up. Gordon is sorting the door lock now. Over.'

Oscar replied, 'We are approaching the rear. There's a goods access door here. Over.'

Kurt continued, 'We're in, there are two dead behind the reception counter. Over.'

They crept towards the door to the conference room, stopped and listened. They heard a scream, followed by an eerie cackle.

'They're inside the conference room,' whispered Kurt. 'We need to move quickly. Over.'

'We're in, there's a rear entrance to the room,' Oscar replied. 'Prepare to enter on our mark. Over.'

* * *

SONIA RETURNED with a set of industrial secateurs. 'I've wanted to try these out for a while, but unfortunately, I don't have a garden. Let's see which of you is the bravest.'

She went straight to Sam and adeptly slipped the blades around the little finger of his bound right hand. She paused for a few seconds to see him register what was about to happen, enjoying the horrified look on his face. Then her fingers closed.

It was a few more seconds before Sam realised what had just happened. The rush of blood and the sight of the end of his finger lying on the floor seemed to delay the onset of the pain. But when it came, his face twisted and a deep moan escaped from his throat. He was desperately trying to keep himself together, but with his hands bound he was unable to give his wound any comfort. He looked helplessly around at the despair on his comrades' faces. He came to grips with the pain, but couldn't take his eyes off his severed finger. His mind started processing the letters on a computer keyboard that he would now be unable to type. He looked up at the Zerot, stalking her next victim, and realised this was just the start of the torture.

Sonia laughed as she strolled around the other three. She was enjoying their undivided attention.

'And don't think your little planet will escape a visit from us. One of our planetary violation teams—Cadre 176—was chased away by your grandparents. After being here for two years, I still wonder how that could have happened. They were here orchestrating the Nazi movement. I recall their pseudonyms were Hitler, Goebbels, Bormann and Schroeder. A standard template used many times, with only a handful of failures. But we always revisit; no one survives the Zerot.'

She stopped at Jon. In an instant, she had the secateurs around his little finger, but this time she cut it straight off.

Jon, having seen Sam's plucky reaction, bit his lip and stared straight back at the Zerot, determined not to react, to deny her any satisfaction. Sonia was ignoring him, though. His gaze eventually came to rest on Mandy. Her determined look surprised him. She stared at him fiercely, the love she had for him manifesting in unspoken instructions telling him to hold it together. A weak smile was his only reply, but that was sufficient for her.

Sonia's short pointed teeth gleamed in the dull light as her thin lips parted. The Zerot's smile brought home—to Amanda and Rob at least—the horror still awaiting them.

'Of course, Cadre 176's failure was a delight to my team, as they are our nearest rivals in the Killing Games. But, in the vast scheme of things, know for tonight, at least, that the fate of your planet is sealed, and it will be a magnificent destruction. I very much hope to be part...' she stopped, stood still for a moment, turned towards the door and activated her full body force field.

* * *

WILLIAM AND KURT positioned themselves on either side of the conference room door. Kurt held his Glock 23 at shoulder level, pointed towards the ceiling. William's laser cannon required both hands. As firepower went, this was the most powerful weapon the group possessed. William whispered to Kurt, 'Open the door, but let me go in first.'

At the rear door, Gordon was marshalling his group. 'Oscar and I will go in first. You girls stay out here until the room is secured.' He grabbed the communicator from Oscar. 'William, as soon as you hear weapons fire, enter. Use the cannon with discretion.'

Gordon took a deep breath, checked his laser stun setting, then crashed through the door.

* * *

ONLY WHEN GORDON had kicked the door down did Grace feel the magnitude of evil nature and power of the Zerot. 'No!' she cried out. But it was too late. Janet stared at Grace then entered the room herself, her Glock 27 trained straight in front of her.

Gordon picked out the Zerot in the middle of her captives and discharged his gun. A visible glow appeared around the strange, insect-looking creature, showcasing the harmless dissipation of the weapon's power. He set his gun to maximum and fired again, only to see the same result. The Zerot's lips rolled back to reveal pointed teeth, leering at his inability to harm her.

Bullets from Kurt's Glock ricocheted innocuously off Sonia's protective shield. She turned her attention to him, willing him to turn the weapon on himself. Kurt had no way of stopping his arm turning the gun on himself or his finger slowly squeezing the trigger. William entered through the front but stopped dead in his tracks. There before him was the horrific sight of Kurt's skull and brains spraying from the side of his head.

As William's eyes met the creature's his hands went limp, and the cannon clattered to the floor. He watched helplessly as the Zerot withdrew an object from her belt that flicked open in segments, creating a sword. She started towards him.

The captives, to a man and woman, were shouting at the Zerot and shaking their chairs. Trying anything to distract it. Sonia ignored them, and carried on towards William.

Nothing was stopping the creature. Grace could feel the futility of everyone's actions. She must distract it. Stepping into the room, she looked straight at it and issued a challenge.

"I CAN STOP YOU, CREATURE."

THE ZEROT TURNED AWAY from William, blood dripping from its sword, to focus on Grace.

"Ha! You are nothing. Your power is nothing. I will show you power, child."

Grace's attention was drawn away from William's fallen body as the creature slowly began sucking away at her will. She resisted, using everything she possessed to fend off the mental attack. Krankel felt the attack on his mistress too, and as with the troll, felt compelled to defend her.

'No Krankel!'

But he was off. The Zerot, seeing the large dog running at her, smiled wickedly and prepared to meet it with its blood-stained sword.

Grace focussed hard and formed a time acceleration bubble; it was all she could think to do.

"Do you try to play simple tricks on me, girl?" It immediately burst the bubble.

But the split second it had taken the Zerot to break the bubble had given Grace a few precious seconds within it, to prepare a wedge node. She deployed it the instant the bubble failed, using all of her remaining concentration to aim it as best she could. *I can't fail Krankel this time.* The dog yelped as it reached the Zerot, glancing painfully off the force field. As the sword arced towards the dog, Grace braced herself. It hit the oblique block of pressurised air from the wedge and was deflected harmlessly underneath. Krankel landed with a yelp, winded. Grace felt the alien's annoyance as it refocussed on destroying the Princess's will.

It crawled deeper and deeper into Grace's mind, sucking away at her. She resisted, but her resolve was weakening.

Gordon had recovered the cannon and with the Zerot now away from the captives, began firing. But its shield held firm.

Grace was losing. Her psyche was slipping away. She was falling into a well, and the light above her was getting smaller and smaller and smaller. Until…

"STAY WITH ME, SISTER."

SHE FELT A NEW ENERGY, recognising the voice from her training session with the troll. An energy that joined with hers, helping to pull her back to the top of the well.

"NOW WORK WITH ME."

HER WILL, combined with the stranger's, was a brake on the Zerot's influence. The balance between the two began to equalise, then, slowly at first, they began forcing it back. Grace felt the panic in her adversary's mind, now doubting its abilities. The gentle strength of the stranger held Grace steady. The creature's concentration was failing, the two-pronged attack too much, and suddenly its control of the protective shield failed, and it blinked off.

The laser cannon now only had flesh and bones in the path of its beam—no match for it at all.

* * *

JANET LOOKED AROUND at the carnage in the room. She had never experienced anything remotely like this.

The Zerot lay dead on the floor.

So did Kurt.

Gordon had William's head in his lap, watching his friend's life ebbing away.

Grace had collapsed, exhausted. No, more than exhausted. A limping Krankel nuzzled her. When she didn't move, he lay down next to her.

Oscar had cut the captives free. Mandy and Jon both ran to Grace's side.

Rob, holding his broken arm, wandered around in a daze, as did Sam, his injured hand tucked under his arm.

She even saw what appeared to be the skin of a human woman lying on the floor.

It was chaos.

How could a single being cause so much devastation? Janet hadn't even fired her gun, though not because she didn't try. The captives prevented her getting a clear shot at the creature. She didn't know what to do. For probably the first time in her life, she didn't know what to do. She could only stare through tearstained eyes.

She heard a noise behind her and looked. More people were entering the room. Five hazy blue shapes were hurrying to assist the injured. Janet rubbed the moisture from her eyes so she could focus. Vercetians, but none she recognised from Cork.

Two went straight to Grace and two to Gordon and William. There was a frenzied exchange between Gordon and the two new arrivals, in an incomprehensible language. The taller of the two, a female, seemed to be giving instructions to Gordon. He deactivated his brooch and gave it to her, reverting to his true form, and helped the other Vercetian pick up William, and immediately carried him outside.

The tall female turned her attention to Grace and the male Vercetian examining her. They conferred, then he picked Grace up and carried her outside. Krankel got up to follow, but the tall female spoke firmly to him, and he cowered back, ears flat, and lay next to Jon.

Jon and Mandy had already stepped back, hoping that Grace would now receive the care they were unable to give. Mandy was looking at Jon's missing finger. The loss of blood was starting to take its toll on him and he dropped into a chair. The fifth Vercetian—who looked to be an elderly male—having stemmed the bleeding of Sam's finger, began attending to Jon.

The tall female was talking to Rob. She held him by his good arm and led him out of the building.

Janet and Oscar followed.

* * *

WHAT THEY SAW OUTSIDE STOPPED them dead in their tracks.

Before them, hovering about six feet off the ground, was what Janet assumed to be a spaceship. A dark silver, forty foot diameter sphere, with a heat haze around it. *What else could it be?* she admonished herself. Two Venetians were carrying a motionless William up a floating ramp, followed by the male carrying Grace, and finally, the tall female escorting the Trun.

Janet shouted over the low hum of the ship, 'Where are you going?'

The tall female turned and looked back at her for a

moment, attempted to say something, then carried on into the ship.

A few minutes later, she returned. At the bottom of the ramp, she passed the remaining Vercetian who had finished treating Jon, and they exchanged words. The elderly male shuffled up the ramp which retreated after him. The tall female approached Janet, and looking down at her, raised one finger while fiddling with Gordon's brooch.

Wait, one something or another unit of time, thought Janet. Apparently a universal symbol. The Vercetian activated the holographic image converter and changed into the most stunning human woman Janet had ever seen. Six feet, two inches, and flawless. She turned to Oscar; his jaw had dropped.

She spoke, her soft deep voice again seeming perfect. 'My apologies. Without the image converter, I was unable to access the speech translator. My name is Dom Kobios. I'm the Chief of Security of the vessel that you see here. It is preparing to take off. I suggest we step back into the building.' The three of them re-entered the hotel as the noise from the Sphere began to increase.

Inside, Janet asked, 'Where are you taking Grace, Gordon and William?'

'Those names mean nothing to me,' replied Kobios. 'If you mean Princess Tauriar, Seca Mika and Dom Seca, to another of our ships here on your planet, where there is medical help.'

'To Douglas, sorry, Prime, in Ireland?' Janet asked.

Kobios cocked her head to the side. 'How do you know about Bala Prime?'

'I've met all of the Life Team in Cork. I know all about the plight of your people, and the war with your neighbours. Your princess is Grace to us. Gordon was attending to your dead comrade William.'

'Dom Seca—William— is not dead yet. He is on the edge of

323

death, but is now in stasis in our sphere, until our medic can assess his condition.'

'Why have you remained?'

'We have no pilot. Seca Mika is infinitely superior to me, and I need to find my young Prince. We dropped him off about forty miles away. I need transportation to get me there.'

'Oscar will drive you,' Janet offered. 'What do I do with the alien—the weird looking one?'

'The what?' replied Kobios.

'That!' Janet pointed at the dead creature still on the conference room floor.

'What is it?'

'I don't know,' said Janet.

Amanda joined them. 'It called itself a Zerot. They're in the process of taking over your home world. They intend to destroy Earth as well if she,' she pointed at what was left of Sonia, 'is to be believed.'

Kobios looked at them, then at the Zerot, then back to them again. She shook her head as if trying to shake her brain into comprehending what was going on. All she managed to do was shake the strange hair into her eyes. She awkwardly pushed the strands away and said, 'This will have to wait until my team return for me. I need to get my Prince.'

'I need to go with Grace. Back to Ireland. My mother and father are there with Prime.' Amanda was looking up at the Vercetian security chief. 'I need to go on your ship, now. Check with Gordon—Seca—he'll vouch for me.'

Kobios concentrated, looking at nothing for a moment, in communication Mandy assumed, then she replied, 'Go. The ramp is back down for you.'

Mandy nodded in thanks to her before turning to Jon. 'I'll be back for you as soon as I can.' Jon nodded to her and smiled. She leant forward and kissed him on the cheek. Lingering, she whispered in his ear, 'I love you.' She stepped away, her eyes locked on his, then she turned and walked outside, the others following her.

Kobios made sure Mandy was safely on the sphere before turning back to Oscar. 'Come then.' She walked toward the only object that could be a vehicle, then turned back to Janet. 'You need to get back inside.' Her tone changed from instructional to questioning, 'Is this human form an acceptable one for me to integrate into your species?'

Janet replied, 'Yes, no one will give you a second look, you should blend in nicely.' She turned to Oscar, closed his jaw with two fingers and with her other hand, gently pushed him off after her.

CHAPTER 42

*T*he Reunion
   Earth - The Republic of Ireland - 2013, Tuesday

GORDON GINGERLY RAISED the sphere off the ground, using only thrusters. He was the reserve pilot for his Life Team but hadn't had any flight time since their arrival on Earth. Even before that, Peter would rarely give up the helm.

To avoid detection, he kept the vessel within a few feet of the ground, ramping up the speed as his confidence grew. The route he plotted to Ireland would give the African locals a fantastic view of this exotic mode of transport.

At his shoulder, Stevos was fussing about and helping where she could. 'Can we make contact with Prime yet?' she asked him.

'Not advisable, Madame.' Gordon couldn't bring himself to be any less formal with this legendary Life Team leader. 'You may need to wait until you are in telepathic range.'

'Understood.'

'Any improvement in Princess Tauriar's condition?' he

asked, knowing it had been precious little time since he had placed her on the recovery bed.

'None,' Stevos replied. 'Hondry will inform me of any changes.'

They had his security chief and friend William in stasis. His life was in the balance but suspended until James would be able to assess him. Gordon hoped he would be at the Hall and not in Cork. He could not park the sphere outside of the busy city residence.

Stevos, looking at the landmass flashing by below them, said, 'What are the chances of the Trun picking us up?'

'If we stay this low, with shields on, we should avoid detection,' Gordon replied. 'It's when we move higher. That's when they can find us.'

Two hours later they were over the south coast of Ireland. Stevos was concentrating hard, apparently now close enough to be in contact with Prime. Gordon was still just feet above the ground and had slowed down to less than one hundred miles per hour. The sight of the sphere gave the locals of Ireland a visual treat. If the last few days or so hadn't quite convinced the population of Earth of the existence of extraterrestrial beings, he was indeed reinforcing that fact now. He smiled to himself at the frenzy there would be on social media in the next few hours.

Stevos had finished with his leader. 'Prime wants us to head for Harewood Hall, your country residence, I think he called it.'

'Yes, Madame.'

'Does sound a lot nicer than our rudimentary, unfurnished monastery,' She looked directly at him for the first time during the journey, and couldn't hide the hint of a smile.

ancer's Fighters
Earth - 2013, Tuesday

Flight Commander Armoury reported back to Rapha. 'No sign of the sphere, sir, but we have picked up two Vercetian signatures at the stop they made forty miles back.'

'Send Lampard down to investigate, Commander, and you keep an eye out for any signs of the sphere.'

'Yes, sir.'

* * *

Flight Commander Lampard landed his 3W fighter on the African plain, a hundred feet from the two figures trudging north. He jumped out of the cockpit and loped over to them. An adult female and an adolescent male. The woman was brandishing a weapon that the boy immediately took from her and threw to one side. He could make out a dust plume from a land vehicle heading for them—probably still two to three miles away.

'Names please?' he snapped. Not trying to frighten them, but conscious of the vehicle heading towards them.

'Prince Ventar of Verceti,' the Prince said, taking charge. 'And this is my mother, Maot.'

Lampard spoke quickly and excitedly into his lapel communicator. The reply was instant.

'Come with me now.' Lampard had his weapon in his hand. Ventar stepped forward obediently.

'You have to take me as well,' said Maot.

'I can't,' he replied, feeling a certain guilt. 'There are only two seats.'

'But you don't understand,' Maot pleaded, 'I'm a Tr..'

'Mother!' Ventar shouted.

She stared at him, eyes wide and begging.

His voice softened. 'I'll be all right, mother. Kobios will be with you in a couple of minutes. I must do this.' He smiled at her and silently said, '*I love you.*'

They boarded the fighter and lifted off just as the Earth vehicle arrived.

* * *

'HAVE YOU GOT THE PRINCE?' asked Rapha.

'Yes.'

'Then get back here, immediately,' he said. 'You too, Armoury.'

'Understood.'

CHAPTER 44

race's Sphere
        Earth - The Republic of Ireland - 2013, Wednesday

ON THE EDGE of the lake on the grounds of Harewood Hall, the escapees were shuttling down to Grace's sphere in pairs via the entry bubble. Douglas and Gwyneth went first, followed by Gordon supporting Grace. Next were Grace's parents, Mr. and Mrs. Shaw, Amanda, and finally, Helen escorting Rob.

But they weren't able to go anywhere just yet. They were waiting for Peter, who had still to leave the Hall.

He jumped on his bike and raced down to the lake. On arrival, he summoned an entry bubble, transferred through the sphere airlock and sealed it behind him. He strapped himself into the pilot's seat and slipped his feet and hands into the controllers.

He concentrated, ignoring everything around him. He hadn't flown a sphere in years, and this needed to be perfect. *Just one shot at this, they depend on you*, he told himself.

He set the vibration mechanism. He had lake silt to shake free of before going anywhere. Once free, the sphere bobbed up, breaching the surface of the lake. He activated the navigational drive, hoping for the best. It started the first time. Vertical thrusters slowly raised the ship out of the water. Once clear, he was able to engage the drive and moved swiftly to about 50,000 ft. He held it there while he plotted his escape arc out of the Earth's atmosphere. He needed a steady and gradual ascent if he was going to avoid detection for as long as possible. The drive kicked in, and four vessels appeared on his monitor, assuming a standard attack formation.

* * *

CAPTAIN VINCENT HARDY eased his Typhoon into position and waited for a few moments for his team to do the same.

'Attack formation Delta 7. You're first, Simon.'

The first of the Typhoons moved in and released two Meteor air-to-air missiles. Lieutenant Simon Jenkins watched them track seamlessly towards the spherical alien vessel before he veered away to make way for his team members. Vince was the last to fire his missiles, hoping he would have more success than the others before him.

'Okay, chaps. Let's back off and let the Yanks have a go at this tricky bastard.'

* * *

PETER FELT the missiles detonate harmlessly on his shield. His monitor showed six more Earth aircraft about to engage him. His shield could take this assault from their military, but it would be a beacon for the Trun cruiser.

Safely through the next onslaught, he had reached an altitude at which the Earth aircraft couldn't follow. A few minutes later and he'd escaped the clutches of planet Earth and was in space. He enabled his star drive and set a course for the nearest wormhole. At maximum speed, he would be there in forty-five minutes. All he could do now was hope.

Ten minutes into the dash to safety, his screen showed four more small dots rapidly closing in on him. These weren't Earth vessels though. These were Trun 3W fighters, followed closely by the battle cruiser.

* * *

THE FIGHTERS TOOK turns sweeping in on the delta sphere, attacking its shield with concentrated ionised particle beams.

Peter was doing the maths. At this rate, his shields would fail two minutes out from the wormhole. He wondered if his attackers were aware of this. Nothing he could do but keep heading towards the wormhole and hoping.

He needed to get there first.

* * *

MANCER STOOD DIRECTLY behind his captain, watching the images relayed by the fighters.

'The sphere's shields are critically low. Failure is imminent.' Captain Rapha was giving him a dispassionate, running commentary.

'Time to wormhole?' Mancer asked.

'Three minutes, sir.' Rapha waited a few more seconds. 'Shields are down.'

'Tell the fighters to stand down.' Mancer instructed. 'Let's give them a moment to consider their options.'

They watched in silence as the sphere headed doggedly towards the wormhole.

Rapha broke the silence. 'The orbiting surveillance drone

has confirmed detection of Vercetian life forms entering the water in transit bubbles. A female of the Princess's age amongst them. According to its flight path, this sphere left from that location.'

'Understood.' replied Mancer. 'They're not going to stop, and we can't follow,' he muttered under his breath.

'Thirty seconds, sir.'

'Resume attack and destroy it.' Mancer turned and walked away from his captain, cursing the Vercetians stubbornness.

The first fighter strike disabled the sphere, taking out part of its lower hull, sending the vessel spinning off course with chunks of hull drifting outwards. It would never reach its destination now. The second strike targeted the drive system and fuel cells. The result was the complete destruction of the ship, with fragments radiating out in every direction.

Mancer had turned around to watch this second strike, wincing at the spectacular light display. He'd seen a lot of death in his long military career, but he would never get used to the senseless loss of life.

Rapha turned around, his face ashen. 'Analysis of the remaining occupants is coming through.' He looked away, then back again, his face nearly white now. 'Sir, your son was on board.'

CHAPTER 45

*T*he *Death Sentence*
Outside of the Solar System - 2013

THE TC BATTLE cruiser had left the Solar System two months ago, and was on route to wormhole Toraxi 4, one of the few large enough to take a ship of this size. Mancer wouldn't need to leave with the Prince for a while yet.

He sat in his quarters with a glass of whisky from the bottle given to him by Zander. 'From me, old friend, for you to enjoy on your return journey, after the conclusion of a successful campaign.'

It had been successful. One Princess dead and one Prince here on board with him—a bonus. But the cost? His son dead, and a chasm in his heart that would never heal. Damn, he hated this war. This was not how it was supposed to end. Where was the glory in this?

He drank some more, wondering if there would be any solace in drinking the whole bottle. There was a knock on his door. 'Come in.'

It was Casma, his petty officer. 'Sir, an FYE only message has just arrived from Premier Gor.'

He accepted the orb and stared at it. 'What now?' he shouted. Premier Gor's ghostly image appeared as soon as he docked it into the holo-projector console.

'CONGRATULATIONS, *Commander. The elimination of two Royals is an excellent result. The War Council have asked me to extend their profound thanks.'* His voice was an unfeeling monotone. *'We have one more duty for you to perform. With the Princess tragically killed, the Council has decided that the best resolution of the whole affair is to eliminate the Prince as well.'* Mancer sat up straight, *What the hell?*

'Please be in no doubt that this order requires your immediate action' Mancer stared at the holograph, speechless. *'The war is at a critical stage. Your battle cruiser is urgently needed back in Trun space. We need you to ensure this happens. Do not return using the sphere as originally planned. I repeat, stay with the cruiser. Again, congratulations. Gor out.'*

* * *

MANCER AND CASMA walked down the corridor to the detention centre that was holding Ventar. An execution required two officers in attendance. He was confused why Zander had not given him the message personally. What was going on at home? And why make him stay with the cruiser? The excuse given was lame. And now he had to execute a boy!

They arrived at the makeshift execution chamber, normally a common room. The engineers had rigged up a plasma chair, ensuring a quick death, with no pain for the condemned. When they entered, Ventar looked pathetically small in the chair.

Though his hands and feet were secured, he still appeared calm.

They both sat down. Mancer stared at the boy, wondering to himself what the hell he was doing. He had never disobeyed an order in his life—he didn't know how to. He told the executioner to proceed, not wanting to drag this out any longer than necessary.

A rough-looking soldier stood by, but it was evident from his demeanour that his heart was not in this. 'Ventar of Verceti, you are charged with war crimes, and the War Ministry of Trun Rizontella decrees you will be put to death by any reasonable means. You have two minutes to make a declaration.'

The young Prince smiled at the soldier and then looked directly at Mancer.

'Firstly, I would prefer not to be executed. Secondly, I go by another name—Camerra Kalter of Trun Rizontella. I'm not in your database, but my parents are: Camerra Maot and Camerra Jake of the KBS. A simple DNA test will prove that I am their son.'

Stunned silence fell over the room.

He continued. 'Thirdly, the leadership of Trun is now deeply infiltrated by an evil race known as the Zerot. They are perpetuating the war between our two nations ahead of an invasion force that is coming to annihilate any of us left and rape our planet. The Trun and the Vercetians need to stand together. It is my intention to unite them. This foe is deadly.'

A completely dazed Mancer looked at Casma then back to Ventar. 'Er, anything else?'

'Yes. You haven't killed Princess Tauriar either.' His sudden smile was wickedly devious. 'A ploy set up with the help of the people of Earth. You destroyed the wrong sphere.'

'Oh, and your son Kean is still alive too. He should be in the sphere with the Princess heading back to our home world.'

'Commander Mancer. This is one order you can disobey.'

POSTSCRIPT

Katie walked into the dining room of the large detached house in Cork, with a tray of food prepared by her own fair hand. It was just the two of them now, her and James. No more Vercetian food ever, now that the others had all left. The thought made her a little sad. In her eleven years on Earth, there had always been the promise of a return home. How far off never seemed to matter, their primary goal was always to train and protect their princess. She just knew that one day she would go home. But now that would never happen. She would never see Preenasette again, her friends, family, or any other Vercetians for that matter.

James was at the dining room table marking test papers for his students at the university. He took his work very seriously and wanted to carry on lecturing. She placed the tray on the table. He looked up. 'Just a few more minutes, sweetheart.'

'Take your time. Nothing here will spoil.' She loved the way he used English colloquialisms. "Sweetheart" on Verceti meant a Zakat meat delicacy. He had immersed himself into life here, especially since he began working at the university. He wouldn't have a problem living out the rest of his life here, and she wouldn't have a problem spending the rest of her life with him.

But, Katie had a secret—a big secret. One she would never be able to reveal to James. One she would now, never have to.

She knew he was a Trun. The spy in their ranks.

* * *

She had witnessed him dispatching the message orb eight years ago. The one that was subsequently reported missing. He had been so moody during the weeks leading up to it, as though he was carrying the weight of the world on his shoulders. She had gone to find him at his favourite spot in the woods to talk to him, to see what was on his mind, only to stumble on him in the act of dispatching it. She understood immediately. Lots of small things falling into place that only a loved one would notice. He appeared to have taken the attempt on Grace's life harder than anyone, and he took little trips away that had no real rhyme or reason to them.

She had immediately gone to Prime and Temper and told them. The three of them had spent all night discussing it. They had all finally agreed to leave things as they were. Knowing about the spy would mean they had the upper hand in managing sensitive data. They would be able to keep him at arm's length but still within reach. Moreover, what could they possibly do with him? They had no justice system here, or anywhere secure to hold him. They couldn't hand him to the authorities of Earth and say. 'Lock him up; he's a dangerous alien.' No, watch and wait was the best policy, and they thought it best to keep this information between the three of them. Katie had agreed to to keep up the illusion that they were still together. But how could she not? She loved him, and her love was unconditional. She'd watched him over the next few weeks. He was in turmoil; she knew that. But as the weeks and months passed everything returned to normal. They had announced to everyone at dinner two months earlier that they had deep feelings for each other.

His mood had dramatically changed with the detection of the Trun cruiser. A full diagnostic was carried out on the sphere in preparation for departure, and a major software failure discovered. Prime's first thought was sabotage. It would take time get to the bottom of it and effect repairs, so Prime and Temper started working on a backup plan for their escape from Earth. Meanwhile, Mandy and the CIA agent Janet Kilkenny had discovered a Trun agent with Jon, and formulated a rescue plan. When Janet had mentioned she thought the spy's ship might be near the Gearagh, they had immediately surmised that the sphere was in the reservoir. Prime now had the means of initiating a far better plan. Katie would be needed to feed misinformation to James.

Peter and Helen who were at Harewood Hall trying to fix the software problem, were diverted to the site of the Trun sphere at the Gearagh, near Macroom. But they couldn't get past the Trun security system and it appeared their new plan would fail. But with the arrival of the other sphere at Harewood Hall, Prime's plan was back on course. A software link from Ventar's ship and a reboot, meant Grace's sphere was operational... and sabotage was not the cause.

Just before the escape, Prime had asked James and Katie to remain. It was imperative that Earth be unaffected by the Vercetians visit—they would need to react to any unforeseen consequences. Not the real reason, of course, but it was what Katie wanted, and for Prime, it was a good solution to his unsolvable problem. They would send a ship back to them one day.

Together, they watched everyone board the sphere. James and Katie made their separate ways back to Cork, giving James a chance to inform the cruiser that the other sphere, with the

Princess, had taken off. They had, in fact, boarded Ventar's sphere, but it was Grace's sphere, piloted by Peter, that left the lake, hoping to lead the Trun a merry chase through as many wormholes as he could. Grace—with Ann and Janet's assistance —had requested the military forces of Earth attack the sphere when it entered their airspace. She had told them that they would be unable to damage it because of the superior shielding, but what it would do was to alert the Trun ship to their location.

Katie monitored James carefully and, to her complete relief, he did not make contact with the Trun ship. Meanwhile, with the Earth and the Trun's attention on Grace's sphere, Grace and the rest of the two Life Teams at Harewood Hall made a cloaked getaway in Ventar's ship.

So, no more Vercetian food.

'Come on now, darling,' she said to James, who was shuffling his papers in order to put into his briefcase. 'Our salad is getting cold.'

* * *

Prime finally had the ship to himself. They had just passed through the first wormhole of their journey and now had a period at sub-light speed and required semi-stasis travel. He'd closed Temper's stasis pod and carried out the safety checks. Just him now, but he would enjoy a brief time to himself first. He had much to contemplate.

They needed to go home, that much was clear.

Tauriar had locked horns with this creature that had appeared to be a Trun but wasn't. She had been mentally traumatised, left in a coma and showed no signs of improving. The only thing she had managed to say as she was carried onto Kobios's sphere was, "He called me his sister." What did that mean? She had no siblings. Could it be one of the princes?

There had never been any previous use of the term brother or sister between the Royals. There had always been ten years between them, so it never seemed appropriate. Prince Camcietti was who knows where, and Prince Ventar was still a boy. It all baffled him.

William, near death. The creature had tried to kill him. A Zerot, Gordon had told him, posing as a female Trun. Only the quick thinking of Kobios had given him the slim chance of life. They had been friends for over thirty years. He didn't want to lose William. His injuries were severe but hopefully, the doctors at home could save him.

Gordon had also explained that the creature had been boasting about how deeply they had infiltrated the upper echelons of Trun society and were manipulating the escalation of the war with the Vercetians. Soon, they would bring their world to its knees before invading and ravaging the remaining population. A tactic they had apparently used on many worlds, over many millennia.

And the young prince, captured by the Trun. He needed to find them and make contact. Convince them who the real enemy was.

He was sorry to have left Kobios on Earth, but the time required to pick her up might have meant the difference between a successful escape or capture. Kobios was first to point this out anyway. He had also told her about James, and Katie's plea for them to be allowed to stay on Earth. He asked her not to make contact and to leave things be. James had the opportunity to betray them but didn't. He told Kobios he would come back for her one day, but for now, his mind was on the threat of annihilation against Preenasette.

And that had Prime at a complete loss.

47851549R00194

Made in the USA
Middletown, DE
04 September 2017